HOTEL 21

D0062028

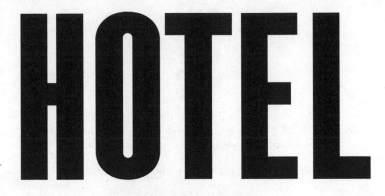

HOTEL 21

SENTA RICH

UNION SQUARE & CO.

NEW YORK

**UNION
SQUARE
& CO.**

NEW YORK

UNION SQUARE & CO. and the distinctive Union Square & Co. logo
are registered trademarks of Sterling Publishing Co., Inc.

Union Square & Co., LLC, is a subsidiary of Sterling Publishing Co., Inc.

Text © 2023 Senta Rich
Cover art © 2023 Bloomsbury

All rights reserved. No part of this publication may be reproduced,
stored in a retrieval system, or transmitted in any form or by any means
(including electronic, mechanical, photocopying, recording, or otherwise)
without prior written permission from the publisher.

All trademarks are the property of their respective owners, are used for editorial
purposes only, and the publisher makes no claim of ownership and shall acquire
no right, title, or interest in such trademarks by virtue of this publication.

This is a work of fiction. All characters, organizations, and events portrayed in
this novel are either products of the author's imagination or are used fictitiously.

First published in the UK in 2023 by Bloomsbury.
This 2023 paperback edition published by Union Square & Co.

ISBN 978-1-4549-5101-8
ISBN 978-1-4549-5102-5 (e-book)

Library of Congress Control Number: 2023930443

For information about custom editions, special sales, and premium purchases,
please contact specialsales@unionsquareandco.com.

Printed in Canada

2 4 6 8 10 9 7 5 3 1

unionsquareandco.com

Cover design by David Mann
Interior design by Kevin Ullrich and Rich Hazelton

For Dave and Miles

Hotel 1

3-star. Hastings. Feb 2011–Feb 2011
Total stay: 3 weeks

Items

Nail scissors x 1
Tester pot of cream x 2
Cigarette lighter x 1
Hair grip with pearl x 1
Tweezers x 1
Shirt button x 1
Gold brooch x 1 (final item)

Chapter 1

I have a first-day rule. Any sign of trouble, even a whiff of a problem and I walk. In hotel 13 I was gone before my first shift even started. I told my supervisor my mother had died and I had to go back to Scotland. I've never even been to Scotland, but I needed to be going far enough away so they didn't expect me to come back. It wasn't the hotel or the way it was run or even the other staff. The problem was the hotel had had someone like me in their midst before.

I don't get nervous on first days. I used to, but I've had so many now I've had to keep a record so I don't forget. This is my twenty-first first day working as a hotel cleaner. So it's a significant milestone and cause for celebration although a very private one. The flutters in my tummy are not the nerves normally associated with starting a new job. Instead, they are the flutters of excitement to get in and get going. Just give me the cleaning trolley, point me in the right direction and I will do the best job in the world cleaning your hotel.

My only hope is that I'm left alone after day one—most establishments "buddy you up" for a few days as part of your induction, to ensure you fully understand how they like things done in their hotel, although there really isn't much difference between one five-star and another, or even one hotel and another whatever the star rating. The only thing that varies is the level of cleaning finish to the rooms. You better make sure you can bounce a coin on a newly made bed in a five-star.

Usually my buddy-up person sees I know what I'm doing and quickly leaves me to my own devices. It's an inconvenience to have someone follow you around all day, watching everything you do, as it means more work and often a longer day. I hate being asked to do it. Having someone looking over my shoulder disrupts my entire routine. The times I have had to supervise a new person, at the end of their first day, whether they're able or not, I tell management they're ready to go it alone. Sometimes they cope with the work-load, sometimes they don't. But there are plenty more hotel clean-ing jobs, so I don't feel guilty, or at least try not to, if they're fired.

My plan today is simple: prove myself quickly so I'm let loose tomorrow. Oh, and most important of all, make sure everyone likes me.

As I approach the slim black door with SERVICE ENTRANCE splayed across it in gold letters, I feel a spring in my step and my heart swells with excitement.

I'm wearing a crisp white shirt under a black hoodie and a smart black skirt with comfortable black shoes, almost a running shoe, which isn't allowed, but I know they're just about regulation enough to get away with. A neat backpack hangs over my shoulder. I look like any other member of staff arriving for work at London's five-star Magnolia Hotel.

Before pushing the door open, I stop for a moment to watch a man and woman dressed in black aprons—the hotel uniform for a classy establishment like this. They are loading an orange laundry truck with large canvas trolleys full of bundled white linens. They look over at me briefly and I nod to them.

The two workers nod back. In a hotel of this size they're not sure if they've seen me before, and they don't really care but there's a code of respect among all members of staff. That's the plus to working in larger hotels. The anonymity is always nice, for a while anyway. Smaller hotels have a friendlier feel to them where everyone looks out for each other and an effort is made to learn a new person's name on the first day.

I tend to last longer in the smaller establishments, once for eight months, which was a record for me. But in the larger hotels, and especially the five-star hotels, I've never lasted longer than a month. While I get comfortable in the smaller hotels and keep the risk low for longer, I tend to become antsy and impatient in the bigger ones and up my game sooner. The guests are also more likely to complain about the smallest thing.

The Magnolia opened in 2016 so it's only three years old. I prefer newer hotels because there's always tons of cleaning equipment and all in good condition, which means there's more than enough to go round. All the vacuum cleaners operate at full capacity, so there's no need for people to secretly swap their rubbish one for yours, which happens in the older hotels. The buckets don't have cracks in the wringer making it impossible to wring your mop head properly, and the cleaning trolleys roll smoothly along the corridors.

In hotel 7, my trolley used to pull to the right all the time. As friendly as the other cleaners were, no one was going to swap with me. I was last in and that was the deal. I only got to upgrade when someone else left and I was allowed to take their trolley and leave the crooked one for the new person.

I like to set myself little challenges. I've decided the extra thrill for starting in the Magnolia is to aim to beat my previous five-star hotel record by lasting longer than a month. So I need to have my wits about me and take it slow.

I did make it to seven months in hotel 15, a four-star in Cornwall, two years ago. My supervisor at the time, Mrs. Gomez, was quite upset when I announced I was leaving "to be nearer my family." No one ever questions that excuse.

I was surprised when Mrs. Gomez's large, wobbly face fell and her already moist eyes filled with tears. She gave me a big bear hug, pressing my cheek into her full soft bosom, which smelled of talcum powder and lily of the valley.

For a moment, in her arms, I wondered what my life would have been like had Mrs. Gomez been my mother. Would I have become a person who stays in five-star hotels instead of cleaning them? Would I want to be different than the way I am now? I normally abandon these thoughts quickly as they're not helpful and don't go anywhere.

Mrs. Gomez finally released me from her bosom and held me firmly by the shoulders.

"You are the best little worker I have ever had," she said.

I smiled at her, genuinely appreciative. It was nice to hear I was good at my job but even nicer to know she didn't suspect me one bit. I was quite sad to leave too. The guests tended to be long-term stayers with mountains of luggage, brimming with personal possessions. The wardrobes were always stuffed full of elegant clothes and fussy designer shoes. And the bathrooms—my favorite space in any hotel room—were strewn with delicate pots of expensive-smelling creams and makeup boxes that popped open to display an artist's palette of eye shadows with elegant brushes and glistening lipstick cases.

One guest had fifty-two lipsticks. Yes, I counted and I couldn't help but be impressed. I had contemplated taking one. I held the black shiny case between my blue-gloved fingers, twisted the bottom and watched in wonder as an untouched ruby red stick slowly emerged, gleaming in the bright bathroom lights. A rush of adrenaline shot up my spine to the base of my neck but with a heavy sigh I put it back in its designated, velvet-lined pouch. A woman with that kind of collection and attention to detail would know in an instant if something were missing. And I'd had a bad experience with a lipstick before and felt it was too risky.

Instead, I slowly unzipped her toiletry bag watching the individual teeth part way as it flopped open to reveal a lucky dip of tubes and pots and shiny plastic containers. I slipped my hand in, pushing down, deep to the very bottom, where smaller items like forgotten lip balms live. I dug gently in and around the pots and tubes until my forefinger landed on a small lid. I ran the tip of my finger around it, getting a feel for the size of the mini container and then carefully lifted it out, all the while relishing the rush of adrenaline thundering around my body, my breathing faster than normal.

It was a small, white tester pot, slightly dirty from being buried in the bottom of the bag for so long and no bigger than the top of my thumb. It was perfect. Not something the guest would notice was missing. I dropped it into the front of my apron and stood for a moment, allowing the rush to subside and my vital signs to return to normal. It didn't matter that I had no idea what was in the pot, as I never use the things I take. I just keep them, like that woman kept her lipsticks.

Nobody's memory is a hundred percent. Even if she had noticed the little pot was missing, she'd never suspect the cleaner. She'd think she lost it in transit or assume she'd thrown it away and forgotten. And if she had noticed and made a complaint, Mrs. Gomez would never have believed that I would steal anything let alone a small tester pot from the bottom of a toiletry bag. And I would swear, forcing fake tears, that I would never even touch a toiletry bag—we're trained not to move guest items unless absolutely necessary.

But the first complaint sets a precedent. What if another was made against me, even if it was, again, over a small item of no value? A flag would be raised. A question mark would appear next to my name and I couldn't risk that.

There's always a complaint eventually, as I inevitably begin to increase the level of risk. It's inevitable. Three weeks after taking the tester pot, I took a little bottle of pink nail polish from a huge, overflowing vanity case. The guest marched down to reception and loudly accused the cleaner of being a thief.

Mrs. Gomez stood by me like a guard dog, teeth bared as she squared up to the hotel manager. As far as she was concerned, I was an angel and so were the rest of her cleaning staff. I got away with it, of course, but it was highly unlikely she would have defended me a second time.

Once a complaint is made against me, I keep a low profile for two weeks and take nothing, which kills me. I bite my nails and lose my appetite and have to force-feed myself buttered toast. Then I hand in my notice with a worthy excuse and leave for a new hotel in a new place.

Not every hotel cleaning job is straightforward and it's not always easy to simply up and leave. I went to work in a small three-star in Jersey once, just to give the English hotel industry a break. Hotel 8. The minute I arrived I knew I'd made a mistake. Not because they were alert to cleaners taking things but because the cleaning team was a well-established clique that was going to be tough to infiltrate. It consisted of eight older women, all from the same Italian family. They spoke Italian among themselves and clearly didn't have much time for the new girl, so my ability to make them like me, and fast, was already severely compromised.

I thought about employing my first-day rule and leaving immediately, but I'd only just arrived on the ferry. It had been my first time on a boat and I'd spent most of the journey with my head over the side vomiting into the wind. I couldn't face the trip back just yet so I was prepared to give it a day or two to see if I could win the women over.

I quickly decided to behave like a scatty, vulnerable soul who leaves my shirt sticking out of my skirt and is always losing things, like the key to my room at the hostel. And that was just my first shift. By the end of the second day they were talking to me in English and giving me hard-boiled sweets to keep my energy levels up. Apparently I was too pale. They even allowed me to join their tip pooling system. Not everybody tips the cleaner and the guests that do leave it at the end of their stay, which means there's a chance you might not be working the day they check out, so you miss the tip that was meant for you. To most cleaners it's simply luck of the draw. Whoever finds it, keeps it. Some American hotel guests tip by the day for that reason.

I liked this new scatty persona for a while, and it helped the women to accept me, and much faster than they normally would, if at all. My supposed disorganization and weakness made them feel good about how organized and strong they were. And I milked it. I became a master at doe-eyes, a new skill I developed and honed while I was there, and I allowed them to tie my apron and tuck in my shirt without asking me first. It was a new experience to be fussed over like a child.

But I still made sure I did my job well, otherwise I would have become a burden and in that instance the women wouldn't have cared if I had a limp and hump. Nobody carries anyone in the world of hotel cleaning.

Still, it was tiring keeping up the pretense. Being constantly babied became irritating and having to remember to be a scatter-brain with a low IQ took great effort, more than I was used to. After five weeks of successfully lifting guest items without any complaints, I took a tiny tin of fruity lip gloss from a bedside table. I knew as I slipped it into the front of my apron it was high risk but I was eager to up my game. Sure enough, the following day the guest complained that the cleaner must have taken it. All the women supported me, as I sniveled my way through a roll of kitchen paper.

"Little, sweet Noelle?" they cried. "She'd never steal anything from anyone."

Two weeks later I handed in my notice. I told them my grand-mother was sick and I needed to go back to England to look after her or she'd be put in a nursing home. The women were horrified—in Italy you look after your elderly relatives yourself. They packed me off home, laden with gifts for my fictional "Nana."

I gave the packets of pasta and bottle of olive oil to the local women's refuge. I'm more of a "beans on toast" person.

The most important thing for me is not to get caught, even once. A criminal record is impossible to come back from and I'd never be employed as a hotel cleaner again. That's why I'm careful only to take small, insignificant items that a guest won't miss or in the very least will question if they had it in the first place. Items like nail clippers, hair grips, a pair of socks (clean, of course), a pen (not an expensive one), an eyeliner (from the bottom of a makeup bag). Sometimes, when I feel like an easy day, I might take a tie from a man's wardrobe or suit bag. The sound of the zip gently parting as I push it up sends shivers down my spine.

Men are much easier to take from because they're far less likely to kick up a fuss. They're often too embarrassed to say a tie is missing. Either it looks like he forgot to pack it or, if he's older, he blames his wife for not packing it. Most of them find it stressful to complain and would rather avoid the hassle, so I mainly stick to female guests—the stakes are higher, so therefore more rewarding when I get away with it, which I mostly do. And I do enjoy a deli-cate rummage through a well-stocked toiletry bag.

In hotel 3, I took a silk scarf from a wardrobe. The guest had a rake of them, about ten in total, bundled together on one hanger. I was eighteen and still learning my craft and thought she wouldn't notice, but she did. I managed to get away with it because her husband, a mild-mannered man who blushed easily, was mortally embarrassed by his wife's flailing arms and shrill voice demanding the cleaner's home be searched and the police called. He apologized for "the misunderstanding" and quickly ushered his wife out of the lobby and into a taxi, her head bobbing and her finger pointing as she continued to complain. I acted like I was offended and hurt by the accusation but the hotel manager, relieved the couple had left, told me not to worry about it and we all went back to work. Still, it was a mark against my name and therefore time to leave.

Later in the staff room, the other cleaners rallied around me in full support, scoffing at the woman's accusation. "Who would want one of her scarves anyway?" The guest had been in her sixties with an old-fashioned style.

I joined in the scoffing. "As if I'd wear something like that." But I wasn't ridiculing the woman. I was amused by their idea of what stealing meant to a person like me. To them the item had to be valuable or beautiful and somehow relevant. How little they knew.

Chapter 2

I don't steal for financial gain. That would make me an ordinary thief and I'm not. I'm a taker of things guests won't notice are gone or I hope they won't notice are gone. I also rely heavily on people being too embarrassed to declare that the hotel cleaner stole their hair clip or tweezers, for example. That's the risk though. But it's also the thrill. I slip these items from under guests' noses and keep them for myself.

The first time I ever took anything was for spiteful reasons, which I'm not proud of—although I was at the time. Alison Rogers was her name. We were ten years old and in primary school together.

She wasn't someone I liked to be around, as I found her irritating. She had a squeaky voice and overpronounced every word as though trying to speak like an adult. She wore her wispy brown hair pinned back with hair clips either side of a center parting and she had a habit of spraying large dollops of saliva when she talked. The only game she ever wanted to play was beauty salon, where she was the owner and everyone else had to get their hair and nails done by her. I'd rather sit in the toilet on my own for the whole break than play with Alison Rogers.

On this hot summer's day, our teacher, Miss Radcliffe, a softly spoken woman in her sixties, had opened every window in the classroom but still the air hung heavy and dry. Alison Rogers seemed oblivious to the heat that day and had been boasting all morning about her one-pound coin zipped up in the pocket of her light blue cotton skirt with a pleat in the front. She was going straight to the sweet shop after school to spend it on toffee bonbons.

She was annoying enough already that having to listen to her showing off made her unbearable and, by lunchtime, everyone was sick to the stomach of the constant unzipping of her pocket to parade her golden nugget of jealousy for all to see.

The other children did their best to act like they didn't care, but I could see the envy behind their squinting eyes. As the day went on, we all began to ignore her, fed up with her nonstop bragging. And it was then that Alison Rogers made a classic schoolgirl error. She held the coin between her finger and thumb and shoved it out in front of her for all to admire as it glowed and twinkled in the hot sticky sunlight.

"So, I've got a pound coin to buy toffee bonbons and maybe some cola bottles," she announced. "Has anyone else got a pound coin to spend on sweets after school?" She looked at everyone, her eyebrows raised way too high in a questioning look. Everyone shook their head.

"Oh, it's just me then," she said, and zipped the coin back up in her pocket, humming to herself.

At that moment, something snapped inside me. Alison Rogers had progressed in a split second from boasting to gloating and I needed to wipe the smug look off her face.

We had painting in the afternoon and I made sure I sat next to her. Alison loved to boss people around in her squeaky voice and I normally ignored her orders until she moved on to someone else, but just for today I was prepared to put up with it. As we painted away, side by side, I asked questions about what she was painting, which looked like nothing more than a mucky swirl of brown sludge. But she was proud of it, declaring it to be a magical wood where a unicorn lived. She leaned back, wiped her paint-covered hands on her plastic apron and blew a runaway strand of hair out of her eyes.

"Painting is so much fun," she squawked. "But there's no money in it. That's what my dad says." She seemed rather proud of this comment and it struck me at that moment that Alison Rogers was in general a little too proud of everything she did.

"How did you get that brown smudge?" I said, pointing at her painting. As she talked about how she flicked her wrist when applying the paint, my right hand carefully unzipped her skirt pocket.

I gently slid two fingers inside her pocket, clamped them gently around the pound coin and lifted it out smoothly and undetected. I carefully closed the zip and then knocked a paintbrush from the table. As I bent to pick it up, I slipped the pound coin into the side of my shoe—no one would think to look there.

Then I waited. And waited. And as we were all busy putting away our painting equipment, my efforts were finally rewarded.

It started as a slow moan and quickly escalated into an almighty high-pitched shriek.

"My pound coin is gone," she wailed. Her cheeks were puffed out, red as sunburn and her eyes were watering, partly with tears, partly with the pressure from puffing out her cheeks. She pulled the lining of her pocket out so it looked like an ear attached to her hip—stiff and unmoving. "See?" she exclaimed. "It's not there."

Miss Radcliffe talked to her in a soothing tone. Maybe it had fallen out of her pocket. She instructed the class to look for it. A proper search, she called it, as she was sure it was in the classroom somewhere.

While Alison continued to sob uncontrollably, the rest of the children, including myself, looked all over the classroom for her missing pound coin. This annoyed me because I was hoping to minimize the amount of moving around I had to do with the coin pressing against the side of my foot. But as we searched under desks and inside crayon boxes, I hid a smile.

Alison Rogers would not be going to the shop after school to buy toffee bonbons anymore and now, finally, maybe Alison Rogers would shut up and stop showing off.

I looked around at the other children, expecting them to also be hiding satisfied smiles, but instead they were all very serious, pulling out books on the shelves and scratching their heads with worry over poor Alison and her lost one-pound coin.

It never turned up, of course. Alison yelled louder, accusing us all of stealing her money. Miss Radcliffe put her straight. It was far more likely that she had lost it while taking it in and out of her pocket all day long. Yes, serves you right, even Miss Radcliffe agreed. I eyed the other children again and definitely detected the smallest of smiles this time.

On the way home from school, I stopped in a derelict shop doorway, reached down to my shoe and retrieved the pound coin. I held it in the palm of my hand—all this trouble just for you, I thought.

I carried on toward home, the coin clenched in my fist, down a narrow, unmade road of small cottages with tiny front-gardens set back from the road. One of the ramshackle cottages was owned by an old man who always waved to me from his front window in the mornings on my way to school. I always waved back and it made me feel grown up. His garden was jam-packed with funny-looking gnomes and was by far the most interesting garden ever to a ten-year-old.

That day, one of the gnomes situated by the front wall of the garden particularly caught my eye. He had a big jolly smile and held a fishing net over a birdbath. His joyful expression reminded me of how I had felt when I heard Alison Rogers wailing for her pound coin.

I looked up and down the street and checked the front window for the old man. Satisfied nobody was around, I leaned over the wall and dropped the coin into the jolly gnome's fishing net.

"You're welcome," I said.

My body was suddenly flooded with a feeling of lightness that made me want to skip and run, although I wasn't in a hurry. The later I arrived home, the better.

I use the word "home" lightly.

Hotel 4

4-star. Brighton. Oct 2011-Jan 2012
Total stay: 4 months

Items

Nail clippers x 1
Small polished stone x 1
Tester pot of cream x 4
Tweezers x 4
Nail file x 3
Razor x 2
Nail scissors x 2
Dental floss x 2
Hair band x 3
Lip balm x 1
Hair comb x 1
Eye shadow x 1
Tester tube of foundation x 1
Tester bottle of perfume x 1
Novelty glasses with
    moustache x 1

Glasses case x 1
Bra x 1
Socks x 3
Concealer stick x 1
Man's tie x 2
Hair grip x 3
Sachet of shampoo x 1
Pad of Post-it notes x 1
Hair ribbon x 1
Plastic mistletoe sprig x 1
Socks x 2
Pencil with fluffy top x 1
Mini hair gel x 1
Passport cover (final item)

Chapter 3

There's always a hum around the service entrance to a hotel, no matter how big or small the establishment might be. In the larger ones it's simply a lot noisier, but it's always there, the eternally grumbling intestines deep within the bowels of the hotel churning away to sustain its existence.

The walk from the service entrance door in bigger hotels is often longer and more hostile and uninviting than in smaller hotels, and is normally through a concrete-clad tunnel with the throb of the generators seeping through the walls and pipes overhead. The Magnolia is no different.

My footsteps slap on the concrete floor, as a heavy, white fire door looms up ahead. I push through letting it bang shut after me and carry on along the corridor, which is a little wider and friendlier now, leaving the hum behind as I head toward the sounds of civilization.

The gentle drone of talking voices, sizzling pans and clashing pots fills my head as I approach the kitchen. I welcome the noises and the hustle and bustle of the internal workings of the hotel.

I peer in through the window in the door as I pass by. A collection of tall white hats bob around the immaculate kitchen as the chefs swivel and dip to open fridges and drawers, never stopping for a moment.

One of the chefs is rolling pastry and glances up at me, intense for a moment. He has a goatee beard and a swirling tattoo on his forearm. He gives me a quick wink and goes back to his work.

I carry on along the corridor. I wonder if I could have been a chef. I once read somewhere that a person can be anything they want to be if they have the will. There should be a warning attached to that statement in big capital letters: WITHIN REASON. It's misleading otherwise. Still, sometimes I wonder if I could have been a lot of things.

When I was a small girl I wanted to be a doctor. I'd been to the hospital a number of times by the time I was eight and everyone always shook the doctor's hand and said, "Thank you, Doctor" or "Thhhank you, Doctor," like they wanted the doctor to know they really meant it. And when I asked why everyone was thanking the doctor, I was told that doctors save lives and I remember thinking that they actually saved them, like the way some children saved pennies in a piggy bank. I had an old jam jar once with a few coppers in it. It never amounted to much.

I remember the way through the hotel to the cleaners' staff room from the information day. There were only three people there, including me. On the way out of the small conference room, one of the other women, tired-looking with sparkly painted fingernails, plodded along beside me. She didn't think the hours suited her anymore. Her friend ran a dry cleaners and she said she might work there instead.

But I knew her real reason for not wanting to work at the Magnolia had nothing to do with the hours. During the presentation

I saw her eyes droop when a slide popped up on screen with the words: *Even when the hotel's not busy, the cleaning staff are.* The Magnolia paid by the hour, not by the room, which I prefer. Even if one of your rooms has a DO NOT DISTURB sign displayed, there are plenty of other things to be cleaning. This woman decided it sounded like too much hard work so good riddance to her. No hotel cleaning team tolerates a slacker.

They also gave us a hotel manual to bring home, which I read cover to cover and was pleased to see that although the Magnolia likes to think they do things differently, they really don't.

I push through the door at the end of the second corridor into a wider corridor where silence immediately descends. Now I am in the hotel. Dark green velvet covers the walls and soft recessed lighting glimmers from the ceiling. Under my feet, a thick pink patterned carpet cushions the soles of my shoes putting a natural spring in my step. I take a sharp breath. The flutters in my tummy rise up, sending a wave of tingling warmth all over my body. It's been nearly two weeks and the longing is becoming unbearable. If everything goes to plan, I might only have to wait a few more days.

The next door has a bar across it and an emergency exit sign. I push the lever down and shove it open, walking through into an airy stairwell, also carpeted with overhead recessed lighting. I check my phone to see the time. I'm twenty minutes early for my first shift, as planned.

I look up the stairwell to the floors above where the luxury bedrooms are located, where rich guests swish up and down the newly vacuumed corridors, their every need attended to. Soon I will be going in and out of their bedrooms with my skeleton key. A shiver of anticipation shoots up my spine.

I turn my head and peer down the stairwell into the floors below where the cleaners' staff room is located. This is where the carpet stops and well-worn linoleum continues. I tidy myself up, smoothing my skirt and pushing stray strands of hair behind my ears. For every first day I have my hair cut into a neat bob. It's become a tradition.

First impressions are crucial. You don't get a second chance. I have to make sure everyone I work with in every hotel likes and respects me, and quickly. I don't have time to repair a bad first impression or to work on slow-burner friendships with colleagues. They have to like me and trust me instantly in case there's a complaint made against me sooner rather than later. Like in hotel 5, a five-star in Birmingham, when I was still finding my feet and finessing my technique. A guest had several worn-looking books shoved into a bag squished down the side of a cabinet, as though forgotten or ready for the charity shop. I took the book balanced on top, not even looking at the title, and placed it carefully under the clean white fluffy towels on my trolley. It was too big to go in my apron, but I planned to wrap it in my shirt later when I changed and sneak it out that way. I assumed the guest wouldn't notice a book missing or even remember if they packed it or not. I don't read books.

It transpired quickly that the guest was a university professor who was researching something to do with the inequality in corporate finance—at least that's what the title of the book was when I checked it the next day.

The guest complained to the manager that the cleaner had taken her very special book. Thankfully, enough of my coworkers— and my supervisor—were on my side and quickly circled the wagons to ensure the manager gave me the benefit of the doubt. But one or two of the cleaners weren't so sure, throwing me curious glances. They hadn't warmed to me and accepted me as quickly as the others, and I hadn't noticed. I realized I needed to be more on the ball.

"Noelle would never steal. She's a good, hardworking girl," harped the women.

"It's too easy to blame the cleaner."

And then . . . exactly the words I always hope for: "Who'd take something like that anyway?"

With my heaving shoulders and red eyes, which I'd rubbed hard beforehand to give the impression of prolonged weeping, and flanked by the cleaners with their arms crossed, the management agreed that the guest had made a mistake and I was cleared of all blame for the professor's missing book.

I'd only been working there for two weeks and I left two weeks after that. My excuse this time: I'm moving to Oxford to help my aunt with my cousin who has Down syndrome.

Everyone was very sweet about my "family situation" and it was one of the biggest donations I've ever received. Even the chefs chipped in. I was actually quite overwhelmed and realized that it wasn't so much the effort I had put in to making them like me, but the fact they were simply a kind bunch of people.

I gave the donation money to a charity for Down syndrome minus twenty quid, which is in and around what I normally get as a leaving present. I was genuinely a bit sad I got caught out so early, but it was a lesson learned.

Make sure everyone likes and trusts me from day one, whatever it takes.

And no more books.

I reach the bottom of the stairs and step onto the raw concrete floor. It's immediately colder and a chill seeps into my bones as the damp smell of the basement parking garage shoots up my nose.

To the left, a heavy white door with a window in it leads to a brightly lit staff canteen with plastic tables and chairs scattered around. I glance through the window and see a couple of straggler cleaners finishing coffee and picking at plates of food. The end of the night shift. Not every hotel feeds their cleaners, but the five-stars do. To the right is another heavy white door leading into a tight corridor with rough brick walls on either side. I walk through to the end and enter a dingy room with gray lockers stacked on top of each other. A fluorescent strip light runs across the ceiling letting out a low humming noise, which I find strangely comforting.

This isn't too bad for a cleaners' staff room. It is, in fact, clean and there's a notice board. I have a quick look—pictures of babies and thank-you notes from guests. I like that. It means the cleaners here take pride in their work, so they'll be easier to disarm. When morale is low and people are unhappy about their working conditions and management, it can be harder to earn their trust and friendship quickly.

For now, I am alone in the staff room. I sit on the bench with my legs crossed and wait. I am fifteen minutes early. I hope someone will arrive soon to witness my promptness so my efforts don't go unnoticed.

I need to decide which Noelle I'm going to be. Will I be scatter-brain Noelle, or sweet, smiley Noelle, or low self-esteem Noelle or one of my others? Suddenly I'm exhausted by the thought of pretending to be someone else again. Being on my guard all the time and going to great lengths to make people like me takes effort.

A huge sigh escapes my lips and I slump a little on the bench. Maybe I'll be injured Noelle, which has been very useful in the past in emergency situations when things weren't going the way I planned. Cleaners always feel sympathy for an injured colleague, especially when they soldier on regardless of their pain. It's important no one needs to pick up their slack. But it does require a careful balance of hobbling and wincing and rubbing of the lower back. You don't want to overdo it and look like you're making a meal of it, which will annoy people, and you don't want to underdo it either or they'll forget you even had an injury in the first place. I could mix it up, I suppose. Start with injured Noelle who is also sweet Noelle.

My gut tightens. Why am I questioning this? I normally slip into whichever Noelle suits the mood. And I enjoy this part of a new job where I'm getting the other cleaners on my side as the anticipation builds to taking my first item. I let out a long steady breath to collect myself. I'm pleased to be in the Magnolia with its two hundred and fifty luxurious bedrooms just waiting to be cleaned. So why aren't I more excited? I tell myself I'm exhausted, especially after the last hotel I worked in.

Hotel 20 was a disaster from the moment I tied one of their flimsy aprons around my waist. And it was my own fault. It all started when

I spotted what I thought was a genius shortcut to gaining the supervisor's trust quickly so I could start taking things sooner.

Fernsby Manor is a three-star hotel in the Worcester countryside where I stayed for four weeks, although it felt like four months.

I had interviewed with the manager and the supervisor a week before I started and had generally felt good about working there. Bernadette, the supervisor, was a tough-looking woman in her forties, with broad shoulders and short brown hair with bangs. She pinned the bangs off her face with a little hair grip that she fiddled with a lot as it kept unclipping. She had a wide, open face and smiled a lot during the interview showing a set of small teeth. I thought the smiling was a good sign, but I should have been more careful.

My first day was like any other. I was already familiar with some of the hotel after a brief walkabout and I found the cleaners' staff room easily; it resembled a dusty store cupboard, with shelves on the wall to keep our bags and jackets. This was normal in smaller hotels—only the bigger ones tended to have nicer staff rooms. Hotel 5 even had a microwave and a little table. It was a shame I only lasted three weeks there.

Fernsby Manor had thirty rooms, most of which were in a modern block to the back of the main house, so the cleaning team was just six cleaners. We also took turns to vacuum the lobby and restaurant and bar areas too, which happens in most hotels, though I made sure to find out if the shift system was managed properly before I accepted. I'll clean any part of a hotel as long as I get my fair share of time in the guest rooms.

The other cleaners seemed quiet and distant, even with each other. I thought the lack of conversation and avoiding eye contact simply meant they weren't the sociable types. You expect some cleaners to keep themselves to themselves, of course, but an entire cleaning team, especially one so small? It should have been a red flag but I didn't see it. I told myself I'd get under their skin no problem and decided instantly to be scatterbrain Noelle, which had worked so well with the Jersey cleaners.

I went to tie my apron, dropping it on purpose. One of the cleaners glanced up and I gave her an embarrassed look—like I was mortified I'd dropped my apron. She gave me a small smile and went back to folding her jacket neatly to put it on a shelf. It was something, I thought. They're not totally impenetrable.

I was about to ask the woman who had smiled at me where I could find the duty roster, which I knew was pinned on the inside of the staff room door, when Bernadette bustled in wearing a stiff white shirt, straight black trousers and flat black slip-on leather shoes with tassels on the front. She stood in the middle of the room with her chubby hands on her waist, pushing her large hips out in front, like she was trying to bend her spine backward. It looked lazy and uncomfortable all at the same time.

"Good morning," she boomed, like a schoolteacher telling her class to stop talking. The other women mumbled "good morning" back.

She turned to me. "Welcome, Noelle. It's good to have you on the team. Have you met everyone?"

The women glanced at me, their faces shrinking into their shoulders like retreating tortoise heads. For some reason they didn't want to do introductions.

"Yes, I have," I said, covering for them, which I hoped would score me some points.

She eyed my apron. "Who gave you that old rag?" she said with disgust.

"It was in the locker," I said.

"I think we can do better than that. Follow me," she barked.

She turned and marched out of the staff room. I glanced at the other cleaners but they were looking anywhere except at me. I quickly ran after Bernadette, confident I'd win over the other women later.

The corridors in country hotels are often narrower and the ceilings lower than the bigger more modern hotels. They usually feel cozy and safe, but as I followed Bernadette along the hallway, I felt a little stifled and claustrophobic. I told myself I was missing the glassy wide open spaces of hotel 19, the four-star I was in before. I lasted four months there.

Bernadette entered a brown door under a staircase and I followed her in. It was a poky room with a desk and chair wedged into more than half of it, with a bent-looking plastic chair set in front of the desk. A large wooden crucifix hung on the wall and a cute little frog ornament on the desk smiled up at me. I peered closely at it and saw the word FROG engraved on the gray stone base and then the words below that said, FULLY RELY ON GOD. I realized then that the frog was in a praying position. Beside the frog was a small, well-thumbed copy of the Bible with red-colored edges.

While she rummaged through her desk drawers, I considered the crucifix, the frog and the Bible. I'd met religious people before—the Italian women in Jersey had been regular church goers. They would arrive into work after a Sunday service wearing silk dresses and jackets with shoulder pads looking fresh with makeup on and washed hair. They'd often be singing together and would give me a hug when they arrived. Watching them made me realize how going to church can make people happy. But it was different with Bernadette. It felt dark and heavy to be in her office. But again, I ignored the signs.

"Here we are," she said, pulling a new apron from the drawer, still in its plastic wrapping. It was then that I noticed the silver crucifix on a chain around her neck.

"I like your frog," I said sweetly, as though I was shy to say it.

Bernadette turned her eyes on me, assessing me.

"If only more of us did," I said. "You know, fully rely on God."

Her face transformed before me, as though melting away to reveal the real Bernadette.

"We're going to get on great," she said, beaming at me.

I beamed back at her and, in that moment, religious Noelle was born.

It was easy to keep it up for the first couple of days. I found some religious sayings online in case I needed to prove my religiousness.

I had a situation with a double occupancy where the guests had squeezed three more occupants into the room than was allowed. I could tell they'd had a drug party from the white powder remnants on a mirror, which they had ripped off the glass table. Bernadette came to inspect the room.

"God hates the sin, but loves the sinner," I said with a sad smile, dropping in one of my one-liners.

"Only if they're a Christian," said Bernadette. "Otherwise they go straight to hell." She was very unforgiving, I thought.

I took something on my second day, just a pair of tweezers from the bottom of a scummy toiletry bag that was unlikely to have been cleaned or checked in about twenty years. The tweezers were a safe bet. And after that I was on a roll, taking one item a day, confident that Bernadette would defend me to the death if a complaint came in.

I went about my cleaning business quietly and methodically, just like the other cleaners appeared to be. I didn't give them much thought and by the end of the first week I had taken a further six items, including a pair of ladies' clean white socks—no one's ever sure exactly how many pairs they've packed unless it's a small amount. If it's over five I assume they won't be keeping count. Nail scissors—a guaranteed favorite, especially in the early days in a new job. A green highlighter pen from a work bag—there were six inside, so I was sure the guest wouldn't notice. A small, tester-sized pot of foundation from a makeup case, never used. And a novelty cuff link that I found under a bed. It was one of a pair with red double-decker buses on them. It reminded me of London. Part of me missed London. Part of me was still afraid to go back.

But it didn't take long for Bernadette to begin to wear me down. I had become her instant new best friend, a role which included other responsibilities and activities.

She liked to start the day in her office reading to me from the Bible. She also insisted I spend my breaks with her and would bring an extra sandwich in her lunch box for me. I could just about stomach the cheese and ham, but the egg mayonnaise made me gag and I would have to say I'd finish it later and then flush it down the loo.

I was putting up with Bernadette to keep her placated so I could take things freely, which was all I wanted to do. It was the perfect scenario. I had written the other cleaners off as possible allies, but anyway it wasn't what I was used to and something at Fernsby Manor wasn't sitting well with me. There was something missing. I always talked to the other cleaners I worked with, and the supervisor was someone we normally talked about behind their back, even if we liked them. Yet here I was, in Bernadette's pocket like a pet hamster, storing all her religious teachings in my cheeks. If only I could spit them out.

I had never been as free to take things as I was in hotel 20, so I decided to stop feeling sorry for myself and just get on with it.

Then came a revelation and not one of a religious kind. It was the end of week two and, after successfully taking seven more items and suffering more Bible readings and smelly sandwiches with smug Bernadette, I was returning to the staff room after my shift when I heard chatter and laugher coming from behind the door. I stopped in my tracks and listened. It was the other cleaners talking and laughing among themselves. They sounded happy and fun, like cleaners normally do.

"She brings him home for the first time last night, right?"

"Your Chloe?"

"Yeah, the new boyfriend. So I shake his hand and say, goodbye."

"Huh? What did you say that for?"

"I don't know, do I? I think it was brain fog. I got goodbye and hello mixed up."

"That's like me the other night with Lenny. I got blow job and watch telly mixed up. He wasn't very happy."

They went off into peals of laughter.

"Yeah, he wanted to watch telly."

Even louder hysterics followed.

I stood there, listening at the door, feeling dizzy as the blood rushed from my head to my feet. The women did talk to each other. They were sociable. There were friendships and relationships here. I was suddenly annoyed, although I wasn't sure why. I didn't even know their names.

I was surprised I was so upset. I usually do everything I can to avoid social occasions and work nights. I should have been pleased to have saved myself the extra effort of becoming their trusted friend. But I wasn't. Instead, I felt betrayed. In that moment, I'd have given anything to be in the staff room chatting with the other women instead of hanging out with Bernadette in her office, no matter how much easier it was for me to take things.

I waltzed into the staff room ready to slap a smile on my face and say hi; ready to revisit plan B and become scatterbrain Noelle. But as soon as I set foot in the room, the chatter stopped dead.

I had been there for two weeks and they had pretended to be boring, quiet women with no personalities. And I had fallen for it. Me, the biggest pretender of them all.

"Hi," I said, determined to make conversation, if only to prove a point. "I lost my skeleton key. Will I get in trouble for that?"

One of them shrugged her shoulders but none of them even glanced at me.

I had been pushed out of the cleaners' circle, probably on day one, and I hadn't even noticed.

Apart from hotel 4, all the other cleaners I've ever worked with have been decent people. There's always a feeling of camaraderie—that we're all in it together. We support and help each other when needed and, even though I'm always a fake Noelle, that feeling of togetherness is part of the whole experience. I had raced headlong into creating a "special bond" with Bernadette, seeing it as a short-cut to what I wanted, and in the process I had pushed the other women away.

It was too late to change the situation. I couldn't admit to lying about being religious, and I was in too deep with Bernadette. She was now my only line of defense for when a complaint came in.

But as the beginning of week three loomed, I started to lose patience. Her constant talk about hell and damnation became more agonizing and I was sick of the Bible readings and the sound bites, not to mention the sandwiches. I wanted to tell her I had been to hell and looked the devil in the eye, so what does that make me?

Some days I felt sorry for her. Most of the time she was so afraid of Satan that she forgot to enjoy the good bits. Breaking point came in the middle of week three. We were in her office and she had just finished reading from her Bible when she looked at me sideways with a little smile.

"You feel it too, don't you?" she said.

I didn't know what she was talking about, so I just smiled.

"That feeling of belonging, of being part of something. It's what pulls us closer to God. You're the same as me, I can tell."

"Am I?" I managed to say, desperately trying to keep things vague.

"We were lost souls who found each other through Jesus. And now we have our own little community. You, me and Jesus. We should give thanks to the Lord for bringing you to me."

She bent her head and closed her eyes, in a prayer position.

I looked on, horrified. I was not like Bernadette and I certainly hadn't been sent by anyone to work in this hotel just for her benefit.

But Bernadette had been right about one thing. It was important for me to belong—just to my fellow cleaners, not to her.

Religious Noelle had turned me into a lonely outcast, and I was emotionally drained and exhausted from keeping up the pretense. For the first time in eight years, I started to wonder if I could continue going the way I was. Suddenly, the idea of moving to a new hotel filled me with weariness not excitement, which worried me. Had hotel 20 broken me? Had Bernadette sucked the life out of me forever? I knew at that moment I had to get as far away from Fernsby Manor as possible.

The following weekend the hotel was taken over by a wedding party. The hotel buzzed with squeals of raucous laughter and echoes of footsteps on the stairwells.

The women's rooms were bursting and sparkling with cosmetics and shoes and hair grips and fake eyelash and tanning kits. There was so much to choose from. I was assigned the job of preparing the bridal suite, which basically amounted to sprinkling rose petals on the bedspread and putting an ice bucket and champagne glasses in the room. But it was the bridesmaids' rooms I had my eye on.

They had interconnected rooms with four bridesmaids sharing two double beds. Clothes were draped over every surface with heaps of shoes everywhere, and they hadn't fully unpacked. The scent of perfume and hair spray was intense.

I flipped open one suitcase and spied a pair of delicate, cream pumps lying in among the sparkly tops. I picked them out and held them in my hands. They were soft and silky to touch, like shoes for a fairy. I put one pump carefully back where it was and pulled the suitcase lid over again. The other I wrapped in a cleaning cloth and carried out to my trolley where I slipped it under the dirty towels I had collected. All I had to do was finish my shift and get home with the shoe before the complaint was made either that night or in the morning. I knew, without a doubt, that the woman who owned the shoe would complain. And I was relieved. This was my exit strategy. The time had come to reap the benefits of my hard work and sacrifices in Fernsby Manor by taking something high risk and getting away with it. My body tingled with adrenaline and anticipation. I knew I would need my best excuse yet for leaving the hotel. Not only did it need to be convincing, but it also needed to be good enough to get rid of Bernadette for good.

When I arrived into work the following morning, Bernadette came rushing up to me in a sweat and ushered me straight to her office. I managed to look innocent, as she launched into an angry explanation about how the woman in room 17 had accused me, the cleaner, of taking her shoe. I opened my eyes wide, as though horrified and tried to muster the energy I needed to pretend to sob and cry, but Bernadette didn't give me a chance. She carried on talking, hardly coming up for air, about how she had put the manager in his place and that I had absolutely nothing to worry about. Sweat trails glistened on her forehead.

"I told him, in all my twenty years in this industry, if there is one cleaner that would never take anything from anyone, it's Noelle," she said, spitting as she talked, her self-righteousness spilling over into the stale air in her office.

I made my lower lip wobble, which was just enough for Bernadette to recite religious sayings about strength. "God gives his hardest battles to his strongest soldiers." I quite liked that one. I'd won the battle of childhood, if winning meant I was still alive.

Two days later I woke up early in my flat and heaved myself out of bed, troubled and unsettled. I gazed around at the dirty plates and cups lying on the thin carpet. Work shirts scrunched up and left on the floor instead of in my plastic bag for dirty clothes. This was not like me at all. I keep my flats and rooms clean. I was slowly falling apart and all because I'd become disconnected from the world I knew of hotel cleaners. I had no group, no team. Only Bernadette and her controlling ways. That was the day I left hotel 20.

I rushed in through the service door and straight to Bernadette's office. I stumbled through my words, trying to explain what was wrong, making my hands shake. Bernadette took charge straightaway and instructed me to breathe deeply. There was something about her manner that told me she was delighted to be the first port of call for my problem. A chance for her to be a savior.

"It's my little brother," I whispered. "He's been killed in a car accident."

Bernadette's hands rushed to her face, speechless. I was pleased I'd managed to shut her up for once. I told her I had to go home to Cornwall to be with my family and that my mother would need me to care for her now as my dead brother used to do it. Bernadette took my hands in hers and looked me in the eye.

"Ask Jesus to take the pain away."

"I will," I said, sniffling. And in that moment, as quickly as religious Noelle was born, she died, never to be seen again.

Bernadette wrote me a glowing reference and, to be honest, after everything I had put up with, it was the least she could do. I cleaned out my shelf in the cleaner's cupboard, ignoring the other cleaners who I could see hovering in the corner of my eye. They wanted to say something kind about my fictional dead brother, but I didn't want to hear it. Not because I was angry with them, but because I didn't deserve it. They had been right to treat me like an outsider. I abandoned them first.

I had already seen online that a cleaning agency was looking for staff for the Magnolia Hotel. I hadn't been back to London for years and my mind wandered to my mother. Was she still alive? Even if she was, London was a big enough city to hide in. I'd been away long enough and it was time to go back.

I yearned for the freshness of a five-star hotel with its wide corridors and high ceilings. I longed to vacuum luxury shag pile carpets and run my hand along the bottom of expensive toiletry bags. And I needed to be part of a cleaners' staff room again where I was one of the girls.

I sit up tall, pulling myself together. I smile a few times, warming up the muscles in my face, like an athlete preparing for a sprint. Forget about hotel 20 and focus on the present. You can do this, I tell myself.

Finally, the door swings open and a woman I recognize bustles in. She's in her mid-forties with light wrinkles around her brown eyes and heavily penciled eyebrows, which give an overly dramatic look, although I'm sure she was aiming for dynamic. She wears a dark blue dress suit, pressed to an inch of its life. Her hair is scraped up in a bun and her high-heeled court shoes clatter on the concrete floor. A hotel pass swings proudly around her neck and she carries a piece of paper and a large file in one hand. I take a glance at her neckline and I'm relieved to see no crucifix.

She stops when she sees me. Her face breaks into a well-practiced smile. I smile back at her, not just with my mouth but my eyes too—I read how to do that online. If you slightly squeeze your eyes together it endears you to people.

I spring to my feet.

"Hi, I'm Noelle. You're Julia, the supervisor?" I've decided to go with low self-esteem Noelle, for now anyway.

"That's right," she says.

"We met at the information day." I say it like I don't want to take up her time, that I understand she's busy.

"Of course I remember you, Noelle." She holds her hand out to shake mine. I act a tiny bit surprised, like I'm flattered she remembers little old me. I shake her hand, still smiling with my eyes. Her forehead crinkles in kindness. Score: One point.

She checks her watch and pins the piece of paper to the notice board.

"You're early," she says. Score: Two points.

"I wasn't sure how long it would take me to get here on the bus in rush hour traffic, so I gave myself plenty of time," I say, still beaming.

"We like staff who can think ahead, so keep it up." Score: Three points.

She taps her index finger on the notice she's just pinned up. It says: *The Magnolia voted 9/10 for cleanest hotels in London.*

"Wow, that's amazing," I say.

"Yes, I'm very proud of our staff." I manage to look eager and excited. She eyes me for a moment, deciding whether she likes me or not. Then she smiles, her mind made up. "Do you fancy a quick coffee before your shift?"

Score: Four points.

I follow her out of the staff room, back along the brick corridor and into the canteen. Julia waves over at the straggler cleaners; they half attempt a smile in return, but it tells me straightaway that there's little respect for Julia among the troops. I'm pleased to be having a coffee with her to ensure she likes me, but as soon as she's on my side, I'll pull back and put the necessary distance between us. I'm not risking a repeat of hotel 20.

Julia grabs a hot coffee pot from the top of a coffee machine. The smell of the overnight food in the serving trays mingled with the moldy scent from the cold walls makes my stomach turn. Julia fills two paper cups and passes one to me. She leans against the counter, apparently happy to stay standing.

"I remember your CV," she says. "You've worked in a lot of hotels and you're only twenty-five or something."

She has no idea how many hotels I've really worked in.

"We're delighted to have someone with your level of experience on our team."

"Thanks," I say.

"Are you a bit of a nomad then with all this moving around? Jumping from pillar to post?"

Great, the probing questions, exactly what I want on my first day. Better to get them out of the way as soon as possible. I drop my smile for a moment, as though I've been taken over by an uncomfortable memory.

"I've had to move around, mostly for family reasons."

"Oh, sorry to hear that. I hope everything's alright now."

She looks at me, expectant. She's fishing for personal information and makes no effort to hide it.

It takes a split second to decide which story to feed her. It needs to be the right story, one that will connect us on a deeper level. I glance at her left hand and see a gold band on her wedding finger. I swallow, as though mustering the strength to discuss a painful event.

"The last place I worked, well, that was a boyfriend thing," I say, adding a slight sadness to my voice. "We broke up and it was too difficult to stay."

"Were you working in the same hotel?" she asks, her forehead wrinkling with sympathy.

"No, he worked in a restaurant nearby." I look down for a second, signaling it's hard for me to talk about this. But she's all in now and wants to hear my sob story and be the person whose advice helps me move on from my emotional trauma.

"Breakups can be very painful," she says, looking into my eyes. "I've had my heart broken." Bingo, I think. The sharing doors are thrown wide open for us to step through into the bonding room, friends forever. Score: Five points.

"Really?" I say, as though anyone could dump Julia.

"Oh, yes," she says, like she agrees that it is unlikely anyone would do that to her. She tops up our coffee cups. Score: Six points.

"Before I met my husband, I was totally in love with this guy, a musician. He played the trumpet in this big orchestra. Anyway, he started coming home late from practice, you know?" I nod, like I know.

"Transpires he was fiddling one of the fiddle players." I look shocked. She smiles, pleased with her one-liner, which I'm sure she's used many times to tell the same story.

"I knew the girl," she says. "Nancy Tunes, can you believe it? That was her name. We went to the same school."

"That's awful," I say. "What did you do?"

"I packed up his gear in trash bags and chucked it and him out on the street." I open my mouth in awe, supposedly impressed by her audacity and bravery.

"I could never do that," I say. She squeezes my arm, a signal that the next thing she's going to say is of huge importance.

"You can't take shit from men. First rule of being a woman."

I nod, as though it's the best nugget of wisdom I've ever heard.

"But I got over it and you will too."

"I'm not sure I'm as resilient as you though," I say.

"I'm not resilient," she says. "I just met someone else."

She smiles at me, proud to be the one to pick me up off my feet and give me the strength to carry on with my life. Then she raises an eyebrow. It's my turn to share now.

"Mine's similar to yours," I say. "But she was a waitress not a fiddle player. I knew the girl as well." I take a little pause for effect. "She was my best friend." Julia's hand shoots to her mouth. The injustice of it.

"You poor thing. No wonder you had to leave," she says, oozing sympathy. Score: Seven points.

She grips both my arms now. "Right, forget about those bastards and make a new home for yourself here. Come and meet the rest of the team. They should be in by now."

"Okay," I say, making my eyes shine with appreciation. Julia nods, approving but firm. As much as she likes being a mentor to a younger woman, she doesn't want someone blubbing on the job.

"We're like one big happy family here," she assures me. She puts our paper cups in the recycle bin and walks out. I follow her.

I've actually never had a boyfriend, but that's not to say I've never had sex. I met a man in a pub once named Colin. He was a banker, five years older than me. Textbook good-looking with a firm body and a face like Action Man, which made me assume he was boring. How can you be interesting if people have looked at you with admiring eyes your whole life?

I don't think I'm unattractive, but I don't think I'm what some would call pretty or hot. My nose has a bump in it and there's a small gap between my two front teeth, although the rest are fairly straight. I've got high cheekbones and brown eyes with a small scar just above my right eyebrow. I'm more kooky, I suppose. And on this occasion, handsome Colin, his pockets stuffed with fifties, seemed to think I was a right sexy thing.

I let him buy me a drink and within minutes he had his arm slipped around my waist. He told me he'd seen me across the bar and couldn't take his eyes off me. I found that hard to believe, but I had the sense not to say it. I'd read online, by accident really, about how to attract a partner and it said to act aloof and not to give too much away, which wasn't hard for me. But I thought it was odd that he fancied me. There I was in a back street pub with my coworkers and Mr. Money Bags wants to buy me a drink. I'd only agreed to come to the pub to keep my colleagues happy.

I was working in hotel 9 at the time, a boutique three-star in Manchester, and the cleaners had insisted on a "work night out." Normally I excuse myself politely from any social activity as I worry about letting my guard down and revealing too much of my real personality, which is not something I can afford to do with colleagues. I work so hard to be a particular Noelle and win their trust that I have to protect it at all costs.

I agreed to join them on this particular night as I was planning to take from room 17 the following day. I had my eye on a light blue silk belt on a silk dress hanging in a wardrobe. I knew it was risky, but who would take the belt and not the dress? Well, someone like me would.

I was about to leave the pub, satisfied I'd spent just enough time with my colleagues to solidify their loyalty ahead of a possible complaint the following day, when Colin had sidled up to me.

I told him straight away I was a hotel cleaner, sure that would send him running for the hills. But he said it was interesting and I told him it really wasn't. But he still wanted to know all about my life as a cleaner and what it entailed. So I told him a fake story about the manager of a hotel being caught in bed with a well-known politician, an ex–prime minister. The next thing I know he's pressing me against the wall in the pub parking lot, kissing me hard.

His lips were full and soft and probing and I liked the feel of his tongue inside my mouth. My body tingled all over and the hardness in his groin made me breathless. With my coworkers in the background wolf whistling and cheering, I jumped in a taxi with him and headed back to his place.

He had a penthouse apartment in the city with a view directly over the river. It was a large glass box with floor-to-ceiling windows and reminded me of a giant fishbowl. He popped a bottle of champagne in the kitchen, while I squinted out of the window, opening and closing my mouth like a goldfish. In the distance, the river snaked its way through the twinkling night lights of the city. So this was how a city boy lived. It was okay, I thought, but in this world can you find a buzz that provides a rush so powerful you have to sit naked in a cold shower to avoid overloading your brain with chemicals?

That's how it feels sometimes when I take things and get them home. Maybe it was the same for Colin when he closed a big deal. I eyed him in the kitchen as he steadily poured the champagne. I didn't think so. He passed me a glass, which I took a sip from to be polite. I'd had two beers at the pub and that was my limit.

"You should probably know this is my first time," I said.

He'd just taken a huge mouthful from his glass and nearly choked. He coughed away the bubbles.

"First time in a penthouse or first time first time?" he asked.

"First time having sex," I said, to be perfectly clear. "Is that alright? Because if it isn't, I'll just call a taxi."

"Fine by me," he said. "I'm happy to show you the ropes."

Although I wasn't expecting much, I was hoping for a little more than what was offered.

I lay on his super king-sized bed, legs splayed as he stretched his body over me, panting, thrusting forward and backward inside me. It was a strange sensation but not one I could say, with confidence, I was actually enjoying. His face was screwed up and toward the end he was grunting. I stifled a laugh. Then it was over. Phew, I thought. He rolled off me and lay on his back. He asked me how it was, putting his hands behind his head, clearly happy with his performance. I told him it was wonderful, not to save his ego, but to save me the embarrassment of crushing his ego.

I waited until he fell asleep, slipped on my clothes and let myself out without making a sound.

After that experience, sex wasn't something I was keen to try again. And anyway, I got my kicks in other ways; the silk belt was beckoning me.

I follow Julia back into the staff room, which is now full of women jostling for space around their lockers, changing shoes and putting on aprons, getting ready for their shift. It's warmer now and the air is sticky with mingling droplets of deodorant and hair sprays. The women don't stop or look up as we walk in.

Julia grabs a newly pressed apron from the top of a locker and passes it to me. I put it over my head and tie it at the sides. It has the Magnolia flower crest and name on the front.

Julia puts her arm around my shoulders. Although I'm pleased she is acting like a friend already, I duck away from her, pretending to tie my shoelace, not wanting to give the other cleaners the wrong impression. I'm one of them, not one of the management.

"Everyone? This is Noelle. She's new," says Julia, loud enough so they can't ignore her. There are a few mumbled hellos, some even muster a smile, others barely give me the time of day. I don't mind—this is what it's like in big hotels. People come and go so you don't get excited when somebody new starts, as they probably won't last. I smile back at some of the women then drop my eyes, like I'm a little shy and overwhelmed.

"You'll be working on floor seven," says Julia.

"Whaaat?" comes a shrill voice from the far end of the staff room. Julia sighs. The other cleaners roll their eyes, some of them smile. A small woman gives Julia a fierce look. Julia nods to her, like she's got this.

The woman with the shrill voice, about my age, pushes her way from the back of the staff room to the front. Her thick dark curly hair is tied up in a ponytail that flows down her back, the ends fluttering against her slim waist. She has full pouting lips, a large chest and heavy eyelids. She's what I would term pretty. She speaks with a foreign accent and is articulate and passionate in her delivery.

"I thought I was being moved to floor seven," she says, her hands on her hips.

"I never said that," says Julia, keeping her voice calm.

"When Marguerite left, I asked you specifically to move me to floor seven."

"And I said I would think about it."

Now I'm wondering what's so special about floor seven and why I've been put there on my first day.

"Can we talk about this later, Fatima?" Julia says, a tad authoritative. She obviously feels at liberty to be tough on Fatima without being judged by the other cleaners.

"This is bullshit," says Fatima, flicking her ponytail back over her shoulder.

"That's enough now," says Julia. "You know we don't move people around willy-nilly."

Fatima scowls at Julia, looks me up and down and then turns on her heel and marches back to the end of the staff room, her ponytail swishing as it goes.

"I'm going to be on floor one forever," she grumbles.

"Stop your moaning" another voice says.

"Yeah, what's wrong with floor one?" pipes up another cleaner.

"I want better views, okay?" she says in a whiny voice. "It's not fair."

"Okay, thank you, Fatima," says Julia, smiling, hoping nobody else has a problem with me replacing Marguerite on floor seven.

"I don't mind which floor I go on," I say to Julia, just loudly enough for the other cleaners to hear.

"It's not your decision either, Noelle. Now, there are five of you on floor seven on rotation. We stay in our teams here. It gives our hotel a unique sense of togetherness."

"Yeah, right," shouts Fatima. Julia waves her hand in the air, ignoring Fatima.

I'm a little thrown. I didn't know I was going to be part of a permanent team that works together every day. At the induction day they had talked about teamwork being important, but I thought that was just in general. As much as I want to belong to the cleaner's inner circle, I don't really want to be stuck with the same people all day every day. It's more effort to keep up the pretense.

"This is Mali. She's one of the floor-seven team," says Julia, indicating the small woman who had seemed ready to take on Fatima.

"Hi," says Mali, holding out her hand.

"Nice to meet you," I reply. She squeezes my hand, shaking it hard, nearly crushing the bones in my fingers. Her English is clipped and confident. Her eyes assess me.

"She's too skinny," Mali says to Julia. "You need to eat more fat. Keeps you healthy," she says to me.

"Okay," I say, secretly delighted that she's made this comment. I'll be able to engage with Mali now on diet advice, which will help us to bond and make her like me. Hopefully, she'll be my buddy so I can build on it some more.

"You and me are going to get on fine," says Mali, pleased I've taken her comments in good spirit. You better believe it, I think to myself.

Another woman steps forward. She's tall and slim with an elegant frame and thick, silver hair in a high bun on her head, probably in her fifties. She smells a little of cigarette smoke and has a mischievous look in her eye.

"I'm Rose," she says. I shake her hand. It's an even, steady handshake, which tells me Rose is probably like that too.

"Pleased to meet you," I say.

"If you have any questions, ask me. The rest of these bitches don't know shit." She gives a deep throaty laugh. The other women give her a dismissive look, but there are faint smiles on their lips. Mali shakes her head, fondly.

"Only joking," says Rose. "None of them are bitches, only me." And I instantly like Rose too. Not only because I appreciate her humor but because she'll be very useful if and when I'm accused of stealing. Comedy can help to take the heat off. "And don't worry about Fatima," she says, lowering her voice. "She's always moaning." I give her a relieved look, like I had been worried about it.

The door to the staff room bangs open and a large woman sporting two double chins, thick glasses, and long mousy brown hair in a messy ponytail comes in. She stares around the room, flustered, her glasses magnifying her eyes.

"Sorry I'm late. My washing machine broke down and there was water all over the kitchen floor. If I didn't mop it up it might have seeped down to the flat below." Her bottom lip quivers as she blunders her excuses.

"It's alright," says Julia, a little tight-lipped. "This is Noelle. Noelle, this is Gaby, she's also floor seven."

"Hi, Gaby," I say and hold out my hand. She slips her hand into mine where it hangs squishy and limp. It's up to me to do the shaking, which I do gently, squeezing just enough to show warmth. She smiles at me but she looks sad and distracted. She shuffles along to her locker and the other women step aside to let her through. I'm not worried. Anyone with a handshake like that is not going to be a problem.

There are five on the team. That's four including me, so where's number five?

"Phil is also on your team," says Julia. I glance around at the sea of women but no one's looking up.

"Phil?" says Julia. I follow Julia's gaze to a woman with her back to us, rummaging in her locker. She has sleek, shiny black, shoulder-length hair and already has her apron on, which has been pressed very neatly.

"Phil," Julia says again, trying to hide her irritation at being ignored. This time Phil turns, a black headband in her hand.

"Hi," I say, shooting forward, big smile, hand outstretched. She eyes me, guarded, shakes my hand quickly and pulls away to put the headband on her head, which pushes her sleek hair off her face.

She's a little taller than me, about five foot six, with a petite figure. She has a pretty face; by that I mean it's symmetrical and doll-like with round open eyes and a heart-shaped mouth. Her lips have a light gloss on them and her sleek hair falls like silk curtains either side of her face. But rather than return my smile, she eyes me with interest, like she's appraising me.

I'm annoyed with myself. Meeting Gaby, Rose and Mali was so straightforward that I assumed meeting anyone else would go the same way. But Phil is what I call "a curious." She doesn't take people at face value and prefers to take her time before deciding if she likes someone. My overly friendly greeting could have made her suspicious and question whether I'm genuine.

I quickly look away and focus on Julia, but I can feel Phil watching me. Julia explains how we are one of many cleaning teams at the hotel, and floor seven should be our pride and joy. She points at Mali and tells me to buddy up with her. I'm relieved it's not Phil. I need time to think about how to handle her.

The service lift door rattles as it limps open and Mali, Rose, Gaby and Phil go to climb in.

"Penthouse!" a woman's voice calls out. We all step back from the lift as a team of five cleaners, looking immaculate and confident with their hair tied in neat buns and their shoulders pushed back, swish up to the lift.

"Running late again, girls?" says Phil, teasing, as the women enter the lift ahead of us. They give Phil a smug look as one of them presses the button for the penthouse. The lift doors close.

"Stuck-up cows," says Rose.

"I could be a *Penthouse* girl," says Mali, sucking in her cheeks and pouting.

"You better get yourself a pair of jack boots then," Rose says, laughing.

"I don't want to be on their team. Everyone hates them," says Gaby.

"Statistically there's more puke to clean up in penthouses, so they're welcome to it," Phil says.

I've never worked in a hotel with such a clear hierarchy among the cleaners. Floor one want to be promoted to floor seven. And the penthouse cleaners look down on everyone else.

The lift returns, the doors open and Mali, Rose, Gaby and Phil clamber in. I follow, stepping into the small, white, musty space. The lift wobbles as it takes the weight of us all. We squeeze up close to each other to ensure we all fit. I avoid looking at Phil. I'm planning on getting some information out of Mali before I try to connect with her again. I also have to prove myself to Mali so she recommends to Julia that I'm able to go solo from tomorrow.

The lift door shudders as it shuts and Gaby bursts into tears.

"Oh, for fuck's sake. What's happened now?" snaps Phil, but her forehead is wrinkled to show concern.

"Sorry, sorry," Gaby blubs, wiping her tears.

Rose looks at Mali and pulls a pained face, feeling sorry for Gaby.

"Gaby has a teenage son," Mali whispers in my ear and then gestures like she's injecting her arm.

"That's awful," I whisper back.

"He needs a good kick up the ass," sniffs Mali.

"What's he done now?" Phil says to Gaby.

"Last night he came into the flat and took the television. Now he won't pick up his phone. It's on layaway, so it's not like I can get another one. This one won't be paid off for nine months."

"What did I tell you?" Phil crosses her arms.

"Change the locks," sniffles Gaby.

"And did you?"

Gaby shakes her head. "It's expensive to do that, you know?"

"Is it as expensive as a new TV?"

"It's not the TV," says Gaby, looking at her feet. "It's the fact he took it."

"Call the police and report him," says Mali.

"He's my son," says Gaby, appalled at Mali's suggestion.

"No, he's a junkie," says Phil. Gaby resumes sobbing.

Rose puts her arm around her and talks in a low, steady voice. "I don't know why you're so surprised, honey? Everybody knows kids fuck up your life and your body. I mean, you still can't sneeze without a bit of pee shooting out, can you?" Gaby nods and wipes her tears. "It's just the way it is," says Rose.

But Phil shakes her head, not agreeing with Rose. I sneak a glance at Phil, intrigued. The other women look up to her, which means her opinion of me matters even more.

She turns and peers at me, assessing me, almost amused. I look away, my heart beating faster but not in a good way. I need a plan to get her to like and accept me. I won't be able to take anything until she is firmly in my friend zone.

The lift door slides open and we bundle out, immediately speaking in hushed voices. Hotel cleaners should be seen but not heard. Even though we're not on the main guest corridor yet, the rules apply from the basement up.

I give Gaby a sympathetic look. Gaby manages an apologetic smile. Showing compassion is a good way to curry favor but I also feel genuinely sorry for the woman.

Phil's already at the service supply cupboard riffling in her apron pocket. We all hurry to catch up with her. Phil pulls out the key to the cupboard and opens it.

So, Phil has the key to the supply cupboard. Julia trusts her. She's one step up on the hotel cleaner's ladder of respect. But this doesn't bode well for me. If I need anyone on the team on my side, it's Phil and so far she's a complete mystery to me. Just keep smiling, I tell myself.

Phil opens the cupboard and flicks the light switch on the wall. Inside are five cleaning trolleys, lined up like soldiers, locked and loaded. Rose offers to take care of the linen and towel trolley.

"Don't make it sound like you're doing us a favor," says Phil. "It's your turn anyway."

"Hey, anything I do for you bitches is a favor," replies Rose with a big grin.

Mali pulls her trolley out first. Then Rose. Gaby, who has stopped crying now, smiles sheepishly at Phil. Phil gives her a big hug, holding her tight, which makes Gaby look like she's going to start crying again. Phil holds a finger up indicating to Gaby to stay strong. Gaby swallows, managing to hold back the tears. She yanks her trolley out, and then Phil rolls hers out, leaving one left at the back of the cupboard. Since I'm Mali's buddy today, I figure I don't need it.

"No one's going to get it for you, princess," says Phil, her eyes laughing at me. Suddenly I'm struck dumb. Which Noelle should I be now? Low self-esteem Noelle or sweet Noelle? I feel like none of my previous personas are going to work. I'll have to wing it.

"But I'm only helping Mali today," I say, trying to keep my voice level, not too shy, not too confident.

"Yeah, well, she doesn't like anyone touching her trolley," says Phil. I glance over at Mali. Mali gives a shrug.

"It's an OCD thing," she says.

"I've told you, you want to sort that shit out. That kind of thing is contagious," says Rose.

"You can't catch OCD. It's not like smallpox," snaps Mali. Rose grins at Mali. There's no malice in her words. She just enjoys winding Mali up.

"I don't want any of your OCD germs falling onto me, right? I've got enough problems," Rose says. Phil and Gaby grin. This is everyday banter to them.

"No problem," I say, bright and breezy. I stroll into the cupboard, pull my trolley out with one hand, swivel it around and proceed to go through all the compartments to see what's missing. I know they're all watching me—I've clearly done this before. I pull out a handful of colored cloths.

"It's green for glass and blue for wood here, right?" I ask. I know full well that it is, as I was told at the information day. Some hotels use different colors for different surfaces, but it's generally the same across the board. Red is always for toilets. I don't want to seem over-confident and asking questions can make people like you.

"Didn't they tell you that at the information day?" says Phil, locking the cupboard door. "And it's in the hotel manual."

"Yeah, I'm just checking," I say.

"So it's a stupid question then," says Phil.

Mali, Gaby and Rose drop their eyes. My face falls. I wish it hadn't, but I'm too surprised to stop it.

"Leave the new girl alone," says Mali.

"Yeah, it's her first day," Gaby says, joining in. Good, Mali and Gaby are on my side.

"She's got to be able to take a ribbing if she's going to be working with us," says Phil. "Can you take a ribbing, Noelle, or are you a bit precious? Do we have to watch what we say with you around? Are you going to go running to Julia?"

"No," I blurt out, genuinely appalled, hoping I didn't overdo it earlier with Julia and give the wrong impression. "You're the one with the key to the cupboard. If anyone's going to go running to Julia, it's you."

The words leave my mouth in a panic. I sound defensive, which is not in keeping with any of my Noelles. I manage to look awkward, hoping to portray a sense of vulnerability. At least they're talking to me, I think.

There's a pause. No one says anything. Then Phil raises her eyebrows at me. Mali grins. Gaby waves her finger in the air and does a twirl—a celebration of the put-down. Rose grips her chest, pretending she's been stabbed in the heart. Phil runs her eyes over me, assessing me.

"You're not a doormat then?"

"No," I say. I have to own it now and hope I can move on from it quickly.

"Then why are you acting like one?"

"I'm not," I bluster. Phil turns to Mali, Gaby and Rose.

"What are you standing around for?"

"We're waiting to see if you have a fight. My money's on Noelle," says Rose.

Mali grabs me, pushing her trolley ahead. "Let's get cleaning, baby." I pull my trolley along beside her. Phil looks on after us, with a furrowed brow.

One of my colleagues is suspicious of me. If I don't reverse that soon, I'll have to invent an emergency excuse and leave. First-day rules.

Chapter 4

Mali parks her trolley outside room 703. The doors are clad in a dark brown cushioned material. If you laid it on the ground you could sleep on it. Mali nods to the area in front of her trolley. I slide my trolley ahead of hers.

"Not touching," she barks at me.

I make sure it's at least a foot in front. I'm acting like I totally accept this quirk about her, which I do, but I want to make sure she knows I do.

She takes a black skeleton key card from her apron, attached to a plastic cord, and presses it against the small, silver scanner box on the hotel room door. It clicks and Mali pushes the door open a little, staying outside.

"Hello, hello, room cleaning?" she calls. She waits for a moment and then happy there's no one inside, she goes to her trolley and moves around it like an octopus, quickly grabbing antibacterial sprays, cloths and her vacuum cleaner from its bracket. She enters the room and I follow. I'm about to close the door behind me leaving it ajar when Mali shakes her head at me.

"No, no, no. We leave the doors wide open here. Julia prefers it. It keeps us safe from any guest who wants to, beep beep." She grins at me, squeezing her own breast, like it's a horn.

"Sure," I say, not missing a beat and opening the door.

Panic bubbles up inside me. Like the working in teams thing, this also wasn't mentioned at the information day or in the manual either. With the door wide open anyone can walk in without warning, so I will have to be extra vigilant. When the door is only ajar, most people knock first, even guests.

But then a surge of excitement rushes to my head and I'm surprised. Do I like this complication? With the chance of being caught red-handed the stakes are raised and the thought of it makes my body tingle all over. Nothing seems to be going according to plan in the Magnolia, so I might as well embrace it, especially if I have to leave by the end of the day.

The room is huge, at least three times the size of a regular hotel room in London with a four-poster bed and a grand, velvet chaise longue positioned at the foot of the bed. A giant chandelier hangs from the ceiling. Its glass droplets glimmer in the sunlight poking through the slither of a gap in the closed curtains. Mali fully opens the thick silk curtains using the cord string and then fixes each side in place with the ties made of the same material. Compared to hotel 20, this is the height of luxury and my heart swells, grateful to be here.

Mali glances around the room and sighs. "Rich people," she tuts, putting down the vacuum cleaner. "Dirty bastards sometimes."

Clothes are strewn on the floor and the bedclothes have been rolled up in a ball. Smeared glasses and used cups have left circular stains on the sideboard and marble table, and the garbage can is overflowing with junk food wrappers and beer cans.

We put on blue gloves and start to pick up the clothes. Tracksuit bottoms, one leg inside out. Black socks, also rolled into balls. A scrunched-up dark blue shirt. This is a single occupancy, one man.

Taking from male guests isn't normally enough of a buzz for me, but with the door wide open and Mali in the same room as me, I might get more out of it now. Maybe even without Phil on board, I could take a risk. The mere thought of taking something on my first day, something I have never done before, awakens the flutters in my stomach. I glance up, feeling Mali's eyes on me. I'm aware that my cheeks must be flushed from the rush of adrenaline just thinking about taking something so soon. She tips her head back laughing hard although it sounds more like a clown's giggle.

"You're squeamish," she says. "Did you think a fancy hotel like this didn't have filthy guests?"

I'm not sure why she's saying this to me until she points at my right hand. I look down to see I'm holding a pair of white Calvin Klein boxer shorts. They are inside out and along the gusset is a brown smudge. I pull a face of disgust.

"No one likes the shitty pants," says Mali giggling again.

I quickly fold the pants up and put them in the pile of folded clothes on the chair. "I'll check the bathroom," I say.

"I hope there's no little presents for you in there," she says, still amused.

I go back to my trolley outside the room and select the bleach, my own antibacterial spray, more blue gloves, and a couple of red cloths. I also grab some small garbage bags and kitchen towels, just in case Mali is right and there's a turd on the bathroom floor; that's only happened to me once in my cleaning career and it's not something you forget.

I move around to the back of the trolley, take the mop and bucket from its holder and wander back into the room all the while contemplating if I should take something now.

Mali looks up at me as I walk in. It's a hard look that makes me stop in my tracks. She eyes the spray in my hands and the mop and bucket.

"I didn't touch your trolley," I say.

"Good girl," she says. "You learn fast."

I lower my head, not wanting to seem smug, and scuttle toward the bathroom as Mali gets on with making the bed. I hear her mutter the words "filthy" and "son of a bitch."

"One day I will be the supervisor then the manager, you know?" she calls out to me. "That's the only reason I'm here and the only reason I do this shit. Reach for the stars."

I smile to myself. There's something about Mali that's growing on me—she seems to have determination and probably doesn't let anything get in her way. It's the same for me with taking things.

I push the bathroom door open and peer inside. The floor is clear, not even a wet towel and all the guest's toiletries are in a bag made of soft floppy leather.

"It's okay. No presents," I call out to Mali.

And no need for clean towels. Towels on the rail mean the guests will use them again. Towels in the bathtub mean they want them changed. Most guests keep their towels for a couple of nights at least in an attempt to help the environment.

"Hurry up," Mali shouts. "We're behind schedule now." I hear the vacuum cleaner start up. Good, I think. As long as it's on, I know where she is.

I move quickly to the toiletry bag and carefully part the zipper so I can see inside. Sitting on top of the toiletries is a six-pack box of condoms. I open it carefully and see there are five left. Mr. Skid Mark got lucky. Shall I take one? Is he going to say a cleaner took one of his condoms? Will he notice?

Taking leave of my senses, I slip one of the blue, shiny squares into the front of my apron and take a deep breath.

"What are you doing?" Mali barks at me like a sergeant major.

I flick around to see her standing in the bathroom doorway, a fierce look on her face and the drone of the vacuum cleaner ticking over in the bedroom behind her. My heart hammers hard in my chest.

"This was on the floor," I say, keeping calm, referring to the toiletry bag.

"I told you to hurry up," says Mali, her forehead wrinkled in irritation.

It's funny how a wrinkled forehead can mean different things. Sometimes concern and compassion, other times deep concentration and effort. When my mother wrinkled her forehead it signaled rage. But right now, with Mali, it was definitely irritation.

"I only said you could buddy up with me because I thought you would be fast. Julia said you were experienced."

"I am. I am fast. Give me five minutes."

"I'll set my watch," she says. And I know she means it.

"If you're too slow, I will tell Julia you are rubbish." She returns to the bedroom to finish cleaning. Suddenly I'm not so fond of Mali.

I pull the front of my apron open a little and glance down at the single condom packet, shimmering under the bright halogen lights. All things considered this is probably the riskiest "lift" I have ever done, excluding Alison Rogers, of course, but that was more of a pickpocket situation.

I get to work on the bathroom and I know I'm good. I have speed, precision and attention to detail. Five minutes later, Mali is at the door again, tapping her watch as I finish mopping the floor, the last thing you do when cleaning any room. You don't want to undo your hard work by walking all over your just-cleaned floors. Mali has a quick glance around and nods, impressed.

"You're safe, for now," she says.

Mali strides along the corridor to the next room, pushing her trolley in front of her. If it wasn't for the thick pile carpet under her feet, it would sound like marching. Farther down the corridor I see Gaby and Rose buzzing around their trolleys, while behind them, Phil collects linen from the supply trolley full of fresh towels and bed linen. Her head flicks up and catches my eye. She gives me a wry smile, as though she's got my number.

Is it possible for someone to be able to see through another person and know what they're thinking? I need to get a grip. Of course she doesn't know what I'm thinking. I'm the one in control here. I'm the one with a condom in my apron. Phil's probably just a bully. I've dealt with bullies before.

Hotel 4 was a smart, four-star in Brighton where I nearly didn't make it through the first day. It took all of two minutes to realize one of the women was a bully, but not the type I was used to—she was more of a stealth bully, or at least she thought she was. She lacked subtlety in my opinion.

I met most of the other cleaners on my first morning in the staff room, which was a small single bedroom with the furniture taken out and replaced by lockers and benches. The ensuite was the cleaner's toilet. I had read in their guidelines that the cleaners were expected to clean the staff room. But it didn't look like that happened very often, given the huge cobwebs and black dusty corners.

It was a medium-sized cleaning team, nine in total, and they seemed friendly enough, although maybe a little guarded. I had decided to be sweet Noelle and asked the other women about the schedule and supply cupboard locations, like I was nervous I would mess up. A couple of them answered my queries but didn't take it as an opportunity to make further conversation with me. I didn't think much of it and remained confident I'd get in their good graces easily enough. Maybe even take something by the end of my first week.

But my high hopes evaporated when Clarissa, the queen bee cleaner, breezed in, carrying a paper bag and cooing hello to everyone. She had a tiny nose and a round face with freckles. Her brown, curly hair was tucked behind her ears making them stick out. She reminded me of a baby bear.

She quickly went around the room talking to each person.

"Shelley? How's that sore foot of yours?"

"Sarah? Did you get out for your walk this morning?"

She didn't wait for anyone to answer and just moved on to the next person, like asking the question was enough.

She held up the paper bag. "Donuts for everyone at break," she said with a big smile. "Except you, Lucy. You're on a diet, right?"

She turned her eyes on a small, quiet woman in the corner wearing a long skirt with thick ankles squashed over the top of her flat shoes. Lucy, her back to the room, carried on tying her apron. Clarissa pulled a mock sad face and sidled up to her.

"I'm joking. Of course, you can have a donut. We all know how much you like a sugary snack in the afternoon." She then turned to me, with inquisitive eyes.

"And who have we got here?"

"I'm Noelle. Nice to meet you," I said and held out my hand.

She looked me up and down and then took my hand, glancing back at the other women and grinning, like shaking my hand was in some way ridiculous. She took her hand away and wiped it on her apron.

"I hope you're a bit tougher than the cleaner before you. Wendy only lasted three days."

"I'll do my best," I said, keeping to sweet Noelle.

"I'll do my best," she said, mimicking my voice. "Chillax there, I'm not your boss, No-elle." She accentuated the syllables in my name. "You too, Loo-cy?" Lucy still had her back to Clarissa.

Clarissa returned to the rest of the women now in a huddle. She said something quietly to them, something I couldn't hear, and then the women burst out laughing. I glanced at Lucy and saw her face and neck redden. I told myself I'd give it to the end of the day to see if I could somehow make this work, otherwise I would have to leave. First-day rules.

During break, I walked into the staff room and found Clarissa and her posse sitting on benches eating donuts together. There were two tired-looking white roll sandwiches covered in cellophane on a tray. The last of the sandwiches provided by the kitchen. I wasn't hungry and it looked like ham and tomato. Not something I eat anyway.

"Oh, sorry, No-elle, no more donuts left."

"No worries," I said, relieved I didn't have to turn one down. I don't like donuts either. But then I saw her handing out more to her group. She still had plenty in the bag. I realized being denied a donut was supposed to upset me or make me feel left out. It didn't. Instead, I was beginning to think Clarissa was an idiot and the women around her were spineless.

But never underestimate a bully. In the same way a bully should never underestimate their victim, especially when they don't know them.

Lucy was nowhere to be seen during break. She must be hiding, I thought, which annoyed me. I was annoyed with Clarissa for causing this hassle but I was also annoyed with Lucy for letting Clarissa control her like this.

At the end of my shift, I saw Lucy exit the lift and head for the services exit with her jacket and bag over her arm. I ran to catch up with her. She glanced at me but carried on walking. I followed her.

"Do you know where the bleach is? I want to give this a deep clean," I said, indicating my mop, making an excuse to start a conversation.

"Don't ask me," she said. "I just handed in my notice. I'm out of here."

"You're leaving?" I said, genuinely stricken to be left on my own with Clarissa and her goons.

"I don't have to put up with that shit. You saw what Clarissa's like."

"She's a bully, that's all."

"She's more than that. She's a psycho. Good luck."

I looked on as Lucy marched down the dark corridor, pushed the service entrance door open and disappeared into the dusky evening.

I'll leave too, I thought. It's going to be way too difficult to get people on my side. I made my way back along the corridor to the staff room, as Clarissa and three of the other women were leaving. Clarissa blocked the doorway, eyeing me with amusement.

"Sorry, do you want to get by?" said Clarissa, not moving.

"After you," I said, keeping up my sweet girl routine. I wasn't about to blow my cover just for her. I stepped aside giving Clarissa a wide berth. She smirked at me and strutted past, the other women following.

"By the way, the supervisor likes us to keep our lockers tidy," she called back to me with a fake smile. As she marched down the corridor, flanked by her minions, I noticed how her feet turned out as she walked, like a penguin. There was nothing special about Clarissa. She'd just been allowed too much power.

I wandered into the staff room and opened my locker door. Inside was a half-eaten, mushy donut with jam smeared everywhere. Someone had wiped the inside of my locker with the donut like it was a cloth.

It was clearly time to abort. I needed to find the supervisor, Sonya, who I hadn't seen since I'd arrived and only met once at the interview. I'd give her a family sob story and that would be it. Next hotel here I come.

But as I went to pull open the staff room door to leave, my throat tightened and my head felt hot.

I'd already let one person get away with bullying me in my life—I couldn't let Clarissa off the hook too. And if anyone could get rid of her, I could.

For the next few days, I kept up the sweet Noelle routine, ignoring Clarissa's put-downs and cackling laugh, like I wasn't bright enough to see her comments were meant to hurt me. I simply blended into the background, biding my time.

Clarissa had the best job, of course, in charge of cleaning the superior suites on the top floor. Every day she picked one of the other women to help her, like they were her favorite for the day, and today it was Shelley, an older woman with tired eyes and a heavy walk. The rest of her cronies cleaned floors two and one and I was left with the ground floor "family rooms" with their extra daybeds, sticky sweets in the carpet and small plastic toys you could easily slip on. There were only four family rooms so I was left to clean on my own.

During our break, while Clarissa and Shelley were in the staff room with everyone else, I ventured up to the superior suites, taking the back stairs instead of the lift so as not to be seen. I had been avoiding the staff room during breaks to ensure they wouldn't notice me missing. I crept on to the carpeted, light-filled corridor. All was still and quiet.

I used my skeleton key to enter room 301 and closed the door quietly behind me. I had a quick look around. I was disappointed by the lack of luxury in the superior suits. They were too chintzy to be elegant, with brightly colored tasseled cushions that clashed with busy floral wallpaper. The room was neat and tidy. The bed was made and a smell of detergent wafted from the ensuite bathroom. The room had already been cleaned. It was a double occupancy with two sets of luggage. At a glance, I couldn't see anything of great value lying around, only things I might take myself, like a hair bobble with a heart on it beside the bathroom sink. But I wasn't there for me and I needed to be quick. Clarissa could return to the floor at any moment to finish the rest of the rooms.

I decided to try the next room instead and was about to leave when the sun's rays blazed in through the window, just out from behind a dark cloud where it had been all morning. It bounced off something shiny beside the bed, making it flash and glisten, catching my eye.

It was an expensive-looking man's watch, laid out flat on the stainless-steel base of the bedside lamp. I would never have noticed it if it wasn't for the sun. I guessed the watch was worth a few hundred pounds. Anything more valuable than that and the guest would either have put it in the hotel safe or not left it behind in the first place. I slipped the watch into the front of my apron. I didn't get a buzz from taking it as I was only borrowing it.

I snuck out of the room as the service lift door pinged at the end of the corridor and Clarissa and her "helper for the day" stepped out, pulling their trolleys behind them. I dived across the corridor and into the stairwell, leaning against the closed door and listened, waiting for Clarissa to pass by or come after me. If she had seen me, I would have had to put the watch back. But the trolleys trundled past and down the corridor.

After our shift, the whole cleaning team was in the staff room, including Clarissa, who was whispering to the other women. I could hear them sniggering, but I didn't care.

The door to the staff room flew open and Sonya, the supervisor, entered in a fluster. Because this was only hotel 4 and early on in my career, I didn't realize at the time just how bad Sonya was at her job. She was never around, never available and seemed very keen to avoid problems. Her lack of presence was probably why Clarissa had managed to take control.

"Everyone sit down, please," said Sonya in a weary voice.

I did as Sonya said and sat down on the bench in front of my locker.

"We have a staff night out. We can't be late for the booking," Clarissa said as she glanced over at me, a little smug. I managed to ignore her by becoming engrossed in a fingernail. I was relieved I didn't have to go on her work night out. Being the outsider certainly had some benefits.

I did as Sonya said and sat down on the bench in front of my locker.

"We've had a complaint from a guest. He says his watch is missing from his room."

"Which room?" asked Clarissa, like she would sort this out.

"Third floor. 301," Sonya said, looking straight at Clarissa.

"One of mine?" she said, as though this was laughable.

"I just need to check your bags before going home, okay? Manager's orders."

This is what happens when you take a valuable item. The complaint comes in immediately and bag checks are inevitable. This is why I only ever take high-risk items at the end of a day. It gives me enough time to get home and hide it. There's no point checking bags the day after.

"This is ridiculous," Clarissa said. "I don't like what you're accusing me of."

"It's not just you. Everyone has a skeleton key, don't they?"

I could see Clarissa mulling this over. She was getting a bad feeling. The other women sat down too with their bags at their feet. Clarissa stayed standing, too jumpy to sit.

"You first, Clarissa," Sonya said, holding out her hand to take Clarissa's bag.

But Clarissa saved her the trouble, opening it herself and rummaging around inside it. "If it's in here, I've been set up," she said with a snarl.

Her face dropped as she pulled out the expensive watch, holding it in her hand like it was a dead spider. She stared at her posse of women, all of whom looked gobsmacked.

"Who did this?" she spat.

One of the women frowned at her. "I didn't take no watch."

All the women shifted in their seats, moving their upper bodies slightly away from Clarissa. I was shocked to see Clarissa accuse her "loyal friends" so quickly, but not so shocked by how quickly they abandoned her. The women didn't really like Clarissa and she knew it.

"Well, I didn't take it either," she said, almost foaming at the mouth in frustration.

She turned to Sonya. "Somebody went into that room after I cleaned it, took the watch and planted it in my bag."

Her voice went up a couple of octaves, verging on hysterics. She was crumbling, she was breaking. I would have felt sorry for her, maybe even a little guilty, if she hadn't been so mean.

I sat quietly on the bench, innocently observing. Clarissa had gravely underestimated me. She assumed I wasn't a threat—timid, sweet, easy-target Noelle. It didn't occur to her for a second it could have been the new girl.

Sonya snatched the watch from her. "Come with me," she said.

"I just told you, I didn't take it," she yelled at Sonya.

"Let's see what the manager says about that," Sonya said and walked out with the watch in her hand.

Clarissa's face fell and her shoulders slumped. There was nothing she could do. There was no bully tactic she could use to get her own way this time.

She grabbed her bag and coat and bent down close to the other women's faces.

"This is not over," she hissed at them, threatening. The women looked back at her with bland expressions. They had already moved on. Clarissa stomped out of the room, slamming the door behind her.

And that was the end of Clarissa. I was a little worried at first that she'd somehow talk her way out of it and come back and wreak revenge, but rumor had it she'd blubbered like a baby when the police showed up.

The mood in the staff room lifted immediately. The other women felt guilty about being a bully's mate and made an effort to be nice and include me in things. It worked in my favor and sweet Noelle blossomed, along with my confidence to take things, which went very well for the next three and a half months.

Then one afternoon, in my last room of the day, I took a rather worn, leather cover for a passport. The passport was half hanging out of it, so I hoped they'd assume it had fallen off.

I dropped the cover into the front of my apron and felt so dizzy with adrenaline that I had to lean against the desk in the room to steady myself. Then my heart rate slowed as the familiar warm tingling sensation spread through my body.

The guest complained and I sniveled and sobbed, as all the women came to my defense, adamant I would never steal. Sonya agreed. "Who would steal a cover for a passport? It doesn't make any sense."

Two weeks later I was gone. I said my father had had a stroke and I needed to go home and help.

But I learned some valuable lessons in hotel 4. When people feel guilty they'll do just about anything to make themselves feel better. And never let a bully get away with it.

Phil's not a bully, I decide. She's nothing like my mother or Clarissa. She's just smart.

A hard tap on my shoulder makes me jump. Mali's face is only inches away from mine and she is frowning again.

"What's the matter with you?" she whispers. "Are you a flake? Staring into space wondering when your prince will come?" She giggles, again like a clown, which is unsettling but I'm getting used to it.

"I was thinking there are so many rooms to get through, it would be better if I went solo."

"That's not going to happen unless I say so," says Mali, narrowing her eyes. "The last girl who buddied up with me was fired at the end of the day. Julia will do what I say, so focus or you'll be out of a job."

She won't get me fired, but I better play along to keep her sweet.

"Sorry, Mali, sorry."

"Okay, okay," she says, throwing her arms around in exasperation. "I like you, but you have problems."

I do have problems, I think. One big one at the moment, called Phil.

Mali opens the next bedroom door with her skeleton key, just an inch, and calls inside. "Hello? Room cleaning?" She waits a moment and then pushes the door open. She grabs her sprays, cloths and vacuum cleaner again and I follow her inside.

There's a cot in this room and a packet of nappies and baby wipes on the side. It smells sweet, like rooms with babies staying in them always do. Other than that it's relatively neat.

"Ah, nice people, nice people," says Mali. "You can help me make the bed and do everything with me this time so you learn." I nod, feigning enthusiasm, as we pull the covers and pillows off the bed and readjust the sheet.

"Have you worked here long?" I say, putting on my best casual voice.

"Six years," says Mali. "But I am moving up. I'm doing a night course in hotel management."

"That's amazing," I say. And I really believe it is. I've never thought about doing any kind of course. If I did, what would it be in? I have a quick think. Nope, nothing springs to mind.

"Have you always worked in the same team with the same people?"

"No, no, no. Me, Gaby and Marguerite worked together for four years but Rose and Phil started later. Phil has only been here for one year. But we are a unit, like in the army. We cover each other's asses. That's why everyone wants to be on floor seven. Gaby doesn't like Fatima, that's why she didn't get moved. She's too loose with her lips," Mali makes her hand move like a mouth talking.

"You must have been sad when Marguerite left then," I say.

"Her husband got a promotion. She didn't need to work anymore. And she has four kids so she wasn't part of the tequila crew." Mali moves her hips in a circle as she says "tequila crew," and then giggles again.

I wonder if they'll expect me to be part of the tequila crew, whatever that involves. But I'm not worried. I'm an expert at dodging work night's out.

"I thought since Phil had the key to the supply cupboard that she'd been here the longest," I say, still aiming for casual. Mali waves her hand in the air, dismissive as I help her pull the duvet up over the bed and pull it tight at the edges.

"Phil has been to college and she has office experience, so Julia gives her responsibility. But Phil doesn't want to be in management, she only wants to clean."

"What did she do before?" I ask. Mali eyes me with her hands on her hips.

"You talk too much and you ask too many questions. Are you undercover police?" She throws her head back and laughs.

I laugh too but decide to stop asking questions. She shakes a pillow, smooths it out, and then stands it perfectly plumped and upright at the top of the bed. I follow her lead, doing exactly as she did. My pillow, thankfully, is just as perky as hers.

"You want to know about Phil?" she says, lowering her voice.

"It's my first day. I'm getting to know you all."

In answer, Mali singsongs my words back to me, "I'm getting to know you all. I'm getting to know you all." She then says, "Now stop talking and get cleaning," clapping her hands. I rush out of the room. "And don't touch my trolley," she yells after me.

I take a deep breath at my trolley, gathering my thoughts. I need to be careful. Mali is sharp and thinks most things that aren't funny are funny. And Phil is smart and definitely on to me, like she senses I'm hiding something. I need a way in, a point of connection. Rose or Gaby might be better sources of information on Phil. I'm not prepared to leave and start another job somewhere else. It's more waiting and extra hassle I don't need.

But a voice in my head is screaming *abort, abort*. Like in hotel 13, when I heard about the "going home checkout." All the cleaners were searched routinely at the end of every shift—bags, lockers, jackets, and pockets.

From finding out about the "going home checkout" to receiv-
ing the devastating news about my poor mother passing away, took
all of ten minutes. My supervisor was very sympathetic, but before
she could offer to hold my job open for me, I quickly said I'd be
moving home to Scotland to take care of my elderly father. If you'd
looked closely you would have seen the smoke coming from the
bottom of my shoes as I bolted up the road never to be seen again.

So why haven't I received a phone call yet about my mother
dying? Why aren't I running for the hills?

I glance up the corridor to where Phil is riffling through her
trolley looking for something. She doesn't see me this time. As
she searches, her dark sleek hair moves from side to side, like a
gleaming sheet of velvet. She finally finds what she's looking for—
garbage bags. She stops and runs her hand through her hair, parting it for a moment before it falls back perfectly into place. She
turns her head a little and looks straight at me. I feel a jolt to my
stomach, but this time I stare back at her. I don't seem to care anymore what she thinks of me. She flicks her head, tossing her hair
from her face, then turns and walks into the room she is cleaning.
What is it about her? Why am I so intrigued? Is it me that's more
interested in her?

"What the flying fuck are you doing now?" Mali says in a
tight whisper, glaring at me from the bedroom door, toilet brush
in her hand. "You are a liability, you know that? Standing around
doing nothing."

"Sorry, I've got a bit of a stomach cramp," I say, pulling a
pained face.

"Aaah, you got your period?" she says.

I nod, relieved this seems to be an acceptable excuse, but Mali frowns even harder.

"You think you're the only woman in the world that bleeds? We all have to work. Now get a move on or I will tell Julia you are the worst cleaner I have ever seen."

I'm beginning to think it would be better if Mali did that and I have no choice but to leave.

Chapter 5

I put the key in the front door of my flat and turn it, but it doesn't move. The landlady warned me this might happen when I moved in last week. She's a short, stocky woman who wears too much perfume of the floral kind. When I first met her, and she shook my hand, the fumes almost overwhelmed me. I coughed and spluttered for a good thirty seconds making the excuse I had asthma. Maybe she has no sense of smell and had been badly advised by someone on how much to apply.

She demonstrated how to wiggle the key around and pull it toward me to get the door to open. I try this. It still doesn't work.

I lean my head against the plastic-coated front door. It's cool on my forehead and for a moment it soothes my racing mind. I glance down at the carpet by my feet, thin and threadbare, probably over thirty years old. The whole building, I'm sure once a glamorous family home, is now run-down and stuffed full of students. An air freshener hangs from the old light fixture in the hall—an attempt to cover the overpowering waft of damp. Maybe that's why the landlady soaks herself in sweet perfume. It's a cover-up. But this flat is all I'm prepared to pay for rent in London and I'm happy with it. I only need somewhere to sleep and wash.

Work is my life and I'm not ashamed to admit that, to myself anyway. The flat I had in Liverpool when I worked in hotel 17 had been a bit swish for my standards with polished floorboards and a dishwasher. This place was advertised as a flat with an en suite because it has its own shower, which consists of a stall with a shower nozzle you have to hold up over your head with one hand, leaving the other hand free to wash yourself.

On the plus side, all bills are included and there is a washing machine situated in the basement. My day for washing is Thursday. I like that I have my own day. It makes me feel organized and gives me a sense of stability.

Footsteps on the stairs make me stand up straight. I glance sideways as a guy in his twenties, wearing tracksuit bottoms and a hoodie with a picture of a green alien and the words HUMANS AREN'T REAL printed on it, swings past me down the stairs, long unwashed hair sticking out from under his hood. He doesn't look up or acknowledge me. I'm invisible to him and that suits me fine.

I wiggle and yank the key in the door again. This time it clicks and turns. I push the door open and enter. The flat has a six-meter-high ceiling with a large window, dreary brown curtains and a view over a parking lot, which is an acceptable outlook in my opinion.

The flat was also referred to in the ad as self-contained because of its separate washing and cooking facilities, but it's really just a bedsit. The matchbox kitchen and shower stall are in a purpose-built unit made of flimsy timber panels divided into two sections. This is on the left as you enter. The toilet is squished into a cubby by the front door, probably once a broom closet. At the far end of the purpose-built unit is a ladder that you climb to access the area above the kitchen and shower where there is a mattress. This is my bedroom, or rather my mattress space. The landlady called it the mezzanine. I like it. It feels hidden away.

The rest of the room contains two dirty old armchairs with holes in them and a small rickety aluminum table with a dark circle on the top where someone put out a cigarette. Attached to the wall is an old electric heater. I'm not that concerned about heat. I normally come home and go straight to bed anyway.

A single clothes rail is positioned in front of a rickety chest of drawers by the window where my white shirts, black skirts and trousers hang, ready for work. I hardly ever go out or socialize so no other clothes are important to me. I have a couple of emergency tops I can pull on over a skirt if I do need to go on a work night out, which is hardly ever these days.

In the corner of the living area is my trunk, the only large item I ever travel with. Inside it, hidden away, is my collection of success stories.

In the eight years I have worked as a hotel cleaner, I have never been caught taking things and I am very proud of that. I slide the condom out of my pocket and smile at it. It was a new experience for me today. I would never normally take anything under those kinds of circumstances, especially on a first day. For some reason I was reckless.

I step into the kitchen area—only big enough for one person. There is a two-ring cooktop beside a tiny sink that you can just about fit two hands into. Beneath the sink is a little fridge with an icebox big enough for a single ice cube tray. A thin narrow cupboard is attached to the wall over the cooktop and there is one small drawer that doesn't shut properly below it. I open the cupboard and take out one of two mugs. This one has SpongeBob on it. The other is covered in faded brown and white spots. Inside the SpongeBob mug is a small silver key. I take it and go to my trunk, the most expensive thing I have ever owned or invested in. Its hard wood has taken some knocks over the years but it's never let me down.

When I went to work in Jersey, I put it in storage rather than ship it over with me and that was a mistake. I felt lost without it. I could only afford a bed in a hostel, and any items I took from the hotel I had to store in a shoebox in my backpack under my bed. I didn't like the setup at all and felt the shoebox was amateur.

The padlock hangs from the opening clasp at the front of the trunk. I kneel on the floor beside it, carefully unlock it, and slip it out of the metal loop. I take a deep breath, lift the lid and push it back so it leans against the wall behind. I rest my hands in my lap, still holding the condom, and run my eyes over the glorious treasure laid out before me.

To the untrained eye it probably looks like a mass of junk and jumble. But to me every piece is unique with its own story. Every item is a triumph. That's the one thing about my kind of taking that doesn't fit the kleptomania profile. I take pride in all I have achieved. Most kleptomaniacs, according to the little I've read online, only enjoy the taking of the item and rarely enjoy the object itself afterward. And still others make a fundamental mistake in that they focus on taking expensive items from shops.

I read about a woman who only took cashmere woolens from Harrods until she was caught. When they searched her house they found tens of thousands of pounds worth of unworn, still-wrapped cashmere scarves and sweaters shoved under her bed and on top of her wardrobe, covered in dust. I didn't understand it. Why all that risk if you didn't even respect the items? These people need reeducating in the art of taking. You take because you love the sense of achievement it gives you, not because you want to possess something expensive. I felt sorry for that Harrods woman. She had the right idea but the wrong method.

As I trail my hand over the mound of trinkets and objects, the tension leaves my body and my breathing becomes methodical and rhythmic. Little pots, tubes of creams and gels, pens, dozens of tweezers, nail clippers, socks, a key ring, a baby's bib, a lip balm with a faded casing, and a large gold button that I took from a woman's blazer in hotel 6. Belts, large and small. Hats, a glove, a pair of slippers, silk ties, rolled up neatly. I pick up a glasses case, open and close it and put it back. There are a couple of bras and a pair of bikini bottoms.

Slotted down the side in a pouch is my dog-eared black notebook and pen. I pull it out and it falls open on the crinkled pages where I keep a list of every hotel I have worked in including the name, star rating, location, the dates I worked there, and an itemized list of all the things I managed to take while I was there. Some of the hotel lists go over several pages, like hotel 7, a three-star in Nottingham where I lasted eight months, my longest time working in a hotel ever. I got into a rhythm there, taking up to ten items a week, but then I started to get bored with how easy it was. I was restless, and in my last room of the day I spotted a net bag full of hair-extension clips. There were about eight different types, including a ponytail, and right at the bottom were bang extensions, the smallest of them all. I knew it was high risk, but I was hoping the guest wouldn't notice it was gone at least until after she'd left the hotel. But a complaint came in that evening and I was hauled into the supervisor's office the following morning. Apparently the bang extensions were her favorite. I got away with it of course but two weeks later I moved on. I told them my mother had been rushed into hospital for emergency heart surgery and I had to go home to look after my disabled father. It was my most elaborate excuse yet and it caused me problems. People wanted to know what heart surgery she was having and which hospital it was. I learned to keep the excuses short and sweet after that, and to stick to fake dead relatives rather than sick ones. Still, hotel 7 is my most successful hotel to date.

I trace my finger down the first page, feeling the bumpiness of the text where my heavy hand has left an imprint like braille. I flip through the pages until I get to hotel 21. Five stars. London. Feb 2019. No end date yet. I write *condom x 1* underneath *Items*, and then add *First Day* in brackets.

I keep turning, looking at all the empty pages I have yet to fill with hotel names, stars, dates and all the items I have yet to take. Again I am filled with a sense of weariness. It's only because of hotel 20, I tell myself. I turn back to the page for Fernsby Manor. Should I rip the page out and erase it from my memory? I go through the list of items I took while I was there, including the last one, the cream pump, and there's no way I could destroy evidence of my hard work. I need to forget about my experience in hotel 20 and focus on the items I took there instead.

I slot my black notebook back in the pouch. The mound of items is getting closer to the rim of the trunk now. Once it's full I'll have to think about emptying it out, which I can't bear the idea of doing, or getting a new trunk, which would come with a whole load of other problems, like transporting two trunks instead of one.

Whenever I move I have my trunk collected and put in storage until I have a new flat it can be delivered to. Could I really justify the cost of two trunks? I'd also have to make sure there was enough space in every flat for both of them. And what happened when the second was full?

I put this concern to the back of my mind too for now and place the condom in the center of the pile. It's not that it's a condom. It's that it belonged to a hotel guest and now it belongs to me.

There's no light in the shower stall, but the light from the naked bulb in the kitchen seeps through the crack in the ceiling so I can just about see what I'm doing as I squeeze into the small space, my feet just fitting onto the shower pan.

I twist the shower handle on at the wall and the whirring noise of the pump fills my ears. It's not so much a hum as it is a screech, like it's going to explode any minute. I have begun playing a game that I only have one minute to wash and get out before the whole building goes up in flames.

Holding the shower nozzle up over my head, I attempt to lather every part of my body with a block of Imperial Leather soap. As the warmish water trickles over my body, my mind wanders to thoughts of Phil and a shiver darts up my spine, a shiver more similar to the physical sensation I have when I think about taking something rather than being cold. I go to wash quickly between my legs, like I always do, eager to get the job done as fast as possible and get out of the shower, when the soap lingers there for a little longer. It feels nice and I'm not sure why. Thinking about Phil makes me want to keep my hand down there, moving, massaging gently.

I close my eyes for a moment, thoughts of Phil and her inquisitive eyes and shimmering, gleaming hair swirl before me. The soap slips from my hand. It's too small in the space to bend and pick it up. I finish rinsing, turn the shower off, drop the nozzle head on the floor and step out of the stall. I grab my bathrobe—a hotel one I was given in hotel 10 as a leaving present.

I stand in the cold for a moment, wrapping my arms around myself, letting the soft fabric warm my skin. The whirring sound of the struggling pump stops and all is quiet except for the glug of the plughole as the last of the water slops down the drain.

My hand wanders under my bathrobe and down toward the mound of pubic hair but I quickly move it away. Whatever this sensation is, it's not something I'm used to or have control over. It feels like a spark that if ignited will burn the house down. Or maybe it will only set fire to me, heating my body slowly from the inside, like a case of spontaneous human combustion. I read online about a man found in his flat by the police, his body burned to a crisp, but no burned furniture. I quickly push this thought aside. As much as I'm not afraid to die, the idea of melting from the inside out isn't a very appealing one. I pull my mind away from thoughts of smoldering sparks to more urgent problems.

Tomorrow is my last chance to make the Magnolia work for me. If I can't get Phil to like and accept me, I will have to leave. And no more high-risk taking of things either, at least not until I'm sure all the girls on the team are on my side.

Chapter 6

Living alone is the greatest gift you get as an adult, so I'm grateful every day that I come home to an empty bedsit instead of the horrible flat I shared with my mother.

We lived on a council estate called West House in Mottingham in South East London. The kids on the estate liked to call themselves the Westies and formed gangs that didn't get up to much except playing knock down ginger and water bombing people from the top of staircases. I really wanted to be in a gang but they wouldn't have me. I wasn't cool enough.

The estate was ugly, like a giant piece of sticky rocky road mixture, everything thrown together: dirty brown bricks, rickety lifts and concrete stairwells tainted with the everlasting stench of urine. Short steps, long steps, paths that went under walkways, paths that disappeared down alleyways. Walls built so high that anyone under five foot six couldn't see over. There were green patches thrown in with the occasional small tree looking limp and out of place in the colorless surroundings, and the odd graffitied bench no one ever sat on, even for a second.

The flats themselves weren't that bad, as though someone had actually thought about the layout. We had a two-bed on the third floor: one normal size bedroom, one box room. I had the box room. There was a short hallway with a small living room to the right that had a window facing the front of the flat, where people walking by on the external corridor outside could peer in if the blind wasn't pulled down. The living room had a wrinkled and cracked fake leather sofa covered in coffee and red wine stains and a small TV perched on a wooden chair. On the floor was an old beanbag that smelled stale, like wet cardboard and, when it wasn't bunched up to be used as a seat, it lay thin and sprawled on the dusty carpet like a shapeless amoeba.

At the end of the hallway was the kitchen/dining room with brown cupboards and a discolored white plastic table squashed into the corner with two chairs. It was the lightest and most spacious room in the flat. The window was weather-beaten and bleached on the outside from the sunlight, and looked out over a graveyard. My mother, in her fits of fury, would often push my nose against the window, forcing me to look out.

"Is that where you want to end up, is it? Down there, six feet under, in a box with the worms eating you?"

To be clear, I was never afraid she would kill me. I knew it was all talk. If anything these outbursts of emotion that swelled up and exploded from within her were simply confirmation for me that my mother was far from normal. I fantasized she was an alien, and when I was eleven, I decided I needed proof.

One night I waited until she was out cold, after knocking back a bottle of vodka, and then I inspected her. I ran my fingers gently over her right arm, which was rough and freckly and made me feel nauseous to touch. I checked behind her ears for any sign of stitching and inside her mouth, gently pressing her cheeks and gums in the hope purple acid would spurt out and burn my fingers. I looked for seams down her legs—maybe she shed her skin sometimes. Not satisfied with the results of my inspection, and confident she would assume she had injured herself while drunk, I took her nail scissors from the bedside table and carefully nipped the top of one of her fingers, but her blood ran red. I don't know what I was expecting. Green blood? Maybe aliens have red blood too. Or maybe I had to accept that my mother was not an alien but just a hideous human being.

From as early as five years old I knew there was something not right with her. When she got into one of her frenzies, I would hide my eyes behind my hands, refusing to put them down. I believed that if I couldn't see her, she couldn't see me. Then when I felt a whack around my head or my body, I'd tell myself that if I couldn't see her hitting me, I couldn't feel it. It helped me not to cry, which used to drive her even more insane.

"Why don't you cry?" she'd yell at me. "You're Satan's child."

Yes, I'd think to myself, I am and you're Satan. Not crying gave me a crumb of control. I was strong and she couldn't break me.

And she certainly wasn't like the other mums at school, especially Alison Rogers's mum, a combination of over-cheerfulness and panic, all teeth, smiles and waves. My mum never came to collect me from school. When I was too young to walk home alone, she paid Malcolm, the drug addict who lived in the flat below us, to do it. He used to meet me at the gates and then walk on ahead expecting me to follow, crossing roads, without even a glance behind him. I would run to keep up, my tatty school bag bouncing around on my back, staying as close as I could to him, fully aware that no one was holding my hand as I trailed after him through the traffic.

There was a near miss with a truck once on the crossing right outside the school. One of the other mums leapt in front of the oncoming white van, hands in the air, screaming and swept me to safety. When she asked me where my mummy was and I told her she was at home watching telly, I saw the look of disapproval on the woman's face. But I knew, even at that young age, that her judgment wasn't aimed at me but at my mother. I've always been good at reading people. It's been my saving grace.

My father, according to her, left when I was a baby because I wouldn't stop crying and refused to sleep. It was my fault, she said, but by the time I was seven years old, I had the sense to know that probably wasn't true. I knew if it was anyone's fault it was hers.

I didn't feel sad about not having a dad, despite other children asking me why I didn't have one. Looking back I realized they were teasing me, trying to upset me and make me feel bad about myself, but it never worked because I figured I'd got off lightly. What if he had been worse than my mother?

Social services probably should have done more but in fairness to them my mother was a professional when it came to covering up our situation. My injuries were frequent enough to raise eyebrows, so any trip to the hospital tended to be followed by a visit from a well-meaning social worker full of questions but often too tired and too overworked to see the truth that lay beneath. And my mother was well practiced and I was well trained.

Once home from the emergency room, where my latest head injury or broken limb had been bandaged up, my mother would scrub and clean the flat till it shone in all the right places. She'd fill the cupboard and fridge with salad and fruit and biscuits and put flowers in a cracked vase on the table. I was required to stay home from school and lie on the sofa with a blanket over me, convalescing. It was a big show and it suited me fine.

For at least three days my mother was on her best behavior, which meant she didn't drink or hit me, and I got to watch telly all day long. By the time the social worker arrived, concerned with the number of hospital visits and injuries I was clocking up, we presented as a loving, if somewhat struggling, one-parent family, where I was a bit accident prone.

"I like jumping off things," I'd say to the social worker.

My mother, acting like she was at the end of her tether with her adrenaline junkie child, would cry and sob about how she simply wasn't able to watch me every second of the day. The social worker would then comfort my mother, pumping her full of sound bites, like you don't have to be a perfect parent, you just have to be good enough. And how she was doing a great job. Then they'd have a little chat with me suggesting I keep my feet on the ground and help my mother by not leaping off the furniture. And I would solemnly agree, like it was going to be a real sacrifice not to bash my body off hard objects on purpose.

After one of my "falls" the area over my right eye split open and needed stitches (which is what happens when someone throws a pepper mill at your head). When we arrived home from the ER my mother launched into her usual routine. The cupboard below the sink was yanked open and any cleaning equipment hauled out to blitz the flat. I was nine years old and something struck me. A question, burning so hot in my gut I felt I would explode if I didn't ask it.

"Why don't you let the social worker take me?"

My mother stood in the kitchen, her arms full of detergent and sponges and stared at me.

"It's what you want. I don't mind going to live with a foster family," I said in my most helpful voice.

She dropped the cleaning things into the sink and leaned over it. I took a step back, checking my exits. I'd never seen her like this before and I wasn't sure what it meant.

"You ungrateful little bitch," she said slowly, without raising her head.

I edged farther back to the front door. She turned and followed me, the vein in her forehead pulsating, her eyebrows raised.

"You want to leave, do you? You want to go and live with a foster family who will treat you like a sex slave, is that what you want?"

It certainly wasn't, but I wasn't sure the sex slave reference was true. There was a boy in my school who was fostered and he seemed happy enough. He had an older brother who waited for him after school to walk home and even had birthday parties, not that I was invited.

"And what about me?" she said. "Everyone around here will know I had my kid taken off me. Is that what you want? People gossiping. And what about the rent on this place? How am I supposed to pay for that and buy food without my child benefit?"

I kicked myself. Of course that's why she keeps me, the money. If she gave me up, she'd lose all her benefits. She'd told me often enough. I quickly backtracked.

"Sorry, I just thought you'd rather be rid of me."

"I would rather be rid of you. But I'm stuck with you, aren't I? Foster family," she mumbled to herself. "If I don't want you, why would anyone else? Now, lie on the sofa in case the social worker comes round. And get your story straight or the next place you'll be going is that graveyard."

Hotel 8

3-star. Jersey. April 2013-June 2013

Total time: 2 months

Items

Socks x 1

Small pot of cream x 3

AA battery x 1

Tweezers x 2

False nail x 1

Highlighter pen x 1

Bikini top x 1

Nail scissors x 1

Razor x 1

Wrapping bow x 1

Eyeliner x 1

Flip flop x 1

Nail file x 2

Shoe horn x 1

Baby's bib x 1

Small makeup brush x 2

Tin of fruity lip gloss (final item)

Chapter 7

Julia drops her file on the desk and swivels around in her chair to face us. Mali and I are in her office, which is also in the basement next to the staff room. I'm confident Mali will recommend me to go solo after yesterday.

"How did she do?" Julia looks at Mali.

"Terrible. Useless. She daydreams, she talks too much and she doesn't like dirty clothes."

Julia looks taken aback. I open my mouth, as though surprised, and manage to flush my cheeks. I know Mali is joking but I can't let on, as that would make me seem arrogant. Mali glances at me and then bursts out laughing—her most clownish giggle yet.

"The look on your face," she says, pointing at me, doubling over. Julia shakes her head, clearly relieved. Julia isn't the kind of woman who enjoys firing people. She needs to be liked by everyone for her self-esteem to remain intact.

"Don't worry, don't worry. You'll get used to my sense of humor," says Mali, putting her arm around my waist and squeezing me. I put my hand to my heart and blow out a long sigh. Julia gives me a sympathetic look.

"I'm afraid Mali has a dark side," Julia says to me.

"I do, I do," says Mali, wiping tears of laughter from her eyes. "You are too gullible."

"You really got me," I say, but the last laugh's mine, of course. Julia leans back in her chair, relieved this is going to be easy.

"So, I take it Noelle is actually a good cleaner?"

"Oh, yes," says Mali. "She is very professional and experienced. She doesn't need to buddy up anymore. She can clean on her own from today."

I manage to adopt another surprised look, like I wasn't expecting to hear that. Julia gives me a kindly smile. She definitely likes my humility.

"If you impressed Mali you must be even better than she says you are."

I blush on cue again, something that took me years to perfect. It's more about the right body language than it is the reddening of the cheeks. If I have the look of someone who is blushing, people seem to imagine the flushed cheeks. The body language is quite simple but also very subtle. The head lowers but only a fraction. Eye contact must be lost but only by a tiny glance to one side. I touch my hair slightly and then move my hand away quickly, as though moving at all is excruciating for me in this moment. I'm not always able to muster the red cheeks at will, but today I'm on fire.

Julia passes me a skeleton key. "I hope the Magnolia will be a fresh start for you."

"Thank you," I say with meaning and gratitude.

"What I want to see from you now is a little more self-confidence, okay?"

"I will work on her," says Mali who still has her hand around my waist. "And she really is too skinny, like an emaciated horse. I will feed her up."

"Looks like you've been adopted," Julia says to me. I smile, slightly squeezing the corner of my eyes together. Score: One hundred and fifty points.

Mali links arms with me as we wander back to the staff room. "Me, Gaby and Phil, and maybe Rose, have Saturday off so we're going out on Friday night to get pissed off our faces. Do you want to come?"

"Oh, thanks for asking. I think I might be working Saturday though." If I'm not, I'll come up with a good excuse to get out of it.

She tightens her grip on my arm. "You find out and then you come with us. We drink shots of tequila and then pick a fight with someone. It's very funny."

In the staff room Gaby is putting on her apron. She waves hi to me. I wave back. We're good. Rose comes up to me.

"Are you going solo now?"

"I am," I say. Rose pats me on the back. We're good too. I look around for Phil but I can't see her. A small panic sizzles up from my stomach to my throat. What do I care if Phil's here or not?

"Where's Phil?" asks Gaby.

"Running late. She had to do one of her things," says Rose.

I immediately calm down, which troubles me even more. If Phil never turned up for work again, what's it to me? And what does one of her things mean? I'm about to ask but stop myself. I can't seem too interested and I don't want to care about what Phil does in her spare time. Phil's a problem I need to fix, that's all. I don't want to find another job and start over again, waiting for weeks to be able to take from hotel guests just because one cleaner thinks she's a mind reader. I'll show her.

As I tie my apron, the door to the locker room swings open and Phil wanders in—her sleek hair in pigtails and little faux diamond studs in her ears. She has smoky eye shadow on today making her look demure and enchanting. She passes by me and stops, her perfume drifts under my nose, musky yet light and tantalizing.

She regards me for a moment. A charge of energy shoots up the front of my body again, faster this time, hitting my larynx like a freight train sending shock waves all over my body, like I've been brushed with a live wire. Phil grins at me. Can she tell? Does she know? Is my body giving me away? Have I become easy to read?

"You're still with us then," she says, her voice smooth and soothing. My mouth is dry.

"Yeah," I manage to say, but I sound croaky.

"Good," she says and walks on to her locker.

I carry on tying my apron but my fingers are shaking. I imagine lying splayed on the locker room floor with Phil on top of me, pulling my clothes off. She exposes my right breast and falls on it, sucking it, pulling it into her mouth. I'm shocked by the vividness of the image and lean on my locker to catch my breath.

"You okay, honey?" says Rose.

"Yeah, just a twinge in my back. It'll be gone when I get moving," I say, being injured Noelle for a moment. Rose nods knowingly. Body aches and pains are part of a cleaner's life, from corns on our toes to slipped discs that we try to ignore, it's always a point of discussion.

I push thoughts of Phil from my mind and try to focus on my success so far. I'm already going solo on my second day and everyone, bar Phil, trusts me. Although Phil did seem pleased when she asked if I was still here. I decide this is a positive sign. But no more thinking about Phil. Today I'm on my own. I will be able to rummage and carefully take something so small and insignificant that the guest won't even know it's gone.

"Guess what?" Gaby nudges Phil.

"You got laid last night?" grins Phil. Rose gives a whoop. Mali giggles.

"Shut up," says Gaby. "No, I changed the locks."

Phil hugs her tight.

"I told Francesco he's never coming back unless he gets clean," says Gaby, her voice a little wobbly.

"What did he say to that?" asks Rose.

"He told me I was a spiteful bitch who would never have any joy in my life and that I'm not fit to be a mother and never was." We all stop and look at her, wondering what effect these words have had on her.

"But what does he know, right?" says Gaby, forcing a smile, trying to hide the pain in her eyes. Rose puts an arm around her. The general feeling is, what else can you do?

We pile into the lift, making it shunt from side to side. I position myself so I'm as far away from Phil as possible, which means two meters instead of two centimeters. She eyes me from the back of the lift.

"Hey, Noelle?" I look up, pulling an innocent expression. "We're all going out dancing on Friday night. Do you want to come?"

"I already asked her," says Mali. "She doesn't know if she's working Saturday or not."

"She's not. I checked," says Phil.

"Oh, right," I say, my cheeks flushing crimson. Shit. Why am I blushing, and unprompted? "Sounds great. It's hot in here, isn't it?" I say, trying to distract from my red cheeks. Phil catches my eye.

"I'm not hot. Is anyone else hot?" she says. Gaby, Rose and Mali shake their heads.

"Maybe you're sickening for something," says Mali. "You're too skinny to get sick, you know that? You need fat on your bones."

"Ignore her," says Rose. "She thinks she's an expert on everything."

"That's because I am," replies Mali, proudly. "I should have gone to university."

"Yeah, the university of how to be a pain in the arse," says Rose. Mali flips her head back and giggles loudly. Rose smiles. She enjoys making Mali laugh and the two of them spark off each other.

"I'd love to have your figure," says Gaby, wistfully to me.

"Thanks," I say, still feeling awkward about the night out.

I glance up to see Phil still hasn't taken her eyes off me. She's reading me. Does she know I'm a fake? I drag my eyes away. Focus, Noelle, focus. Today you can take something a little more special than a condom. Think about the rush. Think about adding the new item to your trunk.

The lift doors open and I'm first out and down to the service door to get my trolley. My foot taps as I wait for the others to catch up. Phil is right behind me.

"You're eager today," she says.

"Just want to get started, you know?"

The others gather around as Phil unlocks the door and one by one we step in and pull out our trolleys. I spin mine around and march off toward the bedroom corridor.

I have fourteen rooms to clean in seven hours—five leavers, nine stayers. The leavers have checked out, or at least should have by now, so these rooms require a "check in" deep clean and prep, which can take up to forty minutes but I'll do it much faster than that. Rooms devoid of guests' personal belongings are of no interest to me. The stayers normally need less time, depending on the level of untidiness, but even at worst I shouldn't spend more than twenty minutes in each. If I do, I have to make it up in the next room.

Time is always tight, especially when I'm looking to take something, which I am today. I have a system whereby I work harder and clean faster in the leavers so I can rummage for longer in the stayers. I can assess a stayer's room cleaning time in under three seconds. I know exactly how long it's going to take from just a quick glance and therefore how much time I have left to sift and hunt through the guest's belongings.

I knock on room 725, my first stayer of the day. A gentle tap tap and wait. Nothing. I take out my skeleton key and open the door.

"Hello? Room cleaning?"

Satisfied there's no one inside, I enter, immediately sizing up the room as I move through it. This is a couple, probably mid-sixties, given the man's sensible shoes in the hallway and the long, embroidered silk nightdress draped across the partly made bed. The curtains are already open and the room has a fresh, just washed feel about it, but my instincts tell me not this room, not these people.

I always listen to my gut. It doesn't always make sense to me, but if I'm not feeling it then it's not happening. It takes no more than fifteen minutes to whisk my way through the room, wiping, polishing, hanging and making perfect. I flush the toilet, finish mopping the floors and walk out, job done. I check my watch. Ten minutes. I'm ahead of schedule, which means a couple of extra minutes to rummage in the next room. My solar plexus is waking up. The buzz begins to bubble inside me.

I knock on the door to room 727 and wait. I open the door a little and call in.

"Hello? Room cleaning?" No answer. I push the door, leaving it wide open and enter, eyes peeled for garments and items that fit my criteria.

This room is a single occupancy, as only half the bed is slept in and there's only one small suitcase. This is another fifteen-minute room, so there's time to have a look around. The occupant is a woman, probably attending a ball or a wedding, based on the dress bag hanging on the outside of the wardrobe.

I check the hallway to the open door. The coast is clear. The wardrobe is around the corner so can't be seen from the door, which means I'll have at least two seconds to cover should someone walk in. Anyway, I'm only looking. I give the zip a little tug and pull it up watching the teeth gently separate. I slip my hand inside the bag and feel the material of a ball gown. It's made of heavy blue velvet and very soft in my hand. I run the zipper back down to the bottom and leave it hanging.

I open the wardrobe and see an array of plain shirts and skirts, nothing too exciting. There's a pair of court shoes, some pumps and black high-heeled sandals with silky straps that tie around the ankle. My mind wanders to Phil. Would she like these sandals? Would she like them on me with the silk ties snaking up my calves?

I feel hot and flustered again. I shut the wardrobe door and hurry to the bathroom.

My eyes fall on a large, leather vanity case. This woman doesn't just have a toiletry bag; she checks an entire makeup department onto the plane. The adrenaline charges through my veins. I move my head from side to side to loosen my neck, needing to keep calm and in control.

With great care and precision, I unclip the clasp to the case and gently lift the lid up and over letting it hang in the space behind. The top velvet-lined drawer holds loose makeup items like eyebrow pencils and individual eye shadows. There's a little leather loop and I tug it gently, pulling the top drawer up and out, revealing more drawers below, all magically unfolding, glistening with colorful tubes and sticks. But I'm more panicked than excited. This is too complicated. How can I judge in seconds what this woman values and what she doesn't? Although instinct tells me there's no way she keeps tabs on every little item. She has two pairs of tweezers. Would she notice one missing? And if she did, it's highly likely she'd assume she lost or misplaced it. It's the safe option and I normally start small in a new job and work my way up, so why am I hesitating?

I pick out a two-color eye shadow palette, soft green and light pink. She would definitely notice if this went missing, but it's not something I would ever consider taking—so why am I even holding it? Do I want a complaint made against me quickly so I'm forced to hand in my notice and leave? I put the palette back. Stick to the tweezers. No one has ever complained to hotel management that the cleaner took their tweezers.

"Naughty girl, caught with your hands in the cookie jar."

I spin around to see Phil lounging in the bathroom doorway.

"It was on the floor," I say, calm as you like.

It's not the first time a colleague's walked in on me looking through a guest's belongings. In hotel 2, I was caught with my head in a wardrobe and again in hotel 12 with my hand in a toiletry bag. Both times I got away with it by not overexplaining and acting like the person who caught me wasn't even thinking I was about to take anything. I'm good at making up excuses on the spot and I find people buy any story if you tell it in a believable way. It's the performance that matters, not the excuse.

"It was on its side. Isn't it beautiful?" I say, regarding the vanity case. Phil eyes it and then glances at me. "Do you need something?" I ask.

"I was just checking up on you," she says, moving closer. She's a tad taller so can look down her nose at me. I feel my breath quicken.

"Why do you need to check up on me?" I ask.

"I don't know. A hunch maybe."

My nipples tingle and I feel my head getting hot. I turn away from her and quickly engross myself in cleaning the bathroom mirror.

"I'm trying to work you out," she says. "You interest me."

I stop what I'm doing and look at her. I don't think I've ever been an object of interest to anyone before, not in the way Phil is implying anyway.

"I'm really rather boring," I say.

"The fact you say that tells me you're probably quite the opposite."

I swallow, as the blood rushes to my face. Damn those over-trained cheeks.

Then Phil grins. "Mali's right, you're far too easy to wind up. I only want to borrow your mop quickly. Mine's soaking in bleach. I got crap on it."

"Sure, go ahead," I say.

She hovers at the door for a moment. "If you are hiding something, I'll find out what it is." She winks at me and leaves.

I lean my head against the mirror, breathing deeply. I'm in a nightmare. I can't leave, I can't take anything, and I can't get Phil out of my mind.

I lift my head off the mirror and sigh. My forehead has left a smudge on the glass and I have to clean it again. I check my watch. Thirteen minutes. I'm behind schedule now and still have to find something to take, although I'm loath to do it after Phil found me with my hands all over the vanity case. She seemed to buy my story but a nagging feeling tells me only half of what she said was to wind me up.

Phil is interested in me and I'm pretty sure I'm interested in her.

Chapter 8

My mother wasn't a total layabout. She worked part-time in a Tesco in Bromley, a twenty-minute bus ride from where we lived, and had done since before I was born. She worked just enough hours so that her benefits weren't affected. And she even had friends there. She went on work nights out and to Christmas parties and talked to people on the phone named Liv and Mazza. When one of these calls came in she left the room to speak in private. I'd put my ear to the wall and listen—the walls were paper thin in our flat.

Her voice would change instantly, becoming warm and friendly and quiet. She would speak more slowly, taking a tad longer to finish words. If she said really, she would say *realleee*. It had a soothing effect. And these friends from work often called her for advice or reassurance and my mother, the horror of a woman that she was, gave it in bucketloads.

"Oh, that sounds aaawful, you poor thinggg," she would swoon. "Let's meet for a drink, okay?"

I should have been resentful, I suppose. How can she switch on her nice button for her Tesco pals and then switch it off for me? But I wasn't. I was intrigued. She was faking it at work and doing a brilliant job of it. It's the only thing about my mother that impressed me.

She always told me never to come to her place of work on pain of death, but sometimes, after school, I'd get the number 314 bus into Bromley and walk the extra five minutes to the supermarket, where I'd look in through the gaps between the posters in the window, unseen, watching my mother. She'd either be working on a till or flitting from checkout to checkout with her supervisor badge on. And I would observe her, trying to see if the cracks would show. Would she suddenly lose it with a customer? Would her face contort into one of her hideous scowls in front of a colleague, revealing her true nature? But in all the afternoons I stood outside that window, she never put a foot wrong.

She was always sober at work, of course with freshly washed hair, which was fair and thin and scraped back in a bun. She'd add a shiny ribbon, often yellow or blue and maybe a hair clip with sparkly bits on it for a bit of bling. She also applied foundation to her tired, pasty skin, giving her a warmish glow, and light pink gloss to her lips, which gave the impression of a woman with a cheerful disposition. I would peer through the gap in the posters, watching her smile at her fellow workers, making jokes and placing reassuring hands on their shoulders. Who was this woman? Were her jokes even funny? Her colleagues beamed back at her, comfortable in her company. She was one of them and they liked and respected her. This was her other life: the life where she got to be a good person.

I was banned from her place of work because she didn't want me to blow her cover. But one day my curiosity finally got the better of me and, while standing outside Tesco in the rain looking in at my mother checking a clipboard, I took leave of my senses and walked right in.

At first she didn't notice me. I was the last person she expected to see. Surely I wouldn't dare show my face here after the threats she had made. But here I was, ready to sacrifice my own life, or at least risk a trip to the ER, just to see how she would handle it.

I stood on the mat in the entrance to the supermarket, as shoppers streamed in behind me to grab carts and baskets. I must have cut a lonely figure, fourteen years old, in a sopping-wet school uniform, hair stuck to the side of my face from the rain. The security guard, a large, jolly man in his sixties, saw me first.

"You alright, love?" he said.

I was rooted to the spot in panic, not sure what to do now that I was standing there.

"I'm looking for my mum," I blurted out.

"Oh, is she shopping here? Can you see her?"

Then, without thinking, I pointed at her.

"Erica, is it? Hold on. Erica?" he shouted over to her.

My mother turned, ready to be helpful.

Her eyes locked on mine. Her face and body froze, like she'd got stuck in time. I knew what she was thinking as she quickly scrolled through her options in her head. Would she disown me? Would she deny I was her daughter? Would she slip me out the back door with a promise of future punishment for my terrible act of betrayal? Before I could move or talk or do anything, a high-pitched squeal made us both jump.

"Oh, my God. Is this your daughter, Erica?" said a bronzed-looking woman with bleached blonde hair. She tottered up to us in very high-heeled red shoes. She had clearly overdone the fake tan but her eyes were kind and engaging. She looked at me with admiration. "Noelle, isn't it? I'm Liv," she said.

I wasn't expecting anyone to know who I was, let alone know my name. I looked at my mother, surprised. She plastered on a smile.

"Yes, this is my daughter." She put her arm around me, something she had never done before—in fact, she'd barely touched me my entire life apart from when she was beating me. "You're all wet," my mother said, pushing the hair from my face. I did my best not to flinch.

"Char, Mazza, Vicky. It's Erica's daughter," Liv called out to her fellow workers. The women rushed over. I saw my mother swallow, as she plastered on another smile. She didn't know what to do. Her two worlds were colliding. Would this fake one still exist in five minutes?

"We've heard so much about you," gushed Liv. "I mean, I feel like I know you." The other women gathered around too.

"Nice to meet you," I said.

"Is everything alright, Noelle?" interrupted my mother in a kind voice, not daring to drop the act for a second to even shoot me a warning glance. I looked into her eyes and felt sad for us. Wouldn't life be so much better if she could make her fake life her real life?

"I, er, I locked myself out," I managed to mumble.

"But I leave a key with Mrs. Glover next door." There was no Mrs. Glover and you'd never leave a key with any of our neighbors unless you wanted your flat ransacked while you were out. But I played along.

"She's not in," I said.

"Look at the poor thing," gushed the lady named Vicky. She had pink streaked hair and big rings on her fingers.

"Bring her to the staff room, Erica, and let her dry off," suggested Liv.

My mother ushered me down to the back of the shop, her arm still around me. I kept expecting her grip to tighten or for her fingers to pinch me, a warning of what was to come, but she didn't. She was so far into her character that she didn't dare come out of it even for a second.

She tapped a code into a keypad beside a door at the back of the supermarket and pushed it open. I walked into the gloomy, narrow corridor and she followed, shutting the door behind her. It was dark now except for a faint glow of light around the door at the end of the passageway.

"Straight ahead," she said in a neutral voice.

I walked on and pushed through the door into a brightly lit windowless room with a vending machine and a kitchen unit with a kettle and microwave sitting on it. There were two square tables and plastic chairs scattered about with hoodies and jumpers draped over them. Along the wall were coat hooks and a notice board. I had a quick glance at the board. There was a group shot of all the workers with my mother in the middle, smiling at the camera.

I held my breath, unsure of what would happen now. If there had been a trap door that I could shoot down, she would have pulled the lever, I'm sure. Instead, she grabbed a tea towel from the back of a chair and gave it to me.

"Dry yourself off," she said.

I ran the towel over my dripping wet hair, not that it did much good. She came over to me, took the towel from my hand and began to squeeze sections of my hair with it. Her touch was gentle, but my knees trembled in fear. I was standing in a strange room, totally defenseless with no exit plan should she suddenly punch me in the stomach or kick me in the shin.

She moved to the back of my head to continue drying my hair but I spun around and swiped the towel from her, moving toward the door.

"I'll do it," I said, trying to keep the panic from my voice. She stayed standing where she was, hands by her sides.

"What are you playing at?" she said in a measured voice. "I told you never to come here." I shrugged at her. I had no answer and no excuses. It was what it was.

"How come you're nice here?" I blurted out, unable to control myself. "How come you're happy and smiling all the time?"

She looked at me, rigid, only the pounding of a vein in her neck gave away her true state of mind.

She doesn't know what to do, I thought. She doesn't know who she really is. And suddenly I felt pity for her. She was a woman with no identity, which was why she could so easily adopt a new one.

"I'm sorry. I'll go home now," I said.

"You need to say goodbye before you go."

"You mean, to your friends?"

She gave the tiniest nod of her head.

"They seem nice," I said.

She went to the vending machine. "Snickers or Mars bar?"

I was taken aback for a moment. Was she asking me what I wanted? She turned to me, waiting for an answer.

"Mars bar, please," I said.

She put a pound coin in the machine and pressed the keypad. The machine sprung to life and a Mars bar dropped into the drawer below. She retrieved it from the base of the machine and gave it to me. I knew it was for show—she wanted her work friends to see she had given me a Mars bar because this Erica loved and cared about her daughter.

I looked at her searchingly, but she cast her eyes down and opened the door for me to walk through.

At the front of the supermarket, I smiled and said goodbye to my mother's friends. Liv gave me a huge hug and told me not to be a stranger. Then I walked out, looking back as they all waved at me.

I paused at the window and squinted through the gap in the posters once more to watch my mother as she settled behind one of the tills and beamed at a customer. I lowered my head and traipsed back along the road to catch the bus home.

That evening when she arrived back at the flat—the ribbon gone from her hair and the makeup faded from her face—I was on my way from the kitchen to my bedroom. I stopped as she came through the front door. We both stood still. I wondered if I should say sorry again, but I didn't. I waited.

"Never go there again," she finally said and went into her bedroom. She didn't come out again for the rest of the evening. I took this as a small improvement, as she hadn't finished her sentence with "or else."

It was the only time in our whole lives we had understood each other. Of course it was short lived. A couple of days later she had my head in the gas oven and was threatening to turn it on. I knew she wouldn't, but it still wasn't very nice. And it certainly wasn't very "Tesco Erica."

I didn't leave home until I was seventeen. It was the morning of the sixteenth of February and the rain was bashing against our kitchen window in the middle of a gale. With each blast of wind everything in the flat shook and whistling sounds filtered in around the window frames.

There was a leak in my mother's bedroom ceiling and she was frothing at the mouth with irritation. According to her, the whole building was going to fall down. I didn't try to placate her. Not only was there no point but I really didn't care.

I was in the kitchen eating buttered toast when she stomped in, holding a bottle of vodka, already only half full, huffing and puffing, muttering how the council was useless and expected her to live in third world conditions.

I tried to slink out of the way as she put the kettle on, but I could feel her eyeing me as I grabbed my backpack. I didn't look up. Avoid eye contact was one of my earliest lessons.

I heard the fridge open and close and then, as I was nearly out of the door, she threw her arm around my neck, pulled me into a headlock and forced me to the floor.

"Who do you think you are? Taking the last of the milk," she yelled.

I hadn't of course, but experience had taught me not to argue. While I spluttered to catch my breath, she sat on top of me, her knees digging into my biceps, pinning me to the ground. If we had been a couple of ten-year-old kids it would have looked like a play fight. She forced both my wrists into one of her hands and held them in a vice-like grip—she always had amazingly strong hands.

She reached behind her, opened the utensils drawer and grabbed the first thing she found, which happened to be a cheese grater. I looked at it, confused. She looked at it too, somewhat surprised and unsure how to proceed. Then I saw it. Hesitation. She was losing her touch. The tiniest smile appeared on my lips, pure satisfaction.

"You think it's funny?" she snarled. And with that she beat me around the head with the grater, which kept catching on my scalp and drawing blood.

It was at that moment, in between the whacks to my head, that I looked into her eyes, searching for something, a sense of humanity, a sense of Tesco Erica, but all I saw were two black holes embedded in her skull. Her face was screwed up so tightly I couldn't tell where her nose ended and her mouth began. From deep within her throat came a guttural grunting noise, as she channeled every ounce of her energy into pounding me.

I decided that day that my mother had no heart and no soul. The Erica I had seen in the supermarket was an empty person, a pretense, an acting role and nothing more. It was a game she played—a way to reassure herself she wasn't a bad person.

It was a revelation for me and, while she slept off the bottle of vodka, I patched up my scalp, packed an old duffel bag and left.

Hotel 13

4-star. Oxford. Sept 2015-Sept 2015
Total stay: 10 mins.

Items

0

Chapter 9

On Friday night, half an hour before I'm due to meet the girls in the pub for the work night out, I send a text to Mali saying I won't be able to make it as I'm not feeling well. I don't hear back from her which I take as a good sign. She probably hasn't even seen my text and I doubt any of them will notice or care that I'm not there.

Instead, I spend the evening looking through my trunk and updating my ledger with the items I've taken this week. Under *condom x 1*, I add *tweezers x 1*, *hair comb x 1*, *tester tube of eye cream x 1* and *man's handkerchief with butterfly* (clean of course) *x 1*. I never take more than one item a day in case two complaints come in at once. It would be impossible to blub my way out of that. I'm impressed with how well I've done in my first week despite the challenges. I feel I'm on track not only to beat my five-star record, but also my record of all time. Eight months, hotel 7.

It's Monday morning and I'm first into the staff room. I'm relieved to be back at work. I'm going to put my name down for any cover shifts on my days off. I'd rather be working than sitting around my flat feeling empty.

I slip my clean apron over my head and tie it at the sides, as more women stream in to start their shift. Fatima flounces past me, ponytail swinging. She's still annoyed about not getting bumped up to floor seven. One of the penthouse girls swishes by, hair in a neat bun, nose in the air. The superiority thing doesn't really work when there's only one of them. You need the whole posse or you just look stupid stomping about with a snooty look on your face.

Mali and Gaby bustle in together, chatting. Gaby is sucking a lollipop and they're discussing the different flavors you can get. Gaby says her favorite is caramel. Mali says hers is tropical because she is hot.

"Yes, you are very hot," Gaby says, laughing. Mali poses, pouting. I feel like they haven't seen me.

"Hi," I say from across the room.

"Oh, hi, Noelle," says Gaby, smiling.

"You feeling better?" says Mali.

"Sorry?" I say, a bit thrown.

"Friday night. You said you were sick."

"Oh, yeah, just a migraine."

"Really," says Mali, as though she doesn't believe me one bit and turns to her locker, her back facing me. I feel my throat tighten. I wasn't expecting anyone to notice if I was there or not, let alone care.

"It's a shame you couldn't make it," says Gaby, genuinely sorry for me to have missed it.

"Or maybe she just didn't want to come?" says Mali.

"What?" I bluster. "No, I wasn't feeling well."

"It's okay," she says. "Not everyone's cut out for the tequila crew."

"Tequila, baby," says Gaby, putting her hands on her hips and wiggling from side to side. Mali throws her head back and laughs, filling the room with her machine-gun giggles. I'm mortified and suddenly I so want to be one of the tequila crew.

Rose wanders in, her graying hair scraped up in a bulbous bun on top of her head. There's something so still and majestic and solid about Rose. Maybe it's because she's the tallest, but I think it's more than that. She's like the anchor in a storm. If the world was being swept away, she'd stay standing.

"Hey, Rose," says Mali, dancing around in a circle, hands above her head, singing. Gaby bops her head and even Rose snaps her fingers as she opens her locker. I venture a smile, an attempt to join in, but I'm simply not part of this. Rose gives me a smile, hello. I nod back.

The door flings open and Phil appears. Her silky hair clipped up on either side with two hair clips with tiger faces on them. On anyone else they'd look tacky, but on Phil they're stylish and sophisticated.

"Kylie has nothing on you, Mali," says Phil, with a big grin.

"Except one thing," says Rose. "Talent."

Mali screws up her face in mock anger and throws a dirty apron at Rose. Rose grins.

"Just don't be going on any of those *Britain's Got Talent* shows."

Mali sings even louder now and gyrates her hips at Rose. Rose can't help but laugh.

"What's all the noise, guys?" says Fatima, coming from the back of the staff room, tying her apron. She feels left out too, but she's floor one.

Gaby turns her back on Fatima and opens her locker.

"We're still in the Friday night vibe. We went dancing," says Mali, then glances at me. "Just the four of us."

Heat rushes to my head in panic mode. I'm on the outside of the group because I didn't go on the work night out. If I had known it was going to dominate the day and bond everyone like this, I'd have made the effort, at least to join them for a drink.

"Maybe I can come next time. I like dancing," Fatima says, a tad too forceful for my liking.

"Yeah, maybe," says Phil.

Fatima flounces off again. Gaby turns to the girls, with a serious face.

"Don't worry," says Mali to Gaby. "Floor seven only."

"At least she'd bother to come if you did invite her," says Phil, eyeing me. I try to ignore her, but knowing she's looking at me makes my mouth dry and my body tingle. As much as I wish she wasn't suspicious of me, I like it when her eyes travel over me like that.

The door swings open and Julia enters with her clipboard in hand. Around her neck, her hotel ID clinks off the silver necklace she's wearing. She smiles around the room oblivious to the lack of response from the women. Out of all the hotels I've worked in, I've never had a supervisor as proud of their job as Julia is. Or as delusional about their relationship with the cleaners.

"Hello, team," she says, holding up her clipboard, like this should signal silence. There's a murmur of a weak reply, which in Julia's head probably sounds like a round of enthusiastic hellos.

She takes a piece of paper from her clipboard and reads from it. The hotel had a big cancellation last night so some of the prepped rooms on floor seven won't need cleaning today.

"Mali and Noelle, I've moved you to front of house for the morning, okay?"

Mali's shoulders droop a little. I'm not sure if it's because she's been put on lobby duty, or because she has to do it with me. Either way, I'm pleased we've been put together. I have some clawing back to do if I'm to be a part of the group again and having Mali to myself will help.

Mali and I step out the service lift with our trolleys in tow and head toward huge double doors. Mali marches on ahead, humming to herself to avoid talking to me.

We push through the double doors and into the grand hall of the Magnolia lobby. I glance up, giddy as the biggest chandelier I've ever seen hovers above me like a flying saucer. Thick, black marble pillars hold up the ornate ceiling and gigantic flowers on long stalks stretch out of huge vases, big enough to hold a human. It looks like the home of a giant. Brown and cream patterned marble covers the entire floor area with thick rugs fixed down around the lounge and seated areas. The marble-covered front desk is tucked away in the corner and is small in comparison to everything else.

Mali tells me what our duties are. I nod like I'm really listening, though I already know what I'm doing. We have to polish the furniture and fixtures and vacuum and polish the guest lifts as well as the corridors and hallways. Cleaning the floor is not our responsibility as it is polished every night by machine when the hotel is quiet. We also have to clean the bathrooms behind the front desk. Mali looks over at the front desk, where a woman is talking to the doorman.

"That's Michelle," she says to me, under her breath. "Be careful what you say to her. Everything goes back to Mr. Redmond."

I look over at Michelle nattering to the doorman. She has small round glasses pushed right up to the bridge of her nose, like they're stuck on her face, and a single plait snakes over her right shoulder. She wears a suit dress and holds a pen to her cheek as she talks.

"We'll start with the toilets," says Mali. She pushes her trolley ahead and I follow her with mine. We pass the front desk and Michelle sees us.

"Hey, Mali,"

Mali nods to her, polite.

"Oh, are you new?" says Michelle, as I pass by.

I nod too, as though I'm shy. Michelle keeps watching me as I follow Mali down the marble corridor to the toilets.

"I'm happy to do the men's if you want to do the ladies'," I offer, trying to soften her up.

"Fine," says Mali and walks to the ladies' on the other side of the corridor. She's really making me pay for not turning up on Friday. I'll just have to pick my moment carefully to get back in her good graces.

I enter the men's room, putting up a small free-standing sign that says CLEANING IN PROGRESS.

I start with emptying the garbage pails, which barely have any rubbish in them. One has a broken wineglass in it though, which I only see just in time to avoid cutting myself. I sweep the floor being sure to get any other shards of glass.

"What's your name then?"

I turn to see Michelle standing over me as I use a small dustpan and brush to catch the last of the glass fragments.

"Noelle," I say, on my guard. I believe Mali that Michelle is not to be trusted.

"I'm Michelle. So you took the spot on floor seven then?" She doesn't give me a chance to answer. "Fatima's not very happy about that. She's one of the other cleaners. Did you meet her? How do you find working with Mali?"

"Great," I say, standing up. She gives me a smug look, like she has my number but she so doesn't.

"Gaby's funny, isn't she? Always late though."

"I haven't noticed," I say.

"And Phil's a right character. Far too smart to be a cleaner. No offense."

I shrug, giving nothing away. Her eyes narrow a little. She's frustrated she's not getting much out of me. She sniffs and pushes her shoulders back, bored of me now.

"I hope it works out for you. I'm sure Fatima's waiting in the wings to step in if it doesn't." She says this with a kind smile, like she's joking, but she's trying to worry me. It's a power play. She wants me to think she knows everyone and everything and has the ability to change things, so I better respect her or else. But I'm much more skilled at reading people than she is.

"You okay, Noelle?" comes Mali's voice from outside. She appears at the door and pretends to be surprised to see Michelle. "Oh, what are you doing in here?" she asks, friendly.

"Just getting acquainted with Noelle. Keep up the good work, girls. Don't forget to give my desk a little clean—the night porters keep leaving coffee stains all over it." She gives us a sweet smile and walks out. Mali looks at me, eyebrows raised.

"I didn't say anything to her. You told me not to."

Mali nods and swivels around to leave.

"You're a good actress," I say, taking a bold approach to get her to engage with me. She turns to me, frowning.

"*Oh, what are you doing in here?*" I say, mimicking her false friendly tone. Teasing Mali is a risky strategy. Rose seems to be the only one who can get away with it.

Mali puts her hands on her hips, her nostrils flaring a little. Maybe today will be the day I have to leave after all.

Then she throws her head back and laughs, filling the echoey room with her cartoon giggle.

"That woman is a bitch," says Mali.

"She is," I say. "And I'm sorry I didn't come on Friday night," I add quickly.

"You had a migraine," she says, shrugging, still not believing me for a second.

"I lied about that. I didn't come because I was nervous, about going out with you all for the first time."

I gaze at my feet, hoping the shy girl act will work.

"Don't bullshit me," she says.

"It's the truth. I chickened out. And I really didn't think you'd be bothered if I didn't come, okay?"

"I'm not bothered," she says, sniffing a little.

"I said I'd come and then I didn't. It's rude."

"Yeah, it is. If you don't want to hang out with us, just say."

"I do want to hang out with you. I just didn't think you'd want to hang out with me," I say, laying it on thick. Although part of what I'm saying is true.

Mali narrows her eyes again, then sighs, relaxing her shoulders.

"If we didn't want you to come, we wouldn't have asked you."

"I realize that now," I say, rolling my eyes, like I'm the idiot.

"You're either part of floor seven, or you're not."

"I am part of it, I mean, I want to be," I say, dropping my eyes, hoping for sympathy but knowing it's a long shot with Mali.

"Okay, okay, skinny," she says, waving me away as though she can't bear the sight of me anymore. "You come next time, alright?"

I nod, relieved to hear her call me skinny again. I am so back in her good graces.

Up on floor seven, I push my trolley along to room 701. It's after lunch and Mali and I have returned to room cleaning for the afternoon. In the canteen, Mali and I saw Gaby and Rose who were pleased to see we were getting along again.

"Noelle met Michelle," Mali told them.

"Oh, dear," said Gaby as Rose shook her head. But I was more concerned with where Phil was. I didn't ask.

I have five rooms to clean now in two and a half hours. Despite still having to win Phil over, knowing that Mali trusts me again is a real boost to my confidence. A shiver runs down my spine. I'm in the mood for taking something. Keep it small, I tell myself. When I've been in a mood like this before, I've taken something way too risky and ended up with a complaint too soon. My track record with five-star hotels isn't great. I'm nowhere near ready to leave the Magnolia yet, so I need to be careful and stay controlled. Keep it small.

I glance up and down the corridor, checking the coast is clear but also scanning the area for Phil. Rose and Mali are up the other end and Gaby is halfway along. I'm pretty much on my own, just the way I like it. I'm about to enter room 701, when Phil appears on the corridor coming from the service lift, pulling her trolley behind her. My stomach flips at the sight of her. She stops to talk to Gaby but she's heading my way. I bend down behind my trolley pretending to look for something in the lower compartments. I grab the mini dustpan and stand up.

"You sweet-talked Mali then?"

"I said sorry about Friday night, that's all," I say, fiddling with my dustpan as though it's broken, which it isn't. Phil eyes the dustpan, a slight smile on her face. I grab cloths and cleaning products and go to enter room 701.

"Do I make you nervous?" she says, with a playful look.

"No," I say, dropping one of my cloths and quickly picking it up.

She gives me a slow smile. "We're going out again on Friday. Just me, Rose and Mali. Gaby has to work the night shift. Will you come this time?"

"Sure, thanks," I say.

She wanders off down the corridor. "I like your hair behind your ears. It's cute," she adds, glancing back.

I quickly check my hair, which is tucked behind my ears. I hadn't even noticed, but Phil did. She said it was cute. My hands shake a little and my legs feel hollow. My heart is racing making the blood thunder around my body. It's a similar sensation to when I take something but more wild and unpredictable. I don't have control over how I react to Phil and this is definitely a problem.

I enter room 701, go straight to the bathroom and turn the cold tap on to splash my face with water. Maybe it's time to accept that things might not work out in the Magnolia, but this makes me weary again. Something inside me wants to stay put for a while, and I like being part of floor seven. I'm going to have to find a way to control myself around Phil and focus more on taking things, which is the only reason I do this job.

Chapter 10

I twist open the new mascara I bought in Boots this afternoon after work. When I say new, what I also mean is first. It's Friday and I'm going on the work night out with the girls. My second chance. I'm looking at a tutorial online on how to apply makeup. I've never bothered wearing it before but feel I should make an effort tonight considering I was a no-show last time. And I'm ready with excuses to bow out after one beer.

I don't drink as a rule. I got drunk once when I was fourteen. I wanted to see what all the fuss was about so downed three cans of cider that I'd swiped from my mother's Christmas stash.

The alcohol washed through my body all warm and tingly, making me feel relaxed and docile. I remember how relieved I was that it was possible to feel like that, worry-free. But when my mother burst into my room and found the cider cans, it wasn't so wonderful. And because I'd been drinking my reactions were too slow to defend myself and I ended up in the emergency room.

My mother had the perfect excuse for my injuries this time. I was an off-the-rails drunken teen that she was struggling to control. The nurses and the doctor comforted her and gave her support leaflets to read and a cup of tea in a mug from their own kitchen. They frowned at me and raised their eyebrows for splitting the back of my own head open.

After that I decided no more drinking. I needed to have my wits about me at all times and it's a rule that stuck. Drinking equals loss of control and that was not something I could allow to happen, especially around the Magnolia girls.

Under the bare light bulb dangling from the ceiling, using a mirror in a powder compact (also new), I finish applying the mascara and add some blush to my apples. That's what the teenage girl in the online tutorial calls her cheeks. I was afraid of overdoing the makeup, so I've barely got any on, but it's definitely made a difference. My eyes appear bigger and more defined, and my cheeks have a warm glow. I might wear it in the future.

I open the Zara bag beside me and look inside at the rolled-up black T-shirt dress I also bought this afternoon. I didn't try it on before I bought it, so I'm hoping it fits. Although, I'm wondering now if I should even wear it.

I glance over at my clothing rail where a few newly washed work shirts hang limply. The only other pieces of clothing I own are a T-shirt with a Fruit of the Loom logo on the left breast and a black off-the-shoulder top with a small hole under the left arm that I throw on over a work skirt when I've been dragged to a night out in the past. I also have a pair of black jeans that I picked up in a charity shop for five pounds but have never worn. These three items, the sole contents of my non-work wardrobe, lie folded and hidden away in the rickety chest of drawers squashed in behind the clothes rail. Although, the off-the-shoulder top did manage to entice Colin, the banker, so it's not to be totally dismissed. But Phil said we were going dancing, so I want to look my best. Not that I'll be dancing.

I refuse to delve much deeper into my reasons and motivations for wanting to look good tonight. I tell myself it's a matter of pride.

My body lurches forward as the bus comes to a stop in Clapham Junction. We're meeting in a pub here and I'm wondering now if I'm overdressed in my new black dress, which has a lower neckline than I expected. Maybe I should have worn jeans and my Fruit of the Loom T-shirt. I don't want to look like I've made too much of an effort. I catch a glimpse of myself in the doors as I wait for them to open. Too much blush. The bus ejects a hissing noise as the air pressure releases and the doors fold open.

The cold air hits my face and I pull my jacket around myself as I step off the bus rubbing my cheeks to remove the excess makeup. I check my face again in a shop window. I look pale now. Maybe I shouldn't have wiped the blush off. I see the pub up ahead, a mock Tudor building with green shrubs and ivy hanging over the entrance and windows. I think about turning around and wonder what excuses I could come up with that they would believe. But there are no excuses this time. It's only one beer with your work colleagues, I tell myself. Get a grip. If I don't go into this pub right now it's all over for me at the Magnolia. Or at least on floor seven. I'll probably be replaced by Fatima on Monday morning.

A loud wolf-whistle makes me spin around.

"Noelle? Noelle?"

I look over the road and see Rose, waving at me, cigarette in hand. Her thick, silver hair cascades over her shoulders. She is squished into a fake fur cerise pink jacket and wearing a sparkly silver dress with very high black wedges. She struts across the road toward me.

"You look great," I say, and I mean it, she really does.

"This is the real me, baby. Work is the only place I look like shit. You look good too," she says as she takes a short, sharp drag on the end of her cigarette and drops it in the gutter.

"Thanks," I mutter, cursing myself for rubbing off the blush. If this is the effort everyone's making, I am so underdressed. Thank God I didn't wear my Fruit of the Loom T-shirt. Rose takes my arm and marches me into the pub.

"We are going to have a wild night," she says to me. I swallow, dipping my head farther into my jacket to take a deep breath. The plan here is to make sure my colleagues know I'm a team player and that they like and respect me enough to stand by me at work if need be. That is all tonight is about.

The pub is already heaving with people, three deep at the bar and the music is loud. I see Phil the minute we enter. She is sitting at the end of the bar farthest away from us drinking a bottle of beer. Her hair is twisted into two high buns on either side of her head with a couple of loose silky strands sweeping her cheekbones. She has bright red lipstick on, accentuating her heart-shaped lips and she's wearing a red halter-neck dress. She looks like a bird of paradise, wild and unaware of how beautiful she is. She sees us and urgently waves us over to where she is sitting.

"There's Phil," says Rose, only seeing her now, pushing me ahead through the crowd. Phil jumps up from her bar stool and hugs me, her mouth close to my ear.

"Glad you could make it," she murmurs then moves onto Rose and gives her a big kiss on the cheek leaving a lipstick mark.

"For fuck's sake," complains Rose. Phil laughs, using her thumb to wipe the mark off Rose's face.

Phil pats the two bar stools beside her. "Quick, I've been guarding these like a Rottweiler." Rose and I plonk ourselves down on the stools. I sit closest to Phil. Phil asks us what we're having. Rose says white wine, I say I'll have a beer. Two is normally my limit, but I know already it's going to be a challenge to stick to that tonight.

Phil smiles at the barman, getting his attention. His eyes sweep over her, clearly taken with her. He ignores the other customers waiting to be served and comes up to her, leaning in close to take her order.

"Two more beers, a white wine and three tequila shots, please." The barman gives her a wink and goes to get the drinks.

"Bring it on," says Rose.

"I don't normally drink shots," I say to Phil.

"Well, you do now," she says.

One won't do any harm, I tell myself.

"Mali's running late with college," says Rose.

"Mali's going to be president of the world one day, did you know that?" Phil says to me, giving me a lazy look.

"Yeah, she can give us all jobs," I say.

"No way," says Rose. "Can you imagine working for Mali? It'd be like boot camp every day with her screaming in your ear. She'd have you marching and saluting and God knows what else." We all laugh and I relax a little. It's good to be out with them. They're a bit odd and so am I.

I glance at Phil. Her eyes linger on me for a moment then the barman slaps our drinks on the bar. Phil gives him a fifty and tells him to have one for himself. She passes me my beer, Rose her glass of wine and then gives us a shot glass each with tequila. I now have a drink in both hands. Phil picks up her own tequila.

Phil and Rose count to three and down their shots, and then chase them with their beer and wine. What the hell, I think, and down mine. The alcohol hits the back of my throat like a fireball, then slips seductively into my stomach, sending a hot sensation through my body. I wince and my eyes water with the bitterness.

"Tequila virgin," yells Rose as she takes the shot glass from me and puts it on the bar. Phil puts her hand on the middle of my back. It feels hot. I look up at her.

"First time for everything," she says.

I look away, taking a slow breath as the initial effect of the alcohol settles in my stomach and buzzes into my bloodstream. I glance around the bar, brighter now. I notice the barman's T-shirt is a vivid purple as he brings Phil her change. Phil nudges the bottle of beer in my hand and I take a big mouthful. The cool bubbles settle my throat and my eyes stop streaming.

I take another swig of my beer. Rose sees someone she knows and wanders off to speak to them. Phil gets off her stool and stands in front of me.

"Do you like my dress?" she asks, half twirling, looking over her shoulder at me.

"Yeah, it's nice."

"Nice? I don't want to look nice. I want to look fucking amazing."

"You look fucking amazing," I say.

"Thank you." She sits down.

"Stand up. I want to see your dress," she says to me.

But I don't want to stand up. I don't want Phil assessing and rating me. What if she doesn't like what I'm wearing?

"Stand up," she says again, looking at me like I'm acting weird.

I stand up. My black dress falls just above my knees, hugging my hips. I glance down at my beige Converse trainers, which suddenly look more bland than usual. Never, in my whole life, have I felt as self-conscious as I do right now.

Phil's eyes move slowly over me, squinting a little. I take a nervous sip of my beer.

"Turn around," she says.

I look at her. Really? This is agony enough. She circles her finger in the air, insisting. I quickly turn around and then sit back down.

"I like your style. Kind of student chic glam."

"Right," I say. Not sure what that means. She puts her hand on my knee. Flesh against flesh.

"There's something I want to ask you," she says, scanning my face with her sharp eyes. I swallow, my mouth dry.

"Stop the party bus, I'm here, I'm here," comes a shrill voice. Phil takes her hand off my knee and throws her arms in the air.

"Mali," she yells.

Mali stands behind us dressed in leather—mini skirt, jacket and thigh-high boots, which nearly reach her hips since she's so petite. She does a little funky move, contorting her face into an oversized pout. Her hair is spiked and the tips are sprayed red. Now I really feel like someone who didn't get the dress code memo.

Phil and Mali embrace, falling over each other with compliments on how they look. Mali pulls me into a bear hug.

"You don't look nearly drunk enough. Get this girl a tequila shot," she yells over to Phil, who is again ordering drinks from the cheeky barman.

"No, really," I say. "I've had one."

"One?" says Mali. "Make that two," she yells at Phil.

Rose comes up to Mali from behind and scoops her up in her arms, jumping up and down with her.

"Put me down, you mad bitch," says Mali, giggling. Rose puts her down.

"You look like a biker chick on acid," says Rose.

"I know," says Mali, delighted, as she grabs her shot, downs it and then drinks half a pint of beer.

My head's a little woozy as I slip off to the ladies', but I like the sensation. It's as though nothing matters anymore and I'm free.

In the bathroom I peer at myself in the mirror. My eyes are black underneath where my mascara has run. I grab some toilet paper from a stall, wet it under the tap, which makes it mushy, and do my best to dab the smudged makeup away.

"What are you doing that for?"

I turn to see Phil, leaning against the hand dryer. Two girls finish touching up their faces and leave.

"The tequila made my eyes water," I say, aware I sound feeble.

"I think the black looks good like that, under your eyes. Sexy."

Sexy. The word bounces around in my head for a moment. She opens her handbag and takes out a small plastic purse with cotton buds in it.

"You carry those around with you?" I ask.

"I carry a lot of shit around in my bag," she replies.

I like that she has weird stuff in her bag. She comes over to me, close. Carefully she strokes the cotton bud underneath my right eye and then my left.

"There, I didn't wipe it all away," she says. She doesn't move and neither do I. "Where did you get that scar?" she asks looking at the white mark above my right eyebrow.

"I fell when I was a kid," I murmur.

She comes in closer to me, our noses nearly touching now. I feel her breath on my top lip and can smell her musky perfume. I look at her skin, so perfect. Then her lips touch mine, barely a kiss. A small moan escapes my mouth and I look at her, mortified, powerless.

She takes my hand and pulls me into a stall and locks the door behind us. I'm pinned against the wall, unable to move, as she presses her body against mine and kisses me, harder this time, her tongue finding mine. I kiss her back, lost in the moment, my eyes closed, my whole body shaking with anticipation.

Her hands move over my hips, stroking the contour of my body. I want to touch her too, but I don't know how. She moves her hands up my body and grabs my right breast, gently. Blood rushes to my head and my knees weaken a little.

She pushes her hand down the front of my dress and into my bra. I can't bear it. If she touches me like this for much longer

I'm going to scream. She takes my nipple between her fingers and gently squeezes. The rush to my head intensifies and suddenly my body shudders and spasms and I can't breathe. I buckle over, catching my breath, aware of an intense throbbing between my legs.

"I'm sorry, I don't know what's wrong with me," I manage to say. She pulls me up and pushes my sweaty hair from my face.

"You just came," she says. I look at her, confused. "You had an orgasm."

I've heard women talk about orgasms before, but I didn't think they happened to people like me.

"Have you never had one before?" she says. I shake my head, not sure how sad it is to admit it, but my defenses aren't just low, they're nonexistent. "You've got a lot of catching up to do," she whispers in my ear.

I want you, I think to myself. She touches my face like she knows and tells me we'll take it slow but I'm not sure what she means. All I'm thinking is, can we do that again? Will she touch me again?

We wander through the crowds back to the bar where Mali is lining up more tequila shots, singing along to the music.

Rose, glassy-eyed, shoves her shoulders forward and backward dancing to the music, a little unsteady on her feet. All I want to do is be with Phil, to touch her, smell her, feel her next to me, but I know to keep cool. Don't be needy, I tell myself. Don't show weakness. The same rules apply here as they do when I start a new job and I need my colleagues to like me.

"Where've you been?" asks Mali, throwing her arms around us.

"Noelle had to clean her face up," says Phil.

Mali regards me. "You have color in your cheeks. That's good! Come on, let's get really pissed."

We push forward to the bar, Mali and Rose between me and Phil. We each grab our shot glass.

"One, two, three," shouts Mali and we all down it in one. I wince again, screwing up my face, but not as much as last time. I shake my head as the alcohol hits the spot. I look over at Phil. She gives me a sultry look. I scream with excitement inside my head. I don't know what love feels like, but I figure this must be it.

I quickly look down at my feet, afraid my eyes will give me away. Rose taps me on the shoulder.

"Be careful with Phil," she says.

"What do you mean?"

"She's not like everyone else." Rose turns to Mali and Phil. "Right, let's get out of here, peeps. I want to boogie." Phil puts her arm around Rose and dances with her.

"Wait!" Mali yells, her phone in one hand, her other hand in the air, a signal for us all to shut up. We look at her surprised. All joy and color has drained from Mali's face. "It's Gaby," she says.

Chapter 11

The taxi pulls into the drop-off area of the emergency admission. No one has said a word the whole way here. I'm sitting in the front and Phil, Rose and Mali are squashed in the back. I opted for the front seat. I need to think about what happened with Phil and what it means. And I'm worried about my self-control. I don't want to do something wrong, like reach out and touch her. But what if that's not wrong? I realize I have no way of knowing what to do in a situation like this.

We pile out of the taxi, rush through the entrance doors and up to the reception desk where a hard-faced man peers at us over his glasses. We must look quite a sight—we're still drunk and from the way we're all dressed, me excluded, we could easily have come straight from a fancy dress party. Phil takes charge, sober and articulate.

"We're looking for Gabriella King? Her son, Francesco, was brought in. Drug overdose," she says.

Mali, Rose and I drop our heads, all fearing the worst for Gaby. The hard-faced man checks the computer. He points to double doors to the side of the reception desk.

"One of you can go through. The rest will have to wait." Mali, Rose and I step back, as Phil heads toward the doors.

We take a seat among the people waiting to be seen, slumped in their chairs. Beside Rose is a young man with his arm in a sling and a black eye. On the other side, next to Mali, is an older man who has fallen asleep, his head so far forward it nearly rests on his huge stomach.

Suddenly, I feel out of place. I've known Gaby for two weeks. I've only known all of them for two weeks and now I'm having orgasms in toilets and sitting in the ER at eleven o'clock at night hoping Gaby's son hasn't died. I wonder if I should make my excuses and go. But I worry how that would look. I don't want to push myself out of the circle again. And the thought of being away from Phil gives me a tight knot in my stomach.

"He better be alright," says Rose taking out her phone and quickly typing a text.

"Little shit," spits Mali. "He's caused Gaby nothing but trouble and now she's in the hospital looking at her baby, wondering if he's going to fucking die."

Rose and I nod so as not to further upset Mali, not because we agree with her. Mali might be right about Francesco being a little shit but it's not helpful.

The double doors swing open and Phil comes back out, followed by Gaby in her Magnolia uniform, red and blotchy in the face from crying. She seems smaller and shrunken. We all stand, bracing ourselves for the worst. Phil puts her arm around Gaby to support her.

"Thanks for coming," Gaby says. She looks at us, lost and a little dazed.

"Is he okay?" says Mali. She wants to rip the plaster off and hear the bad news now if there is any. We all do, to be fair. Gaby shrugs, hopeless, helpless.

"He's in a coma," says Phil. We all relax a little, although a coma isn't good news either.

"They don't know if he's going to make it," whispers Gaby. "I better get back to him." She turns to go then stops. "Thanks again for coming. It means a lot." Mali hugs her, then Rose. I'm awkward, not sure if I'm close enough to Gaby to be able to give her a hug at a time like this, plus I'm not really a hugs person.

I reach out and squeeze her hand. She grips my hand for a moment then lets go and shuffles back through the double doors.

Phil gives us a grave look. Mali flops down on a chair.

"Not good," says Mali.

"Gaby blames herself, you know, for changing the locks," says Phil. Mali sits up and looks Phil straight in the eye.

"She should have done it sooner."

Phil sniffs and looks away. I can see she's troubled.

"Fuck him," shouts Mali. Phil puts her fingers to her lips to shush Mali. But Mali doesn't care, throwing her arms around as she talks.

"What if he makes it but has brain damage? She'll be stuck at home with him for the rest of her life, feeding him through a fucking tube. It would be better if they just switched the machine off."

"Mali? You can't say things like that," says Rose. I agree with Rose and start to wonder if Mali is heartless. Then Mali drops her head in her hands and starts to sob, her shoulders heaving. Phil puts an arm around her, looks at me and gives a little shake of her head.

"She doesn't mean it," Rose whispers to me. "She's upset for Gaby, that's all."

I'm unsure what to say or even how to behave. I've never been in a situation like this before. The only time I've ever been in a hospital was when I was the patient. I decide to be useful and offer to get coffee for everyone.

I make my way past reception and down a long dreary white corridor. One of the overhead strip lights flickers as I follow the sign that says "Shop/Café." My feet make a slapping sound on the hard plastic floor.

I'm surprised I don't dislike hospitals after all the hours I spent in them growing up. Instead I find them strangely comforting. Maybe hospitals represent calm for me. A visit was always followed by a few days at home where life was just about bearable.

At the café area, the shutters are pulled down. It's dim and gloomy. There is a hot drinks machine and a half full vending machine. I have just enough change for four cups of coffee. I watch in a trance as the thin, brown liquid splutters out into small plastic cups. The cups are piping hot so I pull the sleeves of my jacket down to protect my hands as I try to carry all four at once.

"Need a hand?" says Phil, joining me, her shoulders pulled up to her ears as though she's cold. It is cold, I think, which is unusual for a hospital. I always found them sticky and warm. I pass her two of the cups, which she holds carefully by the rim and we wander back up the lifeless corridor toward the waiting area.

"Don't judge Mali. She wants us to live in a world where no one is ever sad and terrible things never happen."

"That's not very realistic," I say.

"And she knows it. That's why she gets angry."

"I like that about her," I say.

"Me too. She hasn't given up on getting the life she wants. She was married once but the guy wanted kids and she didn't. He went back to Thailand. She stayed."

I love Phil talking to me like this, like my opinion matters. We glance at each other. I look away first, terrified I might blurt out something foolish and embarrass myself.

We don't talk for a moment. It's enough to just be with her, carrying cups of coffee together.

"I don't feel guilty," she finally says. "About telling Gaby to change the locks." But her eyes are cast down, suggesting she does feel guilty.

"She had to do it," I say.

"Something like this was going to happen eventually, I suppose," she says with a sigh. "He was never going to get clean."

"Do you think he will now? If he survives," I ask.

"Maybe. I still think he's too far down that road now. Some people never change, do they?" I nod in total agreement. Although I'd lose the word "some."

We're nearly back to the waiting area. I can see Rose with her arm around Mali, who still has her head in her hands, her red-tipped spiky hair so out of place in the bright, sterile waiting room. Phil looks up at the flickering strip light overhead.

"Hospitals give me the creeps," she says. I wonder why, but I don't ask. I know about Mali and her ambitions and work ethic. I know Rose shares a house with her sister. And I know all about

Gaby. But Phil is still pretty much a mystery to me, and Rose's comment in the pub about Phil being different has only made me more curious.

A chubby woman swimming in knitwear rushes into the waiting room, holding her phone, as Gaby bursts through the double doors also holding her phone. It's Gaby's mum. She holds her arms open for Gaby to collapse into her warm, woolen bosom. She's driven four hours from Devon to get here but you know she'd have walked over hot coals if she'd needed to. She kisses the top of Gaby's head, holding her like she's a small child. What a gift it must be to experience love like that. Whatever happens to Gaby's son, Gaby will always be more fortunate than me and I'm okay with that. I'm not jealous. It's only an observation. I'm happy for Gaby to have a mother like this.

Phil, Rose, Mali and I step outside of the hospital, coats wrapped around our bodies, hands tucked deep into our pockets as the cold wind whips around us. Mali has ordered three taxis, and looking at her phone she can see the first one's only a minute away and the other two are just behind it. Mali lives near Rose, so they're sharing. The other two are for me and Phil.

The disappointment of the night with Phil ending hangs over me like a dark, heavy mist. The uncertainty of where I stand with her makes the knot in my stomach bigger. I glance at her but she stares at her feet, collar pulled up high around her ears. She's showing no signs of wanting to be with me now or ever again. Maybe that's all it was ever going to be between us—a fleeting moment in a bathroom stall. The thought makes me dizzy.

The first taxi pulls up and Mali and Rose clamber in.

"See you Sunday, losers," shouts Mali, waving out of the window. Phil and I wave back but quickly put our hands back in our pockets. We are left alone, waiting in silence. I tuck my chin further into my coat as the next taxi pulls up.

I step away from the curb to indicate Phil can take it. Phil climbs in the back and shunts over to the other side leaving the door open. I'm rooted to the spot. She leans across the seat so I can see her head in the open door.

"You coming back to my place or what?"

I nod and get in beside her, banging my shin on the door as I do. The pain shoots through me, but I don't care. Phil smiles at me as I settle beside her.

"What about the other taxi?" I say.

"What about it?" says Phil.

The taxi turns off the road and into an apartment complex made up of three white square buildings. I climb out of the car, careful this time not to bang my shin or any other part of my body, and gaze at the brightly lit buildings.

It has a modern, industrial vibe and everything looks and feels clean and polished. Compared to the run-down heap I live in it's like stepping into the future. Phil joins me.

"It looks like a hospital, doesn't it?"

"What? No, it's lovely. More like a five-star hotel."

She throws me a quick look. "You're an optimist."

Am I? I think. The taxi pulls away, its tires rolling over the gravelly driveway.

Phil leads the way to the entrance and I follow, still looking around. The plants and trees look too green to be real. She opens the main door and we enter an even whiter, silent space with cream carpet tiles covering the floor. I follow Phil past the lift and through a set of double doors into the ground floor corridor. The air smells like washed laundry.

Phil stops at her apartment door, number nine. She puts her key in the lock and pushes the door open. It's dark inside. She goes in first and flicks on the hall light, which casts a dim shadow on the white walls.

I follow her into a living room where she switches on two floor lamps with gray shades. They illuminate the room, giving it a soft, warm glow. There's a chocolate brown, squishy sofa free from stains or holes and a thick, cream-colored carpet, clean, maybe new. Shelving lines one wall, stuffed full of books. The whole apartment has the scent of Phil and her mildly musky perfume. At the end of the living room is a galley-style kitchen with under-cabinet lighting. I'm struck by how sophisticated her flat is. But then, so is Phil.

"Nice apartment," I say.

"It's not actually mine. Well it is, but I didn't buy it. It was given to me."

"Someone gave you an apartment?" I can't hide my surprise.

"My grandmother. She's dead now. I got it in her will."

"Why are you a cleaner?" I say, immediately wishing I hadn't asked.

Phil moves into the kitchen and opens a cupboard. Inside are tins of tomatoes and beans and little containers of spices and herbs and half-full bottles of various oils. It's a proper food pantry. She reaches into the back and pulls out a bottle of Bacardi.

"It's all I've got, I'm afraid."

She has no intention of answering my question or even acknowledging it.

"I don't really want a drink," I say. She turns to me, holding the bottle in her hand like it's useless now. I shrug, it's the truth—the last thing I want is to gulp down neat rum.

"What do you want then?" It's a loaded question. I want to speak but my throat's gone dry. Maybe I do need a drink after all.

Phil leans back against the counter, eyeing me. I wonder how she did her hair. It's perfect. Even the falling strands that frame her face have stayed in place. I swallow, my cheeks beginning to burn, for real.

"Noelle? What do you want?"

I stare at her, under pressure. I'm going to have to answer. Will I say tea? Water?

"It's a simple question," she says, waiting.

I take a deep breath.

"You," I whisper. She nods, like she's thinking about what this means but the pause in conversation feels like an eternity. Will she ask me to leave? Have I said too much?

She puts down the bottle of Bacardi and without looking at me reaches for my hand and gently pulls me to her, moving me around so my back's against the counter and she's now facing me.

My body trembles. She gently kisses me, and I kiss her right back, groping for her, intense, unable to control the longing inside me. She hitches up my dress but I grab her hand to stop her.

"I want to do something for you," I gasp.

"Plenty of time for that," she murmurs in my ear as she slips her fingers into the front of my knickers.

I sit on Phil's toilet, staring into space, still a bit shaky. I grab myself two sheets of toilet roll, which I notice is the fancy cushioned kind, and dab myself dry. I flush the loo and wash my hands looking around the small but perfect and immaculate bathroom. I run my finger along the rim of the bathtub. Squeaky clean. A bottle of shower gel stands on the edge of the bath. It has an elegant, misty pink bottle so I assume it's expensive. I flip the lid and put my nose to it. It smells like Phil. I put a tiny bit on my hand and rub it in.

I gaze at myself in the mirror. My cheeks are still flushed and I'm not surprised. I also wouldn't be surprised if I woke up the entire building.

I fix my hair so it's pushed close to my face—for some reason I think I look prettier like that—and I head back to the living room to pick up where we left off. But Phil is spread out on the sofa snoring gently, an empty glass in her hand.

I take the glass and sniff it. Bacardi. I put the glass on the shiny, slick coffee table—with no stains or scratches on it.

Phil looks so peaceful sleeping. Her breathing is low and quiet. Every now and then she holds her breath a little longer and then lets it out in a quick puff.

I grab the soft fleece from the back of the sofa and gently pull it over her body. She doesn't move and her breathing doesn't change. I sit back on the coffee table, unsure what to do now. Do I stay? She never invited me to. And she went to sleep so she obviously didn't want to carry on what we were doing. I'm not too worried about that. Cleaners get tired and we should sleep when we need to.

I stand up and wander around the living room. The window looks out onto gardens and trees. I'm pleased Phil has a lovely view. What you see from your window when you wake up every day matters and whenever I rent a new flat it's the first thing I check. I once had the opportunity to rent a brand new one-bedroom apartment. It had been the show apartment so all the fancy furniture was coming with it. But the living room window looked out over wasteland that stretched for miles. An old car tire lay on a mound on the horizon. A rusty bicycle with only one wheel had been dumped in a bush. Brambles and thistles spread over the landscape like a bad rash and there were stray cats wandering around. The lonely, lifeless space reminded me of the graveyard view from the flat in West House. It made me feel hopeless. The estate agent was genuinely surprised when I turned it down. It made me wonder if other people bothered looking out of their windows much.

A light snuffle makes me turn. Phil has moved onto her side and the fleece has slipped off her body. I pull the fleece back over her, grab my jacket and my bag and let myself out of her apartment. My gut feeling is it's the right thing to do. For people to like you it's important not to appear too needy.

Chapter 12

The staff room in the Magnolia is crowded as some of the cleaners finish shifts and others start theirs. Phil, Rose, Mali and I get ready in silence, the shadow of Gaby's plight hanging over us.

I glance at Phil, who doesn't look up. It's Sunday and I haven't seen her since Friday night and I haven't texted her and she hasn't texted me. I wonder if she's okay that I left her sleeping and went home.

Julia bustles in, her hotel pass swinging around her neck. She waddles a little due to her pencil skirt being a tad too tight.

"Any news on Gaby's boy?" she asks.

"No change," says Rose. "There's brain activity, so there's some hope."

"That's great," gushes Julia, as though this means Gaby's life will be back to normal by the end of the day and she'll be back at work tomorrow. We gaze at Julia, slightly perplexed. Julia runs her hand through her hair as though all is right with the world. "Tell her not to worry. I'm keeping her job open for her." I smile to myself. The Magnolia is obliged to do that, but hats off to Julia for trying to win brownie points and make it sound like it's her decision.

I push my trolley along the corridor to room 723. Mali and Rose are both up ahead at their trolleys, pulling on blue gloves. Behind me, Phil leans against her trolley talking to Fatima, who is filling in for Gaby.

I watch Phil's eyes move over Fatima's face as she talks, listening. Fatima pushes her ponytail back over her shoulder, eyeing Phil from under her eyelashes.

Phil glances over at me. I quickly check my trolley compartments, but my cheeks are flushed. I want to run up to Fatima and tell her to back off. Phil's my girlfriend.

I stare at the green and blue cloths in my hand. Is Phil my girlfriend? I'm not sure how these things work, and she hasn't said anything to suggest that. Maybe I should have stayed on Friday night. I could have slept on the floor or in a chair and in the morning we could have picked up where we left off. Maybe she thinks that's what I should have done. Is that why she's not paying me attention today and chatting with Fatima instead?

Rose comes up to me.

"Hi," I say, getting busy sorting through my cloths.

"Don't worry about Fatima, she's married with kids."

"Why would I be worried about Fatima?" I splutter.

"Okay, whatever," says Rose as she goes to walk away.

"Did Phil say something to you?" I ask, as though casual.

"She doesn't have to," says Rose. "Look, she's a good person and a good friend, just don't expect too much."

Rose goes back to her trolley. We're all a little behind schedule this morning. I glance back at Phil who stares right at me.

Fatima pushes her trolley farther up the corridor, her ponytail swinging from side to side. I smile at Phil, an attempt to test the water. She smiles back and, with antibacterial spray in hand, goes into room 715.

I enter room 723, leaving the door open, and stand for a moment, analyzing the clues left by the occupants. A bright pink shirt with big collars is draped on the wardrobe door and a suit jacket and trousers hang over a chair. On the unmade bed a floral dress lies in a crinkled mess and a bottle of perfume sits on the marble desk with the lid beside it. The curtains are only half open and an empty crisp packet and wineglass have been left on one of the night tables. I nod to myself, pleased. I can clean this room in under ten minutes, which gives me time to have a root around. They're messy enough, so unlikely to miss something a little more significant than a pair of tweezers.

I pick the dress up and fold it carefully, placing it over the suit on the back of the chair. Something twinkles and catches my eye—a brooch attached to the dress. I peer at it carefully making sure it's not designer or expensive, as I've had a close call with a brooch before. It's a small diamante encrusted flamingo with a pink glass beak: a piece of costume jewelry, light and tacky and not expensive at all. I turn it over and see the clip on the back is already undone so it could easily have fallen off the dress while the woman was wearing it. This is exactly the kind of item I long to find. And a piece of jewelry is ambitious so the buzz will be very satisfying. But where's the adrenaline rush? Where are the flutters in my stomach?

The brooch detaches easily from the dress and the flamingo now lies in the palm of my hand, glimmering in the light. But I feel nothing. No excitement, no flushed cheeks, no trembling fingers.

I close my eyes and imagine dropping it into the front of my apron. Normally just the thought of taking it would bring the blood rushing to my head. I touch my cheeks. Nothing. Take it anyway, I tell myself.

I slip it into the front pocket of my apron and wait. Still nothing. What's the matter with me?

I open my apron and look inside at the flamingo lying at the bottom and suddenly feel ridiculous. Look at the stupid thing, ugly and cheap. I quickly take it back out and leave it on the table beside the perfume replacing the lid on the bottle.

Maybe I have a thing about flamingos. Maybe it's a dislike I've had since I was a kid and I didn't know. But I've never even seen a real flamingo. It's not like my mother ever took me to the zoo.

I hurry to finish cleaning the bedroom and move into the bathroom.

Hotel bathrooms with female guests always give me a rush. There's so much to choose from with all the trinkets and little pots and makeup bags.

On the shelf in front of the sink is a large, black leather Dopp kit with gold letters on the side that say: MAN'S BAG. My instincts tell me this man thinks he's funny and entertaining, but he isn't. I imagine he has small facial features and screws up his eyes so you can't see them when he laughs, probably at his own jokes. And his wife's not much better. Why has she got a cheap brooch when they're spending six hundred pounds a night on a hotel room? Must be a business trip.

The woman's toiletry bag is nowhere to be seen, but she must have one. I swing around and find it hanging on the back of the door. It's one of those fold-out/flop-down ones that unravel like a tool belt with all the items stuffed into clear plastic pockets.

Scanning it quickly I decide it's too risky due to the transparency aspect. People notice the smallest detail if they have a visual memory of something. Taking from a regular toiletry bag is far easier, as a lot of things lie at the base of the bag in darkness, sometimes unseen for weeks or years. Not that I always want it to be easy. If it's too easy, there's no rush. Maybe I do need to take something from the flop-down toiletry bag.

I run my hand over the bumpy clear surfaces, inspecting the pouches. There's a pair of nail scissors. They would be perfect. Quite likely to be noted by the guest as missing but unlikely she would make a complaint, and if she did, I know Rose, Mali and even Phil would have my back now. I decide to go for it.

As my hand slips into the plastic pouch I stop. Again, where's the adrenaline? I retract my hand like I've been stung, leaving the scissors where they are and lean against the sink.

"What's the matter with you now? Are you sick?" I look up to see Mali standing in the doorway with Phil. They both eye me like I'm a strange insect.

"You've been in this room too long," snaps Mali. "And nothing is clean?"

"I'm feeling nauseous," I lie, to explain the leaning over the sink and the lack of cleaning. Phil comes to me and touches my shoulder, a wrinkle in her brow to show concern. Her touch sends an electrical current roaring through my veins and I have to lean harder on the sink to support myself. "I'll be alright in a minute," I say, gently shrugging Phil's hand away, confused by the feelings I have for her and the lack of feelings I have for taking things.

Working in hotels, cleaning rooms and taking from guests is what I do. This is who I am. What and who am I if I don't do this anymore?

"I'll help you finish the room," says Phil.

Mali throws her hands in the air, annoyed with me. "You do your own cleaning, that's the rules," she says, irritated.

"Go on, get out, we're not in the army," says Phil, shooing Mali out of the room. Mali goes in a huff, muttering to herself.

"Mali doesn't like it when things don't go the way she expects them to," says Phil with a sigh.

"I really am fine," I mumble. But I wish I could tell her that I'm not fine. I wish I could tell her my buzz is gone and I'm afraid. I wish I could tell her who I really am and ask her advice. She brushes the hair from my forehead.

"What happened to you the other night?"

"You fell asleep so I went home."

"I like that. You're not needy," she says. I nod, pleased that my decision to leave was the right one, but inside I'm screaming—I am needy and I need you. She leans in and kisses me on the lips, softly. I kiss her back, my hands running over her body, feeling her energy, her vibration through her shirt and apron.

"Easy," she says. I step away from her, mortified by my lack of control.

"It's okay, I can finish the room on my own."

"Alright," she says and goes to leave.

"Will I see you later?" I blurt out. She turns to me, a slight smile on her lips.

"What did you have in mind?"

I'm speechless now—I had nothing in mind. I'd be happy to spend the night with her in a pub toilet.

"How about dinner at yours?" she says.

"My place?"

"Yeah, I want to see where you live. I'll bring the wine," she says as she slips out of the bathroom.

I look at myself in the mirror. Dinner at mine. Fuck.

Chapter 13

It all began with Alison Rogers. After I dropped the pound coin in the gnome's fishing net, the feeling of lightness that flooded my body and made me want to skip and run, lasted well into the evening. It was a buzzing sensation that sizzled through my veins making me smile and long for more. Considering I hadn't had much cause to smile in my life, it was a wonderful novelty for me.

I lay in bed that night, my head half hanging off the mattress so I could stare out of the hole in my curtains at the slither of a new moon in the sky, as the warm feeling traveled from my feet right up to my head. Is this happiness? I thought.

I leaned up on my elbows and considered the shabby dresser pushed up against my bedroom door. This was a much-needed safety measure I had put in place since I became strong enough to move the dresser by myself. Before I was able to move the dresser, my mother, after a drinking binge, would often storm into my room while I was sleeping, drag me out of bed and slap me around the head, sometimes kicking me. It was always because of "the mess in the kitchen," not that I ever left a mess anywhere in the house. I was the only one who tidied up. But I knew not to argue and felt disappointed in her laziness and lack of imagination to think up a different excuse, even once.

She would launch her body at me with flailing arms and I'd roll myself into a ball with my hands by my head, waiting for it to be over. Sometimes I'd kick her back, hard so she fell over. If she was drunk enough, she'd simply pass out wherever she landed. I'd prod her a few times to make sure she was definitely out cold then drag her into the hallway and leave her there, which wasn't an easy feat for a scrawny child. She was heavier than a dresser so it could take up to thirty minutes to get her out of my room, but my determination was strong—the idea of her sleeping on my bedroom floor beside me was too disturbing. Being within three meters of my mother always made me sick with fear.

If she hadn't smacked me around too much, I'd get a jumper or a jacket and put it under her head, but most of the time I'd leave her in the hallway—a sweaty, dribbling mass, sprawled on the tattered, frayed carpet.

She was never there when I got up the next morning. Somehow she managed to crawl to her bed where she'd stay until the next evening. But on that particular night the dresser was in place and I was safe.

Normally, when I lay in bed in the dark, listening to the sounds of my mother shuffling up and down the hallway outside my room, my mind would wander to grim places, like the graveyard at the back of our flats. Maybe I'd end up there sooner than I thought. I wasn't afraid of dying. There's always death, I told myself when I felt especially desperate. It's always good to have options. I didn't think life had much to offer me and we all ended up six feet under in the end anyway, as my mother often reminded me.

But that night, after taking Alison Rogers's one-pound coin, I had different thoughts, positive ones, concerned with planning and strategy about when I could take something again and from whom. I had enough sense, even at that age, to know that taking from my classmates wasn't a practical option going forward. I had gotten away with it once, but I didn't want to risk it again. Instead, I began to take small items from my mother.

It was a high-risk strategy because she would have beaten me to an inch of my life if she caught me, so there was enough of a buzz to make it worth my while, but in a controlled environment. I knew her patterns and routines and what I could get away with.

I took a button from a cardigan she had bought for work, which drove her insane. "It's bloody new!" she yelled, stomping around the flat. "How could the button have fallen off already?" I agreed with her that it was a disgrace. She took the cardigan back to the shop and they exchanged it.

A few days later, when she came home drunk and passed out in the bathroom, I took a button from that cardigan too. Not from the exact same position, of course. I cut it off with her nail scissors.

I was putting myself in the firing line as it was a lose-lose situation. Not because she would work out that I had taken it but because she used me as a punch bag in moments of extreme frustration, like when the boiler broke and she couldn't wash her hair for work. So I wasn't quite sure how she'd react to losing another button, but the risk that she might take her fury out on me was worth it for the pleasure I felt at snipping it off and keeping it.

For the first time in my life I had something that was all mine and belonged to me, something I was in control of, and I wasn't going to let that go.

Five years later, I had a trash bag stuffed in the back of my wardrobe filled with different colored buttons, single earrings, hair bands, hair ribbons and even the odd shoe. She honestly believed that, on several occasions, she had walked home from the pub with only one shoe on. She didn't tell me that, of course. We didn't communicate on that level—by that I mean we didn't talk. But she never mentioned it or complained about it. Too embarrassed, I suppose. And she never suspected me for a moment. After all, why would I or anyone else take one shoe?

I felt like a genius, but the bag was getting too full to hide properly and had to go before I was caught.

When a dumpster appeared a few streets away from the flats, I saw it as an opportunity I needed to take advantage of quickly.

One night, when my mother was out with her Tesco friends, I carried the bulging trash bag through the streets, in the dark so as not to be seen—a man from West House had dumped his old sink in a dumpster once and ended up with a broken arm when the person who had ordered and paid for the dumpster caught him.

I peered over the edge of the steel container. A small pile of broken bricks and plasterboard lined the bottom in a puddle of muddy water. It was still relatively empty, considering how quickly dumpsters filled up when left on a street overnight.

I held the bag over the edge and let it fall. It felt so dramatic as it slipped from my hand and plummeted down to its final end. It made a sad, wet thud as it hit the bricks. I expected it to be louder and more significant and couldn't help but feel a little disappointed.

I sighed, said goodbye to the little trophies that had brought me so much pleasure over the years and wandered back to West House, a light swelling in my chest. I was proud of myself for getting away with taking things from my mother for so long, but knew it was time to up my game. She was far too much of an easy target now, too drunk and stupid to ever question where all her buttons and hair ribbons had gone. I needed more, but until I worked out how to get it, I'd have to keep taking from her.

The answer came to me a few days later in the local grocery shop while paying for my bread and baked beans. The girl serving behind the till beamed at me. She had buck teeth with braces and was about fifteen years old, the same age as me at the time.

"Alrigh'?" she said.

"Alrigh'," I replied.

But I wasn't paying attention to her face. I was staring at her frizzled blonde hair pulled up on her head in a topknot and held in place by a blue silky ribbon with silver star-shapes running through it. It was definitely one of my mother's ribbons and definitely retrieved from the dumpster.

That summer I got a job in a café in Bromley. If the dumpster-rummaging girl could work the till in a local shop, I could certainly serve coffee and snacks to people.

The café was called the Devil's Corner and had a pitchfork for a logo. One of the girls I worked with, Sophie with bright orange hair and a million freckles, told me how some of the religious people in the community refused to come in when the café first opened and had even protested outside with banners that said THERE IS LIGHT IN THE DARK and REJECT SATAN. Despite that, it had become a busy and bustling hangout for the local yummy mummies.

There were ten tables with low stools, all dark brown fake leather with a red trim. Part of the devil theme. The walls were also dark brown with pictures of Satan in his various forms. One picture was a cartoon of Satan reading the Bible in bed and a thought bubble over his head with the words *Bit harsh.* That was my favorite. Nobody likes to be judged.

It was counter service only and there was always a queue. I didn't work the coffee machine as I didn't have the skills yet to whip up a latte like a professional barista, but I didn't mind. I wasn't there to learn, I was there to up my game, although the extra money was a bonus.

My mother gave me a small allowance to make sure I didn't starve. And if my shoes had holes in them she was forced to buy me new ones or the school might get suspicious and call social services. But I'd never had money to spend on anything but essentials. It was strange and I didn't really know what to do with it so I stashed it in a pocket in an old coat in my wardrobe. I told myself it was my emergency money, although I wasn't sure what emergency I was referring to.

I allowed myself two weeks to settle into the Devil's Corner. I made sure I was friendly and helpful with the staff, swapping shifts when asked and doing the dirty work, like taking the garbage out. It paid off and they quickly liked me and welcomed me into the fold. And I smiled a lot. The manager, a spindly man named Daniel, gave me the nickname "Smiley Pants," which I was pleased about. Someone called Smiley Pants sounded pretty innocent. But I was getting antsy and unsettled and felt the urge to take something and soon.

I wasn't interested in stock. It was tightly monitored and there was CCTV in the public café area. I wasn't interested in taking from customers either—that would amount to pickpocketing, which wasn't my style or my buzz at all. The only option was the staff room, which was a cramped space with no windows and smelled like a rummage sale. During breaks, staff would rather stand outside in the rain than sit in the staff room. However, while it was ill equipped and uninviting, it was well used.

There were two empty lockers stacked on top of each other with their doors hanging loosely open, a wobbly bench and a plastic table. Nobody used the lockers to store stuff. Everyone just flung their bags on the bench and the floor and their jackets on coat hooks attached to the wall.

People were trusting of one another and left purses and wallets on the table and their phones charging on the floor near the power points. I wasn't interested in money or phones either. They were valuable items and too inconvenient and awful for someone to lose. I didn't want to cause anyone grief or get caught.

One morning, while washing my hands in the small sink in the drafty bathroom, I noticed a lipstick lying on top of the hand dryer. Its black shiny casing stood out starkly against the grubby white surface.

A rush of excitement soared from the base of my spine to the top of my head in less than a second, as I picked it up and put it in my pocket. I steadied myself with a few deep breaths and, filled with a sense of achievement, left the bathroom. Yes, the stakes were definitely higher here.

Once at home I took a shoebox—my new choice of storage facility—from the base of my wardrobe and added the lipstick to the few items already in it.

I laid it next to a free key ring my mother had got from work. I had never taken a lipstick from her so this was a whole new experience. That night, with the dresser pushed firmly up against my door, I drifted off to sleep with pride and pleasure coursing through my body. Pure happiness.

The following day, I bounced into the Devil's Corner, smiling even more than usual, calling hello and good morning to everyone. It took me a few seconds to notice everyone was huddled at the back of the café comforting Sophie who was crying. I rushed over, full of genuine concern. I really liked Sophie and I hoped she was okay.

"What's happened?" I asked.

"Sophie's lost her lipstick," said Daniel, almost in a whisper, as if even mentioning the lipstick would send Sophie over the edge.

"Where did she last have it?" I asked.

"In the bathroom," piped up Sophie, wiping her tears away. "Did you see it?" she asked me, hope in her eyes.

"No, sorry," I said.

In an instant, all the joy was sucked out of me, leaving me feeling thin and pale. This was a big reaction to a small item of makeup.

"Was it very expensive?" I asked, kicking myself that I hadn't checked the quality of the lipstick. I just assumed it was cheap because we all worked in a café on café wages.

"It was Chanel," she said through her sniffles. Shit, I thought. That does sound expensive. "I bought it with a voucher I got from my friends for my twenty-first." Shit, shit, shit, could it be any worse?

"Let's have another good look for it," said Daniel. "If you had it in the bathroom, it has to be around there somewhere." I joined everyone in the fruitless search for the precious lipstick. When it didn't show up, Sophie wiped her eyes and put on a brave face.

"It's okay," she said, holding her chin up. "It's my fault for leaving it in the bathroom in the first place."

"But it means somebody took it," said Daniel. Everyone glanced at everyone else. I know I looked the most innocent.

That night at home I lifted the lid off my shoebox and peered in at Sophie's lipstick in its glitzy case. It looked far more special now that I knew it cost a fortune. I opened it and pushed up the glistening, dark pink stick, its point not yet flattened from use. It was clearly brand new. I crawled into bed, as dark thoughts about graveyards loomed in my mind.

The next day in the Devil's Corner I worked the counter with Daniel and another girl named Maeve who talked incessantly about nothing and everything. A lot of her sentences started with *I remember when*. I mentally switched off to the sound of her voice, although Daniel seemed to be hanging on every word.

I focused on serving a woman a caramel cream slice. She looked exhausted and had a baby strapped to the front of her body in a sling. A bang from the back of the café made us all look up; even the baby's head bobbed about reacting to the noise.

It was the sound of the staff room door hitting off the wall as Sophie burst through it and bounded up to us at the counter, unable to stand still with excitement.

"I found it," she said, breathlessly, holding up the Chanel lipstick—the most talked-about lipstick in the world. My eyes followed the familiar black casing as she waved it around in front of our eyes.

"It rolled under the sink in the bathroom. Can you believe it?" she gushed.

"That's great," I said, acting very relieved for her.

"I'm sure I looked there," she said, frowning.

Maeve decided to chip in with a theory. "Maybe it rolled somewhere else and then someone kicked it and it rolled. But then why wouldn't someone notice if they kicked a lipstick on the floor? Maybe someone took it and then put it back." I glanced at Daniel to see if he was buying this. But Daniel just laughed.

"Look at Miss Marple here," he said, nodding his head at Maeve.

"Oh, I love that show," squealed Maeve. How I wish I'd taken her lipstick instead.

"I'm just so happy to have it back," Sophie beamed as she applied the deep pink color to her lips. And so did I. Sophie deserved a fancy lipstick.

I handed in my notice the next day. I made an excuse about going to stay with an aunt in Spain for the rest of the summer. Sophie cried when I told her.

"I'm going to miss you so much," she said.

"What part of Spain are you going to?" asked nosy Maeve. Luckily she didn't wait for an answer as she quickly dived into one of her dull *I remember when* stories.

Working in the café taught me an important lesson: don't take from colleagues. The staff room was not a good hunting ground and people had far more awareness of what they had and where they had left it. I needed a different kind of job, one where I had access to strangers and could work alone. It was a while before I found the job of my dreams.

Chapter 14

The day I left home I headed straight for Bromley South train station. I had 165 pounds in my pocket—the emergency money I had saved from working in the Devil's Corner, which I was very grateful to have.

My plan was to get on the first train to anywhere and by two o'clock on that rainy February afternoon I found myself sitting in a packed carriage on my way to Hastings. For two hours I stared out of the window—half focused on the reflection of my face, which was still bloody from the attack, and half focused on the overgrown hedges and occasional back gardens flicking by outside. All I knew was there was no going back.

As the train glided into Hastings station the rain had finally stopped but everything was dripping and sodden. I stepped onto the platform with a few other passengers who scurried off to waiting cars and journeys home. I stayed on the platform, watching the train disappear down the track. Now I was here, I had no idea what I was going to do.

I found a small B&B on a leafy street on the way into the town center. It was a regular house with a "rooms available" sign in the window. It was twenty-two pounds a night and the owner, a woman with a fake smile and a cardigan covered in dog hair, asked me to pay up front. I didn't blame her. I was a sorry sight with my battered scalp and crappy duffel bag.

Breakfast was a self-service situation with cereal, toast and coffee on tap in a small, stuffy dining room with a local newspaper on the table. I flicked through it on my first morning and found the classified page. Most of the jobs required experience and qualifications and since I'd only worked in a café for three weeks, I didn't feel I had much to offer. But I needed a job and quick if I was going to support myself. I decided that whatever job I got, it would have to provide me with two things: enough money to live off and access to items I could take without anyone noticing.

I spotted an ad for a cleaning job in an architect's office. I wondered if that would suit me. I was the only one who ever cleaned the flat in West House, apart from when we were expecting a visit from a social worker, so I figured it was something I could be good at. But cleaning the same office every day would have the same problems I'd had when I worked in the café. The staff are too familiar and aware of what they have and where it is. There was also an ad for a house cleaner but that felt even more problematic than office cleaning. Anyway, the house cleaning job required references. I continued to trail my finger through the listings until I stopped on the last ad.

Housekeeping Assistant, responsibilities include room cleaning on a daily basis. No experience necessary. Immediate start. Paid weekly.

It was for a small three-star hotel on the Hastings seafront, and a hotel cleaner seemed like the perfect solution. There were enough hours to make enough money to survive, and I'd have access to guest bedrooms and all their belongings. There would also be a constant stream of guests offering an endless supply of new opportunities. I wondered why I hadn't thought of it before.

The hotel had twelve double bedrooms and one other cleaner, a woman in her fifties named Marina, who talked to me like I was six. I played along, already aware I needed her to like me in case a complaint was made against me.

Marina insisted on training me for an entire week, often looking over my shoulder and correcting what I was doing. One day she even corrected the way I was holding a cloth. But I managed to keep nodding and smiling as she explained how to clean a toilet properly for the millionth time. It was more work for both of us and since we got paid by the room, it was more work for no more money. But I used the week's training to get a feel for different guests and the things they brought with them. Marina had names for categories of guests like "messy pups" if their clothes were strewn everywhere, "oranginas" if there was fake tan on the towels or sheets, and "dirty rabbits" if she was particularly annoyed about having to scrub a stain out of a carpet or from a toilet bowl.

While she talked me through how to vacuum the base of a wardrobe, I was busy making mental notes of what there was in the room that I might be able to take without the guest noticing. I spied a small flower pin on a denim jacket while Marina was vigorously wiping over a mirror I'd just cleaned. The sight of the pink and blue flower made my heart race. It was perfect for taking. It could so easily have fallen off the jacket, but with Marina in the room there was no way I could risk it.

Finally, I was let loose to clean on my own. The first time I entered a room alone and shut the door behind me, I felt momentarily dizzy as the blood rushed to my head.

The room was a single occupancy, a woman who had packed light given her very small case. But her toiletry bag was large and bursting at the seams waiting to be opened. Carefully, as though performing surgery, I pushed my fingers through the contents right to the bottom where my finger pricked on something. I clasped the item between my finger and thumb and lifted it out gently pushing the other items aside to make way. It was a pair of nail scissors. I opened the front pocket of my apron and dropped the scissors inside. It was my first item ever taken from a hotel room and, although I didn't know it at the time, the first of many nail scissors. A wave of warm pleasure charged through me immediately afterward. I had found my place in the world as a hotel cleaner. I even went as far as to think things were turning around for me.

But in the third week I messed up. I was cleaning a double occupancy room, a man and woman, and they had a lot of luggage and had hung up most of their clothes in the wardrobe. I could see from the book on the bedside table that they were French. I had learned some French at school so recognized the word Moi in the book title. I had had time that day for an extra rummage since all my rooms were stayers and most of them were very tidy and didn't require linen or towel changes.

I pulled open the wardrobe and eyed the jackets and shirts and dresses hanging up. I gently parted them, feeling the fabrics. Then I saw it, twinkling and shiny. A gold safety pin brooch attached to a dark blue suit jacket. Like the flower pin I had seen before, I was sure an item like this would not be noticed if it went missing, at least not immediately. And even if it was, they would have to assume it could have been lost in transit. I unclipped it carefully and put it in my front pocket. The blood rush to my head was so strong afterward that I had to sit down for a minute.

The following day I was called into the hotel owner's office with Marina. The owner was a tired-looking older man named Mr. Jacobs with short stubby fingers and legs to match. He was weary and kept rubbing his forehead as he talked to us. The French guest had complained about a missing designer brooch. Apparently it was very expensive. I kicked myself. I should have been more careful. Don't take valuable items. That has always been my number one rule, even when I was taking from my mother.

Mr. Jacobs asked who had cleaned the room the day before. I was about to say it was me and deny all knowledge when Marina piped up and said we had cleaned the room together as I was still getting used to the schedule and needed help. Mr. Jacobs had let out a big sigh, relieved. If we were both in the room together there's no way one of us could have taken it without the other seeing.

It transpired that Marina herself had been accused of stealing years ago and was still angry about it. She also said she didn't like French people. They were stuck up in her opinion. It seemed like a huge generalization but I was just pleased Marina had saved my skin.

I handed in my notice a week later and already had a new hotel lined up. Hotel 2, a three-star in Reading. I told Marina and Mr. Jacobs that my mother had died and I needed to move closer to home to be nearer my family. They didn't even ask me where home was, which suited me fine.

Hotel 17

3-star. Liverpool. May 2017-Nov 2017
Total stay: 3 months

Items

Hair clip x 2
Tester pot of cream x 5
Key ring with dollar sign x 1
False eyelash x 1
Tweezers x 3
Nail scissors x 2
Sequin bow from a shoe x 1
Pen x 2
Gloves x 1
Bottle opener x 1
Razor x 2
Nail clippers x 1
Dental floss x 1
Ballpoint pen x 1
Notebook (unused) x 1
Face mask sachet x 1
Small calculator x 1 (final item)

Chapter 15

The aisles of the supermarket loom before me. I've never bothered with large-scale grocery shopping before. I normally stick to local shops for my bread and baked beans. In fact, the only time I've ever been in a supermarket was when I confronted my mother in Tesco.

I head for the fruit and vegetable area first, my basket banging against the side of my leg as I walk.

I glance at a woman sorting through every packet of tomatoes, checking each one until she decides she has the best and puts it in her basket. I like her confidence. It reminds me of my own self-assuredness when I enter a hotel room to clean it.

The niggling knot in my gut returns. It's the worry about what happened today with the flamingo brooch and the nail scissors. A fear that my special thing—my own individual kleptomania—has vanished overnight.

I'm not stupid. I'm fully aware there's a direct link between losing my desire to take things and meeting Phil. Has one really replaced the other? It terrifies me—not because I love taking things more than I love Phil, but because I don't know what it means. What will my life become if taking from hotel rooms no longer makes me happy? Will I still want to be a hotel cleaner? What if Phil doesn't love me back?

The thoughts swamp my mind. Contemplating my life being any other way throws me into a black abyss of doubt and doom. Is it even possible to live a different kind of life than the one I have now? All I know is, if I hadn't discovered the thrill of taking things, I might never have bothered with life at all.

I reach out to touch the tomatoes just so I don't look like a woman in a trance in the vegetable section. Focus, I tell myself. Phil is coming to your flat for dinner and you have nothing to offer her, not even a biscuit.

The thought of Phil with her sleek hair and intense stare, the smell of her musky perfume, penetrates my mind and, slowly, the gnawing gloom in the pit of my stomach shrinks away, returning to its hiding place, for now anyway.

I check the shopping list on my phone for what I need for the dinner I'm planning, since all I have is a two-ring cooktop to work with. Two rings means two pots so I'm making pasta with a sauce and a salad.

There are five things on my list: fresh pasta, ready-made pasta sauce, a packet of salad, fresh bread and a block of ice cream small enough to fit in the freezer section of my fridge. I looked up quick and easy meals online and found a dinner plan on a mum's YouTube channel. She calls herself "Not So Superwoman." She has six children and, apparently, no time for herself, although she still finds the time to post daily videos. Anyway, I'm very grateful for her suggestion.

I select a packet of salad leaves and jostle along to the end of the aisle, looking up at the signs overhead. Will there be one that says PASTA?

Not So Superwoman said to go to the supermarket, as it's important to buy fresh pasta as opposed to dried and you're more likely to find sale items. Apparently, fresh pasta gives a more authentic feel to the meal and I don't like the idea of dried anything, so fresh suits me fine.

Finally, I find the Italian section with a fridge displaying various bags of fresh pastas. I settle on the tube-y ones. Beside the bags of pasta are pots of ready-made pasta sauces. I choose the egg and bacon one. It looks silky and creamy and like it might taste the same way. The bread and ice cream are easy enough, although the fresh bread selection throws me for a second. So many different shapes and sizes, sliced and unsliced.

A man in a suit marches up to the counter, grabs a white country loaf and strides off. I decide to do the same. He looks like the kind of man who knows his bread.

With my basket pretty full now, I wander into the household section. Not So Superwoman serves her easy pasta meal in bowls. I only have one plate and one bowl in my flat and both are chipped and discolored. My sparse supply of cutlery is just as pathetic. I contemplate going with paper plates and plastic knives and forks, but I'm assuming Phil has proper, grown-up cutlery to go with her grown-up kitchen, so feel I should get the same.

I stop in front of a display unit containing bowls and plates and pick up two of each. Phil never needs to know that all the crockery and cutlery I have is on the table in front of her. Table? I bite my lip. Will the small aluminum table in my flat work for dinner? I see a wipeable tablecloth and pick that up too. I move on to the cutlery and pick up two knives, forks and spoons, two dessert spoons, and two teaspoons, just in case we make it to coffee.

Last stop is the herbs and sauces. I randomly grab jars and boxes. Oregano, basil, thyme, curry powder, stock cubes, a box of Atlantic sea salt and a black pepper mill.

I join a short queue for the cash register. The clock on the wall behind the cashier says three thirty. Phil's not due at my place till 7:30 and dinner, according to my Internet guru, should not take more than ten minutes to prepare, so I have enough time to stop by the hospital to visit Gaby. Rose mentioned she likes to have visitors and Mali suggested I should go and see her. When I say *suggested* it was more of an order. I don't want to annoy Mali again by not being a team player, and I'm sure Gaby needs the company. It must be grim sitting beside her son who's in a coma all day.

I feel a twinge in my heart for Gaby. I don't want her to feel bad. I glance at the snack fridge—the supermarket's title, not mine—and quickly grab a cheese and pickle sandwich on white bread and a can of Coke. I've seen Gaby have this for lunch before so assume she'll appreciate it.

My shopping bags rustle as I approach the main hospital entrance. The new crockery and cutlery in my backpack makes a clinking sound as I walk.

The large glass door slides open and I wander into the brightly lit reception area. I watch some chatty nurses rush by. The thing about hospitals is the hierarchy of power. The minute you walk through the door, the doctors and nurses know best. You know nothing. Do as they say and everything will be okay. You will live. Don't do as they say and you are doomed. Sadly, I was doomed as a child either way. But in fairness to the doctors who treated me, as well as the social workers who visited us, my mother and I put on a great after show. Why wouldn't they believe I threw myself down the stairs on purpose?

Hospitals are strange, complicated places where a simple checklist or a ticked box can mean life or death. The thought makes me shudder.

Rose told me to go to the Robertson Ward. I scan the information board and see it's on the third floor. I take off along a corridor following the signs to the lift.

I'm suddenly worried I'm not leaving myself enough time to prepare dinner. I need to clean up the flat and lay the table and have a shower and get ready myself. Not So Superwoman showed a picture of her table set for dinner, with napkins and wineglasses. I stop in my tracks. I don't have napkins or wineglasses. I'll need to go back to the supermarket after seeing Gaby. I'll say a quick hello, give her the sandwich and the can of Coke and then go. I figure I need to be home by six at the latest.

I take the lift to the third floor and hurry along the corridor to more glass doors. The black-and-white sign over the entrance says ROBERTSON WARD. I try to open the doors but they're locked.

I peer through the glass and see another corridor, darker, in shadow. There is a bell beside the glass doors. I press it but I don't hear anything. I wait, wondering if the bell's even working.

A small woman exits the room closest to the doors and approaches. She is dressed in a dark blue uniform with red piping. A nurse's watch dangles from her breast pocket just below her name badge. She pushes open the door.

"Can I help you?" she asks. I see her name badge now: *Sharon Smyth. Matron.* She catches me reading it. She stands a little bit taller. It's subtle but I notice. She's proud of her job and I respect that. I tell her I'm visiting my friend Gaby. She asks me to wait and shuts the door.

I glance around the barren corridor and shudder. I'm warm from walking and carrying my bags but I feel like I should be cold.

"Noelle!" I turn to see Gaby at the door, smiling. She rushes toward me and throws her arms around me.

"Thank you for coming," she gushes.

"No problem," I say, putting my free arm loosely around her to return the hug. The shopping bag hangs heavy in my other hand. She pulls back and holds me by both arms.

"They're going to start waking him up in the morning," she says, beaming at me. "They just told me. I mean, I'm not to get too excited, but it's a huge step."

I wonder if being in a coma is the same as going cold turkey. Will he be free from his drug addiction when he wakes up? I don't ask.

"That's great news," I say, quickly smiling.

"Let's go to the café," she says. "I'm starving and I need coffee."

I glance down into my shopping bag where the white label on the cheese and pickle sandwich peeks out. I suppose I can have it for lunch tomorrow if I scrape the pickle off.

Gaby munches her way through two sausage rolls, taking inter-mittent gulps of her coffee. As she talks, the crumbs from the pastry fall onto the front of her pink shirt. This café has a coffee and food counter with clusters of tables and chairs placed in the middle of a bare space. If the café wasn't here the space would be gloomy and empty like the corridor upstairs. But the smell of fresh coffee and the noise of the coffee machine add a sense of normality.

"They say he'll seem very slow and confused when he first wakes up and that he may or may not improve. We have to see." She pops the last of the sausage roll in her mouth and washes it down with the dregs of her coffee. I sip my black tea, which is still too hot to drink quickly. I'm not sure how to reply to her news. She seems happy about it, but it could mean her son will be mentally disabled for the rest of his life.

"The worst case, according to this other mum I met in the unit, her daughter fell off her horse and is just out of a coma, is that you have to mind them at home, but there's help and support services for that."

"Right," I say, feeling more confused. How can any of this be good news?

Gaby smiles at me, warmly. I notice now how perky she looks. She's wearing her hair down and has makeup on, which I haven't seen her wear before.

"You're wearing makeup," I say, trying to change the subject.

"You get bored upstairs just sitting there. I had to go to the chemist to get a few things and I thought, why not? It's just mascara and some blush."

"It suits you," I say, very aware how inappropriate that sounds but Gaby grins.

"I've lost a bit of weight too, although I'm not sure how. I spend my life in this café. But thanks," she says. "I'm sick of feeling dowdy all the time. How's work?" she asks, pushing her glasses up her nose. "I hear they got bloody Fatima to cover me."

"Why don't you like her?" I ask.

"She nicked my mop once and then denied it. And she's in Julia's ear all the time, telling tales on everyone. I mean, don't even think about eating a cracker or a crisp with her on your shift. It goes straight back to management."

"I'll be careful not to eat on the job then," I say. Gaby nods, pleased I've taken on her advice. Fatima must have gotten Gaby into trouble for nibbling on a biscuit while she was cleaning. No food or drink allowed while working. Those are the rules. Still cleaners don't tend to rat on each other, which means Fatima's not a team player. I'm pleased to hear this as it gives me more reason not to like her.

I consider Gaby as she leans back in her chair, yawns and stretches her arms. She's relaxed and looks well rested.

"Rose and Mali said I should come and see you. I wasn't sure if it was okay."

"Of course it's okay," she says, grabbing my hands across the table. "You're one of us now." I'm not sure what this means. I'm one of the cleaning team but somehow I don't think she's talking about that.

"We're a little family—me, Phil, Rose and Mali—and now you as well."

"But I've only been here a couple of weeks."

"So? We like you," she says and leans forward dropping her voice. "And from what I hear Phil especially likes you." I blush despite myself.

"We're just friends," I say, shifting in my seat.

"Well, I think you make a lovely couple," Gaby says beaming. I'm pleased to hear this but also aware that Gaby's probably just trying to be supportive. I'll leave the straight talking to Rose. Still, it is nice to hear.

Gaby's face breaks into a smile as she waves at someone behind me.

"Hi, Steven. How are you getting on? How's Sheila?" Steven says something I can't hear and I don't bother to turn around. Gaby pulls a sympathetic face in response to Steven's answer. "I'll catch up with you later for a chat," she says to him, putting her hand on her heart.

"Poor man," she says to me, her eyes moist. "They're moving his wife to a hospice today. It's so tragic." I now turn to look at Steven, who has thin white hair and glasses, and is bent over a walking stick. He's about ninety years old if not more. It's sad that people die, of course, but Gaby's situation is far more tragic, well, to me anyway. Her son could have permanent brain damage.

Gaby waves to a nurse walking by, big smile on her face.

"You seem to know a lot of people here," I say.

"We're a little community, all struggling and hoping," she says, slightly wistful. "I'm going to get some cookies to bring up to the nurses. Do you want anything else?" I indicate my black tea is still full. Gaby goes to the coffee counter. I check the time. It's four o'clock. I need to leave soon.

Two hands cover my eyes from behind. "Guess who?"

I pull the hands away and turn to see Mali with Rose. I wasn't expecting to see them and I'm surprised how pleased I am that they're here. They wave at Gaby who comes rushing over. Rose holds up a plastic bag with magazines in it.

"Hardcore porn to get you through the long nights."

Gaby giggles.

"No, it's not," says Mali, pushing Rose affectionately. "It's *Hello* magazine and a book of sudoku."

"Thanks so much," says Gaby. "Now sit down and let me get you a coffee."

Rose already has her purse out, but Gaby forces her to sit and goes back to the counter. Mali and Rose join me at the table.

"She seems in good spirits," says Rose. Mali slaps Rose on the arm.

"What are you talking about? Her son is in a coma. He could die."

"He's not going to die," says Rose.

"They're waking him up tomorrow," I say. "She's not sure how it's going to go yet."

"See?" says Mali to Rose. "She's in denial. But we are here for her and we will get her through this."

"Whatever you say," sighs Rose.

But I agree with Rose. Gaby does seem in good spirits and if this were any other setting, it could easily be her birthday party and we're her guests. Mali takes *Hello* magazine out of the bag and starts flipping through it with Rose.

"Ugly," she says pointing at some celebrity's child.

"Yeah, but rich ugly," says Rose.

I hear laughing and turn to see Gaby chatting with the girl at the counter, her hands moving as she talks, confident and animated. She blows some hair from her eyes, like she's hot. Then it strikes me. Gaby is enjoying herself. She's actually in her element here in hospital.

She waves at a janitor passing by carrying a mop and bucket. Gaby is happy and she wasn't before. Having her son in a coma and possibly a vegetative state is a better option for her than having him addicted to drugs and robbing from her. Her nights are no longer filled with worry about where he is and if he's even alive. She no longer has to answer the door to the police or tell people her son is an addict who steals from her. She doesn't have to live with the fear he'll end up in prison or put up with judgmental looks that say her son's chosen path in life is somehow her fault. She has become a part of a much more socially acceptable group—the parents who bravely face a tragedy that has struck their child and soldier on with a positive mindset. Those people are heroes and Gaby could be one of them now.

Gaby sees me looking and smiles over at me. Shit, she even looks younger.

The shopping bag cuts into my leg and my backpack bobs up and down on my back, clinking loudly, as I rush back into the supermarket for napkins and wineglasses. It's busier now and there are queues at the tills. I might have to muddle my way through the self-service.

I hurry to the back of the store to where the household items are. I grab two wineglasses and search the nearby shelves for napkins.

"Can I help you?" I turn around to see an older woman wearing the supermarket uniform of a T-shirt and trousers. She holds a bunch of frying pans in her right hand, in the middle of hanging them on hooks. She peers at me. I swallow and stare back, frozen to the spot.

Slowly she looks me over as the recognition begins to register on her twisted face. I wish I could move, but my feet are stuck to the ground. My insides feel heavy and weak, like they're about to spill out onto the floor below me.

I manage to speak, doing my best to sound casual.

"I'm looking for napkins," I say.

The woman walks toward me, her gray hair scraped back in a ponytail with a ribbon in it. She's much larger around the middle than she once was and dark, heavy bags under her eyes make her look far older than she is. Her cheeks are sunken and her nose seems bigger and longer. She wears pink lipstick, which only draws attention to her thin, disappearing lips.

I want to walk away if only my feet would move, but our eyes lock. Recognition complete. I have no choice but to look her in the eyes: the eyes of my tormentor, my abuser, my mother.

"Hello," she says in a gravelly voice. "Fancy seeing you here."

Finally I gain control of my legs and start to walk backward, checking my exits. Old habits die hard.

"Where've you been all these years, eh?" she says, looking me up and down.

She follows me as I back myself into a knife display and nearly stumble, which wakes me up a little and brings me to my senses.

"What are you doing with yourself these days?" she says, trying to see what's in my shopping bag. She always had mouse-like features with a smallish sharp nose and round, piercing eyes, at least when she wasn't screwing up her face in a rage, which wasn't very often. But now, with her face close to mine, so gray and knobby, baggy and lined, she's far more rat-like. I instinctively move my bag behind me out of her gaze.

"Working," I manage to say.

I tell myself I'm safe here. It's a public place and she's Tesco Erica. She won't touch me, but my heart is racing and not in a good way.

"It's been a long time," she says. Her voice is gruffer than it used to be, the years of smoking having finally taken their toll. My stomach starts to churn.

"Eight years and two weeks," I say.

"You always were a geek, remembering stupid things like numbers and dates."

Yeah, like my birthday, which she never remembered. I start to shuffle to the side, glancing at the next aisle as a possible escape route.

"Do you live around here?" she asks.

"No, I'm visiting a friend," I say.

"Are you married?"

I squint at her, wondering if I heard her correctly. She thinks I could be married? She looks at my fingers, searching for a ring. I start to feel nauseous. I'm not sure whether it's the sight of her or the smell of her pungent perfume, the same one from all those years ago. I'm surprised they still make it. I'm not so surprised she still buys it.

"What do you work at?" she asks.

The panic rises to my forehead and the nausea's getting worse. She wants to know if I have any money. My hand tires of holding the shopping bag behind me and I swap hands and return it to my side, but she tries again to see what's in it. I move it back behind me again. She eyes the wineglasses in my hand.

"Wineglasses? Bit posh."

"I have to go," I mumble and start moving toward the next aisle, keeping her in my sights.

"Don't be like that. I'm your mother," she says, in a sinister whisper. She glances left and right, making sure the coast is clear and none of her coworkers are in the vicinity. "I can't believe you never even tried to find out how I was. I was sick, you know? And where were you? I had to deal with that all on my own. Do you know what that's like?"

I keep backing away, but she follows. A fellow supermarket worker rushes by carrying a box. She quickly beams at him.

"Careful with that box, Charlie. You don't want to fall over your feet."

"Thanks, Erica," he calls back. Her face drops again as her dark, droopy eyes return to me.

"What kind of daughter leaves her mother like that?"

The kind you beat every day, I want to say. But if the last eight years have taught me anything it's that my mother is abnormal in every way and is incapable of having a rational conversation.

But I do need to say something. Not to hurt her but to show her that there is nothing between us, no love, no connection, no coming back. A surge of energy fills my chest. I'm not afraid of her anymore. If she even tries to touch me, I'll defend myself this time.

"You look like a rhinoceros," I say. "All gray and baggy and ugly and old."

She squints at me and moves closer.

"I hope you rot to death in your own steaming piss, you miserable bitch," I say to her face.

The corners of her mouth drop. Her ears move back, like a beast about to pounce. And with that, I run to the next aisle and head for the exit, my bag bashing against my legs and the crockery clanking in my backpack.

I slow down for a moment to place the wineglasses on the nuts and seeds shelf and dash out through the large sliding door at the entrance, nearly knocking over an elderly man on a walking frame.

"Sorry," I call back.

I make it to the end of the street, dive around the corner and stop, leaning against a brick wall to catch my breath.

I've never stood up to my mother before. When I was younger I needed to keep her sweet or I might have ended up dead or worse crippled by her ever-escalating violence. But I just did and now my chest, my heart, feels lighter. I take a huge deep breath, filling my lungs with satisfaction.

It's six o'clock. I've still got time to prepare dinner, but I'll avoid the big supermarkets from now on and stick to local shops.

Chapter 16

Time check: 6:15. I tilt my head to consider the two saucepans on my two-ring cooktop and cringe. I should have bought new ones. It's only now I see how old and battered they are. Neither of them sits comfortably on the burners. I try to reposition them but they keep lifting on one side. It's the rings, not the pans. They're buckled slightly. I give up and leave them the way they are. I'll make sure Phil doesn't come anywhere near the kitchen. There's barely room for one person in here anyway.

I climb the ladder and check my bed is made. I'm not worried about my bed sheets, as I only changed them two days ago. I know I'm counting my chickens but I'm hoping Phil will stay the night.

I still don't have any wineglasses despite my efforts to buy some. I eye the two chipped mugs in the cupboard, SpongeBob and the one with faded brown and white spots, both with dark tea stains inside them. I remember some plastic cups I took from a room in hotel 11.

I take the key from the SpongeBob mug and open the trunk. Confronted with all my trophies, I'm a little startled to feel nothing, not even pride. I quickly switch my thoughts to Phil and get rummaging, gently sifting through the items like I'm stirring a great bowl of porridge. And there they are—two red plastic cups.

Hotel 11 was in the Lake District and a couple had brought the cups to bring on a Valentine's Day picnic. They had a stack of eight and I took two. I was confident that they wouldn't miss them and they never made a complaint.

I clutch the plastic cups to my chest—while they'll save me the embarrassment of Phil seeing my grotty mugs, do I really want to use them? They look like two regular plastic cups but they mean more to me than that, or at least they did. And I never use the things I take. It's a rule I've always stuck to.

Forty-five minutes until Phil arrives. I need to make a decision.

I shut the trunk lid, click the padlock back into place and carry the red plastic cups to the kitchen. It's a sacrifice I have to make. I take the washable tablecloth from the bottom of my shopping bag and rip off the plastic wrapping.

The tablecloth is stiff and unfolds like cardboard. It has an old-fashioned flower pattern trailing around the edges, which wasn't visible in the package. I hate it and it's far too big for my aluminum coffee table, which is no more than half a meter wide. I scrub the table down to see if I can make it look any better. It's no use, the big, brown burn mark still dominates the surface and now, as I stand back, it dominates the whole room.

I put one of my new plates on top of the stain and that seems to do the trick. I look up at the naked bulb hanging from the ceiling. Should have bought some candles, I mumble to myself. I wonder if it's too late to cancel Phil. I could say I'm sick, but I want to see her, I'm desperate to see her, and I don't want to let her down. I throw the washable tablecloth over the trunk instead, which makes it look like a plastic-coated blob, but better to cover it up so Phil doesn't see it and ask me questions about it.

I jump into my screeching shower, lather myself quickly in soap and shampoo, and hurriedly jerk the shower nozzle over my body, rinsing as fast as I can. While I'm drying myself, I ponder what to wear. I was so caught up in getting the food right that I completely forgot about my limited wardrobe situation. It'll have to be the off-the-shoulder top and my jeans, which I hope will fit me.

I pull the top over my head and it immediately falls snugly into place. As long as I don't raise my left arm too high and expose the hole, it's perfect. I try on the jeans but they're too big and sag around the middle. I quickly pull them off, shove them back in the drawer and put on a clean black work skirt. With the top pulled down it almost passes for a dress. I slip my feet into my trainers and look at myself in the reflection of the window. Is it too much? Is this smart or casual? Do you dress up when someone comes for dinner?

I open the drawer again in my rickety chest of drawers and consider the Fruit of the Loom T-shirt and my black T-shirt dress. I shut the drawer. I'm not really Fruit of the Loom anymore and Phil's already seen my T-shirt dress.

I peer at my reflection again. The top and skirt make me look slim and curvy, but maybe the window's warped. It's too late to change now, not that I have anything else to change into. My short bob has grown out slightly and my bangs are in danger of sweeping into my eyes. I comb it through, making it smooth and then carefully hook the sides behind my ears. Phil said I looked cute like that.

I still have to set the table, without napkins. Maybe she won't notice. My two new pasta bowls will just about fit on the aluminum table with the new white plate in the middle, covering the stain. I'll put bread on the plate so it has a purpose. My new knives aren't sharp enough to cut the bread, so I rip it with my hands, putting four chunks on the plate on the table. I fill one of the saucepans with water ready to boil and pull the plastic lid off the creamy pasta sauce to empty into the other pan, but it's stuck inside the container and I have to shake it. Finally it slops out in one, big glutinous lump, splashing as it hits the bottom of the pan. A speck of white sauce jumps up onto my top. I lick my finger and carefully wipe it off but it leaves a tiny mark. Using a wet cloth will probably make it look worse. I decide not to think about it.

I carefully open the pots of herbs and the curry powder and the stock cubes and empty half of each into the garbage. I rough up the stock cube box, so it looks a bit battered and roll each herb pot around in my hands, taking the shine off the labels before putting them in my wafer-thin cupboard. I close the cupboard door, wait a second and then open it again, to see if it looks authentic. It's way too neat so I move the containers around a bit to give the impression they're put in and out a lot. It's only in case Phil comes into the kitchen and opens my cupboard to look for something. She will see my used herbs and spices and assume I am a woman who can cook up a feast with ease.

With the food prepared, I add the knives and forks to the table and pull the two armchairs in closer. I walk to the front door, turn and survey the room, imagining what Phil's first impressions might be.

Despite my efforts, my flat is still undeniably a dive, but Phil must know I live in a shithole. She probably would too if she hadn't been given a flat. If anything, seeing my horrible bedsit will remind her of how much nicer her place is. I like that. I want Phil to feel good.

My phone beeps with a message from Phil.

Outside!!!

Coming, I text back.

I go to yank my front door open but it chooses to stick. I pull at it harder, hurting my hand on the handle as it gives in to the pressure and flies open. I grab a pair of old socks to shove under the door to keep it ajar and dash down the stairs.

The front door to the house is heavy and old, probably the building's original door but now painted in lumpy white gloss. I click the heavy industrial-sized lock to the side and pull the door open. It's already dark outside and I'm aware how bright the hallway is in comparison to the indigo night sky and the orange glow from the streetlights.

"Hi," says Phil, swaying from side to side, an empty bottle of wine in one hand. Her other hand is draped around the shoulders of a young man with floppy blond hair and the most stunning aquamarine eyes. He has a pretty button nose and wears a parka, jeans, and white Adidas trainers. He holds a brown paper bag with two bottles of wine in it.

"This is Freddy. I invited him. Hope you don't mind. Doesn't he look like an angel?"

"Hello," says Freddy, stepping forward to shake my hand. "Phil said you wouldn't mind, so thanks for having me." His voice is clipped and educated and oozing confidence. Yes, I do fucking mind, I want to scream. Instead I shrug my shoulders, no problem.

"I told you she'd be cool," says Phil, swooning over Freddy. She snakes her arms around his neck and kisses him hard, their tongues probing and exploring each other's mouths. My gut twists and tightens. I want to pull Freddy off her. She stops kissing him and swings around to me.

"Isn't he just so good-looking?" she says.

"She's drunk," explains Freddy. Then he lowers his voice. "I thought I better make sure she got here in one piece."

"Come in," I say, as politely as I can, but there's an edge to my voice.

I lead the way up the stairs. Behind me Phil trips on a step and Freddy catches her. They both giggle.

"What would I do without you, Freddy?" Phil says, nuzzling into his neck.

My stomach churns making me feel sick and I can't bear to watch them. I bound quickly up to my bedsit, slide the rolled-up socks to one side with my foot and push the door wide open. On the plus side, Phil's so drunk she might not notice how awful my flat is.

Phil runs past me into the room, bottle swinging in her hand. She looks up at the bare light bulb and winces in the glare. Freddy follows her. He does a quick scan of the room.

"Nice place," he says. His tone is genuine and warm.

He doesn't mean it, of course, but part of me is grateful. At least he's making an effort. Phil shields her eyes from the dazzling light bulb.

"It's very bright in here," she shouts.

Freddy passes me the bag with the wine in it. "You should probably open the red now and let it breathe," he says, smiling at me revealing a perfect set of pearly white teeth. Maybe he is an angel. Even if he is, I'd still like him to vanish into thin air. No more Freddy.

I take the wine to the kitchen and leave it on the floor, as I have nowhere else to put it. I open my one small drawer and shake my head at myself. No corkscrew. I know I have one in my trunk from hotel 14.

A man had brought his own so he could drink beers in his room. When I cleaned his room it was littered with empty beer bottles and bottle tops and the toilet and bathroom sink were covered in dried-up pieces of vomit. I'll clean up most things without a bother but I strongly believe vomit is something people should clean up themselves. So I took his bottle opener with a corkscrew attachment on it. It was a standard stainless-steel one, nothing special, so I was sure he wouldn't complain and he didn't. Why hadn't I thought of digging it out of the trunk when I had it open?

"Any chance of a glass of vino?"

I flick around to see Freddy. His tall frame fills the narrow entrance to my kitchen, making me feel claustrophobic. I want to push him away.

"I'm afraid I can't find my corkscrew."

"That's okay, have you got a wooden spoon? I'll push the cork in."

"Oh," I say, genuinely surprised. Freddy has his uses then. I pass him the one wooden spoon I have, which on close inspection is warped and stained, possibly burnt. Freddy doesn't notice and even if he did, my instincts tell me he'd pretend not to, and I find myself starting to respect him for that.

He quickly removes the seal from the neck of the wine bottle and places it on the floor, holding it tightly between his feet. He pushes the end of the wooden spoon handle down on top of the cork. He keeps pushing, persevering. It's not going to work, I think. Then suddenly, slowly, the wooden handle lowers as the cork slips from its position, down into the bottle.

"Sweet," he says. I pass him the two red plastic cups. "Good idea. No point giving glass to a drunk person."

He knows, I think. He knows I'm ill-equipped and inexperienced but he's not about to rub my nose in it. I decide to play along.

"Well, I'm not giving Phil one of my crystal numbers," I say. Freddy bursts out laughing. I laugh too. I think it's the first time in my life I've made a proper joke. He grins at me. We have an understanding.

"Where's my drink?" moans Phil. I look at her, now lolling about on one of my decrepit armchairs. She sits sideways with her legs draped over the armrest. Freddy pours the wine into one of the red cups and passes it to Phil.

"Plastic cups? Really?" she says, clearly appalled.

"Safest option for a pisshead, darling," says Freddy. Phil throws her head back and laughs.

"I love you, Freddy. You are the funniest person I know."

Freddy looks at me and rolls his eyes. He pours wine into the other cup and passes it to me.

"No thanks," I say. With the addition of Freddy to the evening, whoever doesn't get a plastic cup gets one of my embarrassing mugs. He takes the plastic cup for himself and drinks.

"Cheers," he says.

"Cheers, you sexy beast. Can we have some music? It's too quiet in here," whines Phil.

Music, shit. Freddy, seeing me pause, jumps in.

"I can be DJ," he says, taking out his phone. He swipes the screen a couple of times and dance beats fill the room. Phil clambers to her feet and throws her arms around Freddy's waist, her red wine spilling on the carpet. She holds onto him, swaying from side to side. Freddy grabs her, pulling her close and they do this kind of grinding dance with Phil pushing her pelvis into his. Phil giggles, staring at Freddy and licking her lips.

"I'll check on dinner," I shout, unable to keep the angry edge out of my voice and squeeze back into my excuse of a kitchen.

I'm never having people to my flat again ever. And why is Phil so drunk? Why has she turned up with Freddy? Who is he to her?

"I'm guessing this isn't the night you had planned." Freddy blocks the doorway again and I wish he wouldn't. His broad shoulders cast a shadow over my simmering pots and I want to shove him back. Behind him Phil continues to sway to the music, eyes closed, in a world of her own. I don't like drunk Phil. She's normally so smart and slick and strong. I go back to my pots, stirring the creamy white sauce, which doesn't look nearly as appetizing as it did when it was in its container in the supermarket.

"How do you know Phil?" I ask, trying to sound casual.

"We grew up together. I went to the school across the street from hers."

"Oh, she hasn't mentioned you, that's all." That's got to hurt, I think. But Freddy's not bothered.

"She mentioned you," he says with a cheeky grin.

I force a smile, annoyed by his self-confidence. I wish he was threatened by me at least a tiny bit.

I move the pasta around in the pan with a spoon. It's soft, which means it's ready. I turn off the burner and stare at the pot. I don't have any way of getting the pasta out of the hot water. I should have bought a colander. I don't even have a lid for either of my saucepans to hold the pasta back while I drain it. Freddy must have seen the worry on my face.

"Use a plate to drain the water out," he says. There's no malice in his voice, he's not even patronizing, just kind, but it makes me resent him even more. I grab my other plate, which is propped up at the back of the cooktop.

"I've only recently moved in. I haven't had a chance to fully equip my state-of-the-art kitchen yet," I say.

Freddy bursts out laughing again. My second joke of the night. I'm quite proud of myself for a moment. Phil sticks her head in under Freddy's arm, putting her arms around his waist.

"What's so funny?" she asks, snuggling into Freddy. Freddy hugs her back.

"Noelle was saying how she's hoping to be on *MasterChef.*"

I smile. Freddy teasing me gives me a warm feeling. But he's still a problem.

By the time I serve dinner, Phil has found her way up the ladder onto my mattress, and has passed out.

Freddy and I sit at the table, each with one of my new white pasta bowls now brimming with overcooked pasta covered in shiny white sauce. Freddy tucks into his like it's the best meal he's ever had. Not to draw attention to how awful it is, I eat mine with enthusiasm too.

"She doesn't get like this very often, well, at least not anymore. She had a bad counseling session at the hospital today, that's all," he says, like it's common knowledge. Before I can hide my surprise, Freddy clocks it.

"You don't know?" he says, taken aback.

"Everyone needs counseling sometimes," I say, like it's no big deal. I heard someone say that once.

"No, I mean, you don't know, about Phil?" he says, holding a fork of gloopy pasta over his bowl ready to eat.

"Whatever it is, I'm sure she'll tell me," I say, faking confidence. He nods, relaxing again.

"Yeah, I'm sure she will. She likes you," he says, popping the pasta in his mouth.

"She seems to like you too," I say, finding it hard to keep the tension out of my voice.

"I'm her boyfriend," he says.

The color drains from my face and I stare at him.

"It's okay, we have an open relationship. I see other people too," he says.

"It can't be that serious between you then," I blurt out.

Suddenly I don't care about hiding my feelings. If I'm going to fight for Phil I need to know what I'm up against.

"We're soulmates," he says, like that answers everything. "I hope that doesn't change how you feel about her. It shouldn't."

"It hasn't," I say, and it really hasn't. Deep down I'm hoping Phil will choose me over Freddy. I decide not to take the soulmates thing to heart.

"Where are you from?" he asks. It's not a probing question. He's seems genuinely interested.

"South London," I say.

"Cool. Do you have family or are you on your own?" he asks.

I stare at him. Now it feels like he's probing.

"I'm on my own," he continues, totally relaxed and at ease. "My grandparents raised me but they're dead now."

"Sorry to hear that," I say.

"It sucks being alone at first but you get used it."

He can tell, I think. He knows I'm on my own in the world. Is it that obvious? I glance around my excuse for a flat. Anyone with a decent family wouldn't be living in a hovel like this, I suppose.

"I used to live with my mother but I left home when I was seventeen," I say. Suddenly I don't seem to mind talking about my past. There's no judgment with Freddy.

"Do you keep in touch?"

"Not really. I bumped into her today in the supermarket. It's the first time I've seen her since I left home."

He stops eating and looks at me.

Now I'm worried that I've said too much, so I carry on eating.

"Fuck. How did it go?" he says.

"Fine, you know," I say, not willing to divulge anything else.

"My parents went trekking in the Amazon when I was a baby and never came back. Vanished into thin air, that's what my grandmother used to say," he says, wolfing down the rest of his pasta. I decide it's impossible not to like Freddy.

After dinner he gives me a hug and goes, saying it's better to leave Phil where she is and that she probably wants to stay the night anyway. I can see why Phil is attached to him, but soulmate or not, I'm not giving up on me and Phil.

The ladder creaks as I climb up to the mattress area. In the dim light I see Phil lying on top of the duvet on her side with her knees pulled up to her chest. I duck to avoid banging my head on the ceiling as I tiptoe to the bed and fold the other half of the duvet over her to keep her warm. Her breathing is once again gentle and uninterrupted. I lower myself down beside her, lying on my back so as not to disturb her by rolling over.

I stare at the stained ceiling. I've never noticed how bad it was before. It reminds me of the damp patches on the ceilings in West House. I shiver, partly with the draft, partly with the memory of the flat I grew up in.

I close my eyes, sending the thoughts away, trying to imagine the stains are balloons and I'm releasing them into the wind. That doesn't work, so I imagine they're watermelons. One of them is my mother's head, and I'm whacking it with a sledgehammer. That seems to work.

I feel a calm descend. Phil is in my bed beside me. Maybe the evening worked out well after all.

I wake with a start and it takes a while for me to get my bearings. My body is cold and my nose feels like ice when I touch it. I reach for the duvet, which is piled up in a lump beside me and my heart swells with anticipation. Phil is here in bed with me. She hasn't moved since last night. I envy her ability to sleep so soundly. I gently push her. She doesn't stir.

"Phil? Phil?" She moans a little as she starts to come around. "Do you want coffee?" She makes a grunting noise, which I take to mean yes.

I climb down the creaky ladder to the living room and slide open the curtains. The curtain rings and rail are made of plastic so they don't make much noise when dragged across but two of the rings are missing, which makes the material bunch up along the rail. I fold the curtains inward toward the window to hide the bunching. The sun streams in, lighting up the room.

My bedsit looks slightly better in the daylight as opposed to the nighttime. I don't know why but the stains on the carpet don't show up so badly. It's as though they sink back into the floor scared of the sunlight like vampires.

The water in the pan on the cooktop begins to boil, making a rattling sound on the uneven ring. I shake instant coffee into my two embarrassing mugs, slop hot water over the granules and stir with one of my new teaspoons. I should buy more cutlery and more plates. Maybe I'll try a charity shop, as I'm never going back to a supermarket.

Using one hand to hold the cups and the other to grip the ladder, I ease myself up to the mattress space. Phil stirs and groans, her hands over her eyes and forehead.

"What's with the bright light?"

"It's morning," I say. Phil forces her eyes open and peers at me.

"What time is it?" she croaks. Her makeup is smudged and her hair sticks to her face, but to me she looks beautiful.

"Eight," I say. We're not due in work till ten.

"Where's Freddy?" she asks looking around.

"He left," I say passing her the cup of coffee. She holds it with two hands and cautiously takes a sip.

"Sorry about last night. Did I totally ruin dinner?" she asks.

"Yes, but it wasn't very nice anyway."

"I'll make it up to you," she says. That's all the encouragement I need.

"Freddy says you had a bad meeting." Phil eyes me and takes another sip of her coffee. "It's okay if you don't want to tell me."

"I don't want to tell you," she says.

"Fine," I say and crawl over to the ladder, the disappointment burning a hole in my stomach.

"Wait," she says.

I turn to look at her. She's frowning, still making up her mind about telling me.

"The meeting was a group counseling session, okay?"

I come back and sit on the mattress. Excitement whirls inside me. Phil is talking to me.

"It's part of my bail conditions."

She pauses, letting this land. I give her a shrug and it's genuine— I really don't care what she's done.

"I have this issue," she continues. "Some people—arseholes in white coats, mainly—call it bipolar. When I come off my meds, which I haven't in ages, I go a bit wild. Last time it was drunk driving. I crashed a car . . . into a police van."

My eyes widen in awe.

"It was more of a bump than a crash. Anyway, I have to go to therapy and stay on my meds or they'll lock me up."

"So what happened yesterday in your meeting?"

I'm determined to keep her talking. Phil drains her coffee, hands me the mug and throws herself back on the pillows.

"There's this dickhead in my group named Marnie. We had a fight. She called me rich and privileged because I choose to work as a cleaner. She said I should leave the cleaning job for someone who really needs it." I nod, showing support and understanding, but deep down I wonder if Marnie is right.

"I mean, who does that shallow bitch think she is?" says Phil, on a roll now. "She doesn't even have a job. And you can't blame everything on mental health issues. Sometimes people are just dickheads who happen to have a mental health problem."

I can see she's getting worked up. She's told me her secret and that's enough. I don't need to hear about dickhead Marnie. I wait for her to take a breath in her rant.

"I went to see Gaby yesterday," I say, changing the subject.

"How is she? Is she okay?" she asks, sitting upright, attentive now. I tell her about Gaby's son being brought out of his coma today.

"Shit," says Phil and flops back in the bed, her arms above her head. I move in beside her, wanting to be close to her. I lay my head on her chest, the soft gentle beating of her heart makes me want to curl up and go to sleep. She rests her arm on my shoulder and runs a finger in circles on my back.

"Freddy says he's your soulmate."

"Yes, he is. Is that a problem?"

I lean up on my elbow and do my best to look cool, but my cheeks are burning.

"No," I say, but I had hoped she'd say they were friends more than anything else.

"Are you sure?" Phil asks. "Because I'm not really the exclusive type."

I nod my head. If sharing Phil is the only way to have her then I'll have to put up with Freddy. Phil pushes the hair from my face.

"I've never met someone like you before," she says. "You're kind of intriguing. I like it."

"And I've never met anyone like you before," I say in a quiet voice, a little embarrassed to be putting my feelings out there.

"Are you in love with me?" she asks.

"I think so," I say, looking her right in the eye.

She moves on top of me, sliding my T-shirt up over my head. I pull at her clothes, trying to unbutton her jeans. Giggling, we strip down to our underwear. My breath is fast and erratic. She traces a finger along my shoulder where there's a long thin mark, then down my arm to a burn scar.

"What happened to you? Were you in an accident?"

"I, er, fell out of a few trees as a kid," I say.

"What? Onto knives?"

I've never had to answer questions about my body before. I'm not sure what to say.

"I was a bit of tomboy too," she says and bends her head, gently kissing my scar. "Let me show you something." She slides her hands down my body and slips off my knickers. She kisses my neck, then runs her tongue over my nipples, making me gasp, then moves down to my navel, still kissing. What is she doing? Where is she going? Then her hot breath hits my crotch.

Chapter 17

I got my name from a woman in the registry office for births, marriages and deaths. That's how my mother told the story anyway. She had to register my birth because it's a legal requirement but when she arrived at the office to do it, she still hadn't given me a name.

She joked that she nearly wrote *Oi* in the first name box on the form. That's all she ever really called me. In fact, the only reason she went to register me at all was because she wouldn't get child benefit unless she did. She said if she could, she'd have left me on the front steps of an orphanage. I kind of wish she had.

According to my mother, while waiting in the registry office to be called to one of the counter windows, she watched a woman beside her filling out her form. The woman's baby's name was Noelle. She thought, what the hell? At least it wasn't more than two syllables.

My birthday is on the twenty-third of December and even though my mother claimed I ruined Christmas, part of me will always hope she had a Tesco Erica moment and named me Noelle because it was festive—that for one brief moment she had actually cared about me.

Chapter 18

The taxi drops us at the service entrance to the Magnolia. It's been pouring rain but it's stopped now and the low-hanging dense clouds are beginning to break up. The ground is still soaked and we have to swerve to avoid a giant puddle as we approach the door.

"Do you want to go in ahead?" I say to Phil. She gives me a funny look. "In case Mali and Rose see us together," I say. She looks over my shoulder at two guys, hotel staff, rolling trolleys of dirty washing onto a truck in the loading bay.

"Hey, Marcus, Tony." She waves over at them. They wave back. She's avoiding my question. Either she doesn't know how to answer it or she doesn't want to answer it.

"I was only asking," I say glibly and go to open the door.

"Look," she says, putting her hand on my arm. God, please don't let her say something I don't want to hear. "Nobody cares what we do. They won't even notice if we arrive together."

"Sorry," I say.

"Don't overthink it."

She throws open the door and strides in. I follow her down the concrete tunnel with the hum in my ears, which seems louder today and more intrusive. Our footsteps slap on the concrete floor. The heavy, white fire door looms up ahead. On my first day at the Magnolia, I had felt confident and filled with excitement as I weaved my way through the network of passages and corridors into the bosom of the hotel. It was familiar terrain and I was the master of my universe. But now, following Phil, I feel lost, like I took a wrong turn, and as we approach the fire door I wonder what will be beyond it. Maybe we'll step out into a black hole of nothingness, plunging into oblivion. I'm not averse to this idea. At least we'd be together. Phil pushes through the door and marches on into the next corridor. No black hole waiting for us. Phil strides on ahead and I have to walk faster to keep up with her as the hotel corridors close in on me, seeming narrower and tighter and less friendly.

Phil pushes open the staff room door and we bundle in. I mutter hellos but keep my eyes down, not wanting to catch Mali's or Rose's eye. Despite what Phil said about nobody caring if we arrive together, if they suspect we did they'll be all over me asking questions the minute Phil's out of earshot.

I go to my locker and dump my bag in, sticking my head in the cool, dark space. I stay there for a moment, feeling hidden away.

"What's the matter with you?" Mali pokes me in the ribs.

"Ow," I say, turning to her, rubbing my side. Rose comes over as well.

"You okay, honey?"

"Yeah, why wouldn't I be?"

Mali slaps a cold food container in my hands. "Chicken curry with cream and peanuts. Get some fat on your boobies."

"Hey," complains Rose. "You've never made me chicken curry."

"I don't do diet food," says Mali.

Rose raises her eyebrows. "Are you saying I'm fat?"

"You have a potbelly," says Mali, patting Rose's tummy. Rose slaps her hand away, pulling her apron tight across her middle.

"I like my insulation," says Rose. "And it's not big."

"Big enough," says Mali, laughing. Rose laughs too.

"Thanks for the curry," I say to Mali.

"I want marks out of ten."

"It better be ten or you won't hear the end of it," says Rose.

I look up as Fatima glides into the room, her long ponytail bouncing along behind her. I take my bag out of my locker again and unzip it to put the chicken curry away. From the corner of my eye, I watch Fatima stop and chat with Phil. They talk quietly for a few seconds, then Phil smiles at something Fatima says and her hand falls on Fatima's waist for a moment. Fatima pushes her chest out and puts her hand on her hip, definitely posing. A shooting pain punctures my stomach like a hot poker and I flick my head away quickly. My chest hurts too. The smell of cold chicken curry wafts up from my bag, turning my stomach.

The lift is more claustrophobic than usual today with Fatima eyeing me across the enclosed space. I stare at the lift buttons, avoiding her gaze. She's working out if I'm a threat to her or not, and I am. Phil stayed at my place last night. She woke up with me this morning.

I imagine Phil and Fatima naked together, Phil's face between Fatima's legs, and my throat contracts like there's a clamp on it.

Phil joins me as I park my trolley and open room 715.

"You okay?" she asks.

"Sure," I say. *What's the story with Fatima?* I want to scream, but I don't.

"You seem a bit off. I mean, we had fun this morning, right?" I look at her, disarmed, putty in her hands.

"Yes," I whisper.

"I like you a lot. I hope that's enough."

"Of course." But it's not enough, not enough by far. She touches my face.

"I'm glad you came to work here," she says and wanders back to her trolley.

I'm stuck to the spot. I can't feel my feet. I sniff and smooth my skirt, aware of the icy vines snaking up around my feet, trying to sneak up on me, making me feel hopeless. I turn to my trolley and grab cloths, gloves, garbage bags and antibacterial spray. Room 715 is a stayer, so there shouldn't be a need to change bed linen.

I wander in, determined to be in and out in less than ten minutes. Judging by the empty cans of Pepsi Max in the trash, they're a young couple. The surfaces are littered with oddball personal belongings: a nail file, a lip liner, a pen with a furry top on the end, half a bag of Skittles, some chewing gum and a club flyer.

Apart from the flyer and the edibles, I'd normally consider taking any one of these items, but the urge still isn't there. I need to consider if it's simply time to up my game. I've been taking little trinkets and insignificant items for eight years. If I increase the risk by taking more valuable items, will the buzz return?

I shake the soft duvet out, ready to make the bed. I know I'm kidding myself—the only rush I get now is when I'm with Phil or even just near her.

I lean against the edge of the bed for a moment, suddenly cold all over. I squeeze my eyes tightly shut, trying to keep the creeping doom at bay.

Phil said she likes me a lot. I can build on that. I can make it work. I hang onto this thought as the warmth returns to my body.

In the locker room after our shift, Mali, Rose and I change out of our aprons but Phil's nowhere to be seen. I daren't ask Mali and Rose where she is, but I don't have to. Rose offers the information anyway.

"Phil finished early and went for a coffee with Fatima." I stick my head in my locker pretending to look for something to hide my flushed cheeks.

"She better come to the hospital," says Mali. "If it's bad news Gaby's going to need us." I had completely forgotten Gaby's son was being brought out of his coma today.

"I told Phil," I assure Mali and Rose.

"Then she'll be there," says Rose. Mali lets out three short breaths, like she's preparing to lift a heavy barbell. Rose gives her a hug.

I turn away. Whatever the outcome for Gaby's son, it is not going to be okay for Gaby. Mali and Rose know it too.

Chapter 19

At the hospital, Rose and I sit in the reception area. We're not allowed up to the ward, which I'm pleased about. There's enough of an empty feeling inside me without standing on the corridor outside the Robertson Ward again. And there are seats here and a potted plant by the front desk struggling to remain green and perky.

Mali marches up and down in front of us, her hands behind her head. She's wearing white skinny jeans, red pumps and a black leather jacket. Her hair is swept back off her face, like a porcupine with its spikes laid flat. She looks tiny but fierce and neither Rose nor I want to say anything to upset her.

Mali stops walking and turns to us, hands still behind her head.

"He must be awake by now," she says.

"Gaby said she'd know something by four o'clock and it's only twenty past," says Rose in her calmest voice.

"Something's wrong," says Mali, shaking her head at us.

"You don't know that," I say.

"Yeah," says Rose. "He'll be back sticking needles in his arm and robbing from her before she knows it." I look at Rose, surprised. It's not like her to be cynical. Mali resumes pacing. I check my phone for messages. Phil hasn't got back to my texts. How long does a coffee with Fatima take?

"Everything okay with you and Phil?" asks Rose.

"Er . . . yeah," I say, as though it's an odd thing to ask.

"She's not someone you should get too attached to, not in a romantic sense anyway."

"I'm not attached," I say.

"That's alright then," she says, putting her arm around my shoulders and giving me a quick squeeze, which only makes me feel worse.

But it's not alright. I am attached and every fiber of my body feels starved of Phil, like I'm wilting.

"Mali?" yells Rose. "Sit the fuck down. You're making me queasy, all this walking up and down."

Mali scowls at Rose.

"And don't look at me like that," says Rose. "You are enough to send anyone over the edge. Now sit your arse down." Mali sits. Then Rose nods to the entrance. I turn to see Phil and Fatima coming through the doors, both still in work clothes.

"Gaby can't stand Fatima," mutters Rose under her breath.

An uncomfortable mass stirs in my gut. I can't bear to see Phil with Fatima. And why has she brought her to the hospital? I attempt to smile at Phil, but only one side of my mouth manages to move, so it must look crooked.

Her eyes sweep over me as she sits beside Rose. Fatima says she's hungry and asks if anyone wants anything from the café. We all shake our heads and she slopes off. Why is Fatima hungry? If they just went for coffee, why didn't she eat there? What have Phil and Fatima been doing? I look at my hands, shaking.

I feel a soft caress of my hair and whip my head around. Phil is leaning around the back of Rose's chair and is now fondling my ear.

I look at her, wishing I wasn't so grateful for the attention. She gives me a lazy smile and I smile back at her, relief flooding through me but more aware than ever at the power she has over me.

Gaby appears, coming toward us with her head down. Rose sees her first and stands up. Everyone quickly stands up too, ready to face the news of Gaby's future.

"Thanks for coming," she says.

"Is he awake?" asks Phil.

"Yes, and so far he seems to be okay." She finally smiles at us, like the news has just sunk in.

Mali claps her hands and hugs Gaby hard.

"When you say okay, do you mean fully functioning?" asks Phil.

"Yep, he's groggy and stuff, but no brain damage," says Gaby, disentangling herself from Mali's grip. We all let out big sighs of relief. Gaby takes my hand, Mali adds hers, then Phil and Rose.

"I've got my boy back," says Gaby. But I can tell she's not being honest. She's saying all the right things, she's smiling, and her body language screams relief, but her eyes give her away. They're expressionless and unmoving. Then I realize what it is.

Disappointment. Gaby knows she should be over the moon that her son doesn't have brain damage, and she is, but part of her had become used to the idea of being a full-time hero mum of a mentally disabled son. It must beat being the mum of a drug addict, recovering or not, for Gaby anyway.

"So you'll be back in work soon then," says Rose.

"That's right. Everything will be back to normal," says Gaby. Her words weigh heavy on all of us. Will Gaby return to sleepless nights and stolen televisions? Will she once again have to contend with abusive and violent threats from her son when he's desperate for a fix? Gaby plasters on a bigger smile, but there are tears in her eyes. Phil, Rose and Mali swoop in for a group hug.

Who am I to be here? Who am I to Gaby or Mali or Rose? Who am I to Phil? I'm nobody. I don't belong here. In fact, I don't belong anywhere. The only time I ever feel like I belong to something is when I take an item from a hotel guest. In that moment, I feel connected and happy and satisfied that something that belonged to someone else now belongs to me. But right now, I feel lost, like I'm floating in space.

I turn and walk out of the entrance doors. I don't expect anyone to notice.

I came straight home from the hospital, scraped the chicken curry Mali gave me into the garbage and climbed the ladder to my mattress. I've been lying on up here ever since, staring at the ceiling.

The sound of a car alarm breaks the silence. I'm not sure what time it is, but it's dark outside and has been for a while and the curtains are still open. I'm still dressed in work clothes but don't have the energy or inclination to get under the covers let alone get undressed. My hands and feet are cold and so is my nose. I stare at the stains on the ceiling above me. Even if you ripped the plaster out and started again with a new ceiling and new paint, the stains would return over time because the problem is not the ceiling but the house, left to drip and sag and waste away.

I hear a shuffling outside my door as someone takes the stairs to the floor above me. The sound of the footsteps reminds me of my mother when she used to prowl up and down the hallway outside my bedroom, like an evil spirit who never gave me any peace.

I close my eyes, desperate to sleep so I can wake in the morning with the day ahead of me instead of the night. An icy breeze grips my heart and I squeeze my eyes tightly shut, trying to force myself to think of Phil, touching me, loving me but all I can see is Fatima sticking her chest out for Phil to admire.

Chapter 20

"Where did you get to?" Rose asks me the next day. I have my head in my locker, fumbling around for my apron. I know my eyes are puffy and red from lack of sleep and I'm finding it difficult to move quickly, as though I'm wading through mud.

"I had a headache," I say.

"Ah, fuck," says Rose. She looks at my eyes and shakes her head. "I'm sorry, Noelle. I did tell you not to let Phil get to you."

"I haven't," I say. "Why would she get to me?" I'm acting bewildered, but from Rose's pained expression I'm not doing a very good job of it. I give up and slump against my locker.

"You just have to learn to handle her properly."

"What does that mean?" I say, suddenly desperate for advice.

"She's a funny fish," says Rose. I glance over at Phil tying her perfectly pressed apron as she chats with Fatima. If anyone's a funny fish around here, it's me.

"She'll grow tired of Fatima," Rose reassures me. Like she's grown tired of me, I think. "She's better as a friend, that's all I'm saying. And anyway, Gaby's back now."

I tie my apron, keeping my head down so as not to make eye contact with Phil by accident. How did I end up in this situation? I'm like a needy stray cat nobody wants to pet. There were plenty of those in West House and if you came too close, they'd scratch your eyes out.

Mali and Gaby come up to me and each put an arm around my shoulders. Rose looks on, pleased. Mali twists my face around to look at her.

"Hey, Skinny, you okay?"

"Yeah," I say, although with Mali's vice-like grip on my cheeks I can barely get the words out.

"Thanks for being there for me," says Gaby, squeezing me tight.

"I didn't really do anything," I say. And I mean it. I only went to the hospital to visit her because Mali told me to. Mali pulls Rose into the group hug, which I now find myself in the center of. I feel claustrophobic and I can't breathe for a moment.

"How was the chicken curry?" says Mali.

"Ten out of ten," I say.

"Are you just saying that?"

"No, it was really delicious." Mali seems satisfied and they all let me go. I take a quick breath, relieved to be free of the huddle. Phil saunters over and hangs her arm over my shoulder.

"Did I miss a group hug?" she says. I keep moving so her arm slips off. I don't turn to see the look on her face. Something inside me has changed. Something inside me is angry. I've become pathetic Noelle and I don't like her one bit. Well, I don't need Phil. I don't need anybody, I never have. It hasn't worked out for me at the Magnolia and when that happens, I move on, starting with taking a high-risk item, which is then followed by a complaint and my speedy departure. I might as well stick to my plan and do things properly. There's been enough of a disruption to my life as it is.

Mali, Rose, Gaby, Phil and I pile out of the service lift. It's good to have Gaby back and Fatima gone. I walk on ahead to the service cupboard, keen to get my trolley. My mouth and throat are dry. I stifle a cough. The others follow and Phil glances at me, but I ignore her. She opens the door with the key.

Mali, Rose, Gaby and Phil wheel their trolleys out first. My foot taps as I wait my turn. I quickly pull mine out and check it over to make sure everything is there as Mali, Rose and Gaby push their trolleys down the corridor. I'm about to follow, when Phil steps in front of me and makes me stop.

"Hey," she says.

"Hey," I reply in a clipped tone, not giving her an inch.

"I never promised you anything."

"I never promised you anything either," I retort then immediately regret it. I know I sound weak.

"Then what's your problem? I thought we talked about this," she says.

I look at her for the first time today. There's no judgment in her voice or her eyes, only confusion, maybe concern. I feel the fight drain out of me, like someone let the air out of my tires. So much for my big talk about sticking to plans.

"It's too hard," I whisper. I can't believe how honest I'm being.

"Then we'll be friends, okay?" she says, smiling at me. I nod, trying to appear nonchalant, but my jaw is clenched.

"I'm sorry," she adds and moves off with her trolley.

That's it, you're sorry? You split my heart open, rob me of the only thing I had in my life that gave me any sense of purpose, and then say sorry, like that makes it okay? And what does she mean, friends? I don't have or need friends. The only people I ever interact with are the people I work with but once I move on, I never see or speak to them again. Phil and the other women are no different.

Pushing my trolley along the corridor, I stare at the floor, watching the carpet flicking past underneath me, the shadows of my feet moving in and out.

It's over. Phil doesn't want me. I wait for the devastation to ravage my body. But it doesn't come. Instead, the old familiar feeling of excitement stirs within me, like someone just lit a sparkler in my gut.

I enter room 726 with an urgency I haven't felt in a while. This is almost my last room to be cleaned today and it's also my favorite on floor seven. It has a view over a small, manicured park with a walled garden where families walk their dogs and eat picnics together.

I peer out of the window for a moment at the perfectly trimmed hedges and circular pond. Large proud rose bushes line the stone pathways as leaves flutter in the wind, reminding me of the flutters in my stomach. Maybe one day I'll have a flat that looks out on a view like this.

A quick scan of the room tells me it's a double occupancy, a couple. Suit trousers in the trouser press. Floral scarf hanging on the wardrobe door. I know they only arrived yesterday, as I had prepared the room. I run my hands over the silk scarf letting it slide between my fingers, as the butterflies in my belly rise up, released from their slumber. I smile to myself out of relief but also excitement.

I need to take something—something big enough to trigger a complaint and significant enough to be a memento of my time at the Magnolia. Once the guest complains to the management, I'll have no choice but to hand in my notice and leave the Magnolia and Mali, Gaby, Rose and Phil behind me forever. The heat rushes from the base of my spine to the back of my neck. Game on.

As I make the bed, my eyes land on the woman's hairbrush lying on the desk beside the hair dryer. It's not new, far from it, and is full of matted brown hair. I pick it up and hold it in my hand.

This is a big item and bound to be missed. I take a short sharp breath and slip it into the front of my apron. I stand still for a moment allowing the tingling sensation to reach its peak before it gives way to the rush of adrenaline, storming my veins like a river that's burst its banks. I roll my shoulders, letting my heart rate slow. I glance in the front of my apron at the hairbrush. It belongs to me now.

The suitcases are closed and stacked upright, which tells me the guests have unpacked. Still in rummaging mode, I open the wardrobe where their clothes have been neatly hung on hangers and put away in drawers. These people are organized, which quickens my heart rate again. This woman will definitely know she left her hairbrush on the desk. No one will be able to convince her otherwise, even Mr. Redmond.

I pull open a drawer and push it back in again, just looking, but something catches my eye. The label in a pair of the woman's knickers is visible and it says Primark. I hear cleaners talk about Primark a lot because of the cheap deals they get there. I close the wardrobe door and scan the bedroom again. I need a second look at who these people are.

On the bedside table are a cup and saucer from the bar downstairs, and a box of tea bags that they brought with them. Rather than pay five-star hotel prices for a cup of peppermint tea, approximately £7.00, they bring a cup of hot water to the bedroom and make their own. I respect that.

I check the minibar to see if it needs restocking. It's not the cleaner's job to do that—there's a minibar trolley that does the rounds in the afternoon—but it's another way to assess the type of guests in a room. Are they willing to pay £3.50 for a can of Coke the size of my thumb?

I open the fridge and find the items inside untouched, which isn't unusual; not many people tuck into the minibar these days. But there's a niggling feeling in the pit of my stomach. I'm starting to like this couple. Despite the amount they're spending on the room, they have a sense of value. Maybe it's a business trip and staying in the Magnolia is a big treat for them. I make a snap decision and put the hairbrush back where I found it. I'll take something from the next room, my last of the day.

I glance at my face in the mirror. My pupils are dilated and my body is sizzling. I'm back, I think to myself. Fuck Phil.

I head to the bathroom, keen to clean it quickly and get out and into the next room. I'm actually looking forward to the commotion in Julia's office tomorrow with my fake sobbing and sniveling as I deny all knowledge of the missing item, and backed up by my good friends, Gaby, Mali, Rose and Phil. I'm confident they will fight to the death for my innocence now.

In the bathroom, I stop in my tracks. Every single towel has been dumped in the bathtub. I pick up the towels to inspect them. They've barely been used. My eyes narrow and anger bubbles up inside me.

I collect clean towels from the towel and linen trolley outside in the corridor and return to the room to stack them in the towel cubbyholes above the sink in the bathroom.

I whip around the rest of the bathroom, polishing the taps and the mirror and mopping the floor. I flush the toilet and leave the room, the barely used towels in my arms for the laundry.

As I pass the desk in the bedroom, my right hand swoops down and, without even looking, I sweep up the hairbrush and drop it into the front of my apron.

In the staff room after our shift, Mali, Gaby, Phil and Rose chat among themselves as we take off our aprons.

"Don't forget my sister's birthday party, two weeks on Friday and you're all invited," says Rose.

"I'm only coming if there's dancing," says Mali gyrating her hips. Rose goes on to tease Mali about being a Kylie Minogue fan.

"If you met her, what would you say to her?" says Rose.

"I'm not going to meet her so it's a stupid question."

"If I met Jean-Claude Van Damme, I'd know exactly what to say to him." Rose and Gaby high-five.

"As if he'd look at you," says Mali.

"Oh, he doesn't have to look at me. We can turn the lights out." Rose roars laughing at her own joke. Mali giggles.

"I like Kylie, but I still prefer Madonna," says Gaby. Mali tuts, disapproving.

"I thought you'd be more of a Madonna-head," Rose says to Mali. "All that S&M shit." Mali slaps Rose on the backside.

"Hey!" complains Rose. Then Mali slaps Gaby and Phil on the backside too.

"You want S&M, I'll give you S&M," says Mali.

I'm tucked away at my locker and manage to escape the crack of Mali's hand. The banter continues but I'm not tuned in. I simply have nothing to contribute. I feel disconnected, like my wires have been cut.

Phil smiles at me, trying to engage, but I look away. I can't help it. I don't want to behave like this, as I need to keep them all on my side until the complaint comes in but, on some level, I've already moved on. These people are no longer important to me.

But when I think about never seeing Phil, Mali, Gaby and Rose again a pang of regret snaps inside my chest, like the ping of an elastic band. I barely lasted three weeks in the Magnolia so I'm not sure why I'm even the slightest bit bothered about moving on. I blame Phil. She's the one who caused me all this trouble in the first place.

I roll my apron up carefully, so as not to disturb the hairbrush, and put it in my backpack. I zip it closed, ready to leave, as a hand lands on my shoulder. The girls have stopped talking.

I turn to see Julia, a serious look on her face. I keep my facial expression neutral, but I know immediately the woman from room 726 has already complained. I wasn't expecting it to happen so soon.

"Can I speak to you for a moment?" says Julia. Phil, Rose, Gaby and Mali look on, intrigued.

"Sure," I say, keeping my voice steady and calm. I casually return my bag to the locker. Julia heads back to her office, her high heels clip clopping on the concrete floor.

"What's going on?" Phil asks me.

"I don't know. Maybe it's a promotion," I say, attempting to distract them with humor.

"It better not be, or I'll kill you," Mali says, frowning.

I enter Julia's office to find her standing behind her desk, unconsciously chewing the inside of her cheek. She's uncomfortable, which is a good sign. She doesn't want to accuse me of stealing, especially if I didn't do it. It could tarnish her reputation with the other cleaners and destroy what trust she's managed to build with them. It could lead to staff gossiping behind her back and a general feeling of dislike toward her. Julia needs to avoid that at all costs. Her self-esteem simply wouldn't survive. I feel completely in control.

"I'm afraid a customer has made a complaint about the cleaner of room 726 today."

"That's me," I say, acting perplexed.

"She said her hairbrush is missing," she says, letting out a long sigh, not wanting to take responsibility for accusing me.

"I don't understand," I say, as though what Julia has said makes absolutely no sense to me. Julia winces, despising every minute of this. She tries to cushion the blow.

"She said it was there before she went out because she used it but when she came back it was gone." I wrinkle my forehead, as though still confused. Julia takes a deep breath. "Did you see it, Noelle? The hairbrush." I feign concentration, acting like I'm trying to remember.

"Room 726 was one of my last ones today. The room was neat, but they'd put all their towels in the tub for changing. They only arrived yesterday," I say, with a grave look on my face. Julia shakes her head, annoyed to hear this.

"Some people. Don't they care about the environment?" she says, relaxing a little, glad to find common ground with me.

"I don't remember seeing a hairbrush, sorry."

"Okay, well, look," she says, leaning on the desk toward me, a sign that she believes me now and wants to ensure the continued love and respect of her team by supporting me. "The problem is, she's saying the cleaner took it."

I act like it's taking me a moment to process this information.

"I don't think you stole her hairbrush," she says, lowering her voice. "That's not what this is about."

"What?" I say, my voice louder than Julia's now. "She said I stole her hairbrush?" I force my eyes to moisten and redden, which involves holding my breath for a few seconds and forcing pressure up into my head, which also makes me feel dizzy for a moment.

"Not exactly," says Julia, panicked that I'm getting upset and look like I'm about to faint. "But maybe you moved it or it dropped into a laundry basket or garbage pail by mistake."

I start to ramble now like I'm trying to make sense of the accusation. "But we don't touch guests' things. We only move them or pick them up if we have to. I don't remember picking up a hairbrush or moving it or anything. The rule is don't touch if possible, so why . . . why . . . would I?" I add a little hesitation to my speech for effect.

Julia nods, relieved she can now be sympathetic. I wipe my eyes, blinking, as though about to cry.

"And what would I want with a used hairbrush? That's crazy."

"I know," says Julia. "I've never heard anything so ridiculous."

I flop down in the chair across from her, like this is the worst day of my life. My bottom lip quivers just enough to make Julia's heart melt.

"Are you going to fire me?" I ask, doe eyes fully engaged.

"Don't be silly," says Julia, rushing to my side, hand on my shoulder. "I have to conduct an internal investigation when there's a complaint, that's all. The chances are the woman never even packed her hairbrush; people always reconstruct their memories to suit themselves."

"But will Mr. Redmond believe me?" I whisper.

"I'll talk to him, okay? But first, with your permission, I have to check your things before you leave, just to be sure." A rush of blood to my head makes me feel momentarily giddy.

"Of course," I say.

I rise from my chair, dizzy with panic and leave the room. Julia follows. Shit, shit, shit. This is why it's crucial the complaint comes after I've left the hotel for the day and the item is back in my flat, locked away inside my trunk. I didn't time it properly. I should have taken from my last room of the day, not my second to last. I should have been long gone from the hotel by the time the guest made a complaint. Instead, I had lingered in the staff room, lost in my thoughts. I'm off my game and out of practice, thanks to Phil. This could be it now: caught red-handed with no way out.

I walk toward the staff room. My hands are numb—so are my cheeks. The sound of Julia's high heels clatter behind me. The thumping of my heart fills my head, boom, boom, boom.

I need to get rid of the hairbrush before Julia sees it. Maybe I can shove it up my sleeve. Or maybe I'll just grab my bag and make a run for it, never to be seen again . . . and never to be employed as a hotel cleaner again. I could try a sob story about how I was beaten as a child and sometimes take things without thinking, swearing blind to having no memory of picking up the brush. But none of these options are going to work and I know it.

The staff room is now empty.

"Let's start with your jacket, shall we?" says Julia in a kind voice.

I swallow, desperate to stop my hands from shaking. I take my puffer jacket off the coat hook and give it to her. She runs her hands over it, squeezing the material and checking the pockets, inside and out. She would have made a good customs official. There has to be a way out of this, but all I can do is look on, helpless. She turns to my locker and nods at it. I open it for her. This is it.

"If you could take everything out for me," she says.

Go with plan B, memory blackouts. She might believe me when she sees how manky the hairbrush is.

I lift my backpack out and Julia takes it. I'm about to say, *I can explain*, when she quickly unzips the backpack, takes out my apron and shakes it. Nothing falls out. I freeze on the spot.

She passes me the apron to hold and sticks her hand into my backpack and sweeps it around inside. Nothing. She checks the outside pockets, running her hands slowly over the entire surface, squeezing here and there, in case I slipped it into the lining. Lastly she glances inside the locker. Empty. She turns to look at me and nods at my skirt.

"Do you mind?" she asks, sheepish. I pull out the empty pockets of my skirt so they protrude like ears, reminding me of Alison Rogers. Julia gives a sigh of relief and passes me my jacket.

"I'm really sorry I had to do that, Noelle."

"No, please, you had to," I say, sitting on the bench, slumped, exhausted as the adrenaline slowly leaves my body.

"I'll tell Mr. Redmond I searched you and your things and that you were 100 percent cooperative, and I will let him know how upset and shocked you are."

"Thanks, Julia," I say, heartfelt, so she knows I believe we were in this together. Julia goes to leave.

"Julia?" I croak, ready to play my last card. "I would never do that, you know? Steal."

"I know," she says. "Some guests are just crazy." She walks away.

I lean the back of my head against the locker door. The coolness of the metal brings me back to my senses. I pick up my backpack and look inside. Did Julia miss it? But the hairbrush isn't there.

My legs feel heavy and tired as I take the stairs to my flat, not caring if I ever arrive at my front door or not. Maybe this is what hell is like, an endless staircase you climb forever, getting nowhere.

I reach the second floor and step back, nearly falling down the stairs I've just painfully climbed.

Phil is sitting on the floor outside my front door. In one hand she holds a half-full bottle of beer. In the other, between her finger and thumb, she dangles the hairbrush.

Chapter 21

I stare at her, my mind racing, unable to find my voice. Even if I could speak, I'm not sure what I'd say. She gets to her feet, blocking the door. She swigs her beer and offers me the hairbrush, handle first like it's a dangerous weapon. I take it. Whatever it is about being found out by Phil, I still want it. It's still mine.

I scramble in my bag for my key and go to open the door. Phil doesn't move, standing in my way.

"Excuse me," I say.

"Why, what have you done?" she says, peering at me. A flutter in my stomach takes me by surprise. I like that she's interested in me again but I shake the thought from my head. Phil is not to be trusted. Phil causes me pain.

"I checked with Michelle at the front desk on my way out," she continues. "She said 726 accused the cleaner of robbing her hairbrush."

I ignore her and try to access my front door again. This time Phil steps aside. I put the key in the lock and go to turn it, but it doesn't move. I grit my teeth. Of all the times I need my door to open, it's now. I hear Phil guzzle more of her beer. I daren't turn around. Instead, I reinsert the key in the lock but again it doesn't move.

"Fuck," I yell out. Phil gently pulls the key from my hand and nudges me out of the way. She reinserts the key herself.

"You have to pull and wiggle at the same time," I mumble. She yanks the door toward her and wiggles the key.

"Like this?" she says, wiggling her hips too. She's trying to get me to lighten up but that's not going to happen.

She tries to unlock the door but the key won't move for her either. I look at her and shrug. See? You don't have the magic touch. Phil takes the key out and kicks the door hard with her booted right foot.

"Oh, yeah, because that's going to work," I say. Phil puts the key in the lock and click—the door opens.

"A bit of force every now and then works wonders," she says. I'm impressed but determined not to show it.

"Thanks," I say, taking the key from the lock. "And bye."

I enter my flat and go to close the door, but Phil wedges her foot in the gap. I feel a tightness in my chest. I want her to leave. I don't care what she thinks of me. I don't need her or any of the girls on my side anymore. My name has already been cleared. I open the door and stare at her.

"I said thank you. What more do you want?"

"A drink, maybe?" she says, waltzing past me into the flat. I stay standing by the open door, a protest to her being in my flat without my permission.

"I didn't say you could come in." I make no attempt to keep the annoyance out of my voice. She flops down in one of my disgusting armchairs and grins at me. Behind her is my trunk, fully exposed without the wipeable tablecloth covering it, rumbling with my secrets. I need to get her out of here.

"I'll talk to you, okay, but not here. There's a pub at the end of the road."

"You'd rather discuss 'the hairbrush' in a public place?"

I drop my head, squeezing my eyes together.

"How about I ask the questions and you answer?" she says.

The tightness in my chest is getting worse.

"I'm not leaving until you explain," she says.

"It was an accident," I say, not caring if she believes me or not.

"So it just fell into the front pocket of your apron?"

"It was on the floor, I picked it up, my hands were full and then it ended up in my pocket. I forgot about it, that's all."

"You forgot about it. Even when you were folding up your apron and putting it in your bag?"

"It was too late by then," I say, deadpan. "If I'd tried to explain to Julia I'd have been fired."

"And it's thanks to me you weren't."

"Yes, thanks to you," I admit, suddenly genuinely grateful. "How did you know?"

"You were acting funny all day and then rolling up your apron a little too carefully." I'm impressed by Phil's observational skills but disappointed in my sloppy performance. Phil gets up off the chair, comes over to me and shoves the door shut. I immediately feel trapped by her presence.

"Just tell me the truth. I told you about my counseling," she says.

Phil's face is close to mine now. I want to kiss her but instead I duck away and walk into the living area.

"So what if I'm lying?" I say. "It doesn't affect you, does it? I mean, thanks for rescuing the hairbrush but I never asked you to do that. I would have handled it myself."

"You did steal it, then?" she says.

I close my eyes feeling the tension move up from my chest to my head. What's the point in trying to explain what I do and why? No one would ever understand. But what if Phil did? What if Phil is the one person I can talk to? I cover my face with my hands, like I used to do as a child when my mother was in one of her rages. If she couldn't break me, Phil certainly won't.

"Take your hands away from your face. You're not six."

"Go away," I mumble. Phil grabs my hands and pulls them down. I have no choice but to look at her.

"Tell me," she says gently. "Why did you take it?" I bustle past her into the kitchen but quickly come out again, not wanting to get cornered in the small space. I edge toward the front door. Running might be my only option here.

"It's no big deal. You stole a hairbrush, so what? Every cleaner sees things they'd like to have, all that luxury thrust in front of us every day, but we don't act on it. You did, that's all."

I sigh. Phil thinks I'm a regular cleaner who had a moment of weakness.

"What I want to know is why you took a hairbrush. It's not worth anything and the woman could have nits. You'd have to dis-infect it before using it." My body is heavy and tired now. Exhaus-tion seeps into my bones.

"It's not about the hairbrush."

"What do you mean?" she says.

"It wasn't a moment of weakness." I look her right in the eye. "It's not the first time I've done this."

"What? You have a hairbrush fetish? My cousin in America collects rubber ducks, you know, the ones you put in the bath. She's got like two thousand of them."

"It's not a fetish. I don't get off on hairbrushes."

"You didn't get off at all until you met me."

There's no malice in Phil's words, only the truth and I agree. I collapse into an armchair, too weak to make a run for it now. And anyway, I've said too much. Phil kneels in front of me, hands on my thighs.

"So, you've taken a few hairbrushes, for whatever weird reason. Just don't do it again. I might not be there to save your arse next time." She leans forward, puts her arms around me and squeezes me tight. I hug her back, feeling the warmth of her body, and I want to stay there forever.

I have a choice now. Let her think I took a few hairbrushes in my eight-year career or tell her the truth. She pulls back and gives me a warm look. I decide she doesn't need to know the truth. She seems happy with her own version of events. All I have to do is go along with it.

"You're one of the team now. Me, Rose, Mali and Gaby. We take care of each other."

I nod, as though I appreciate it—I want to appreciate it, I really do—but I'm not part of their team and there's no way I can stay at the Magnolia now.

"Got any beers?" she says, putting her empty bottle on the table.

"There's some wine left over."

She goes to the kitchen. It strikes me, sitting there in my hideous armchair, that not one person in the whole world knows me properly, not even my own mother.

I look at the hairbrush in my hand, turning it over. Phil comes back and passes me the brown and white spotted mug half full of warm white wine. I guzzle it down. She drinks the rest from the bottle and wanders around the living room.

"We have to get you out of this shithole," she says.

I drain my mug and let the wine dull my senses. Then she turns to me, casual.

"What's in the trunk?"

Chapter 22

"What's in the trunk?" asks Phil again. The fact I'm not answering makes her uneasy yet curious. She runs her hands over the rich wooden domed lid.

"Expensive piece of kit," she says.

"It was here when I moved in," I say.

"Yeah, right," she says.

What the hell? I think.

"Four hundred pounds on eBay," I blurt out. Her eyes widen and she drains the last of the wine in the bottle.

"There's nothing in it," I add quickly. She puts down the wine bottle and tries to lift it. It's funny watching Phil, legs wide, bent at the knees trying to bench my trunk. She can't lift it, of course. You need at least two fairly strong people to do that. Sometimes I take items out, wrap them and put them in my suitcase so the trunk's not too heavy for the delivery guys when I move. She wipes her brow and turns to me.

"Doesn't feel very empty to me. Is it full of hairbrushes?"

I give her a blank look. She swallows. I see her thought process unraveling. She was joking about it being full of hairbrushes but now she has to face the fact that it might be true and she's not sure anymore if she wants to know the truth.

Does she want to discover who the real Noelle is? Opening this trunk will tell her everything she needs to know. If I were her, I'd walk out the door right now and never come back.

"Forget about the trunk. Let's go and get a drink," I say. I get up from the armchair and head for the door. I'm offering her an out, but will she take it?

Phil looks from the trunk to me waiting at the door for her to follow. She has a decision to make: keep pushing until I cave, which I may or may not do, or leave it and me alone and accept that this has nothing to do with her. She puts her hands on her hips, still in decision mode. I stand in the doorway ready to leave.

"First round's on me," I say, mustering a smile.

"Open it," she says. "I want to see."

Phil and I kneel in front of my open trunk, brimming with all my trinkets. She has said nothing for five minutes apart from shit, fuck and Jesus. She slips the little black book from the side pocket and eyes it.

"It's a list of all the colleagues I've killed who found out about my secret," I say.

Phil gives a nervous laugh.

"And you thought I was easy to wind up?" I say. I open the book for her. "It's all the hotels I've worked in and for how long and the items I took. The Magnolia is my twenty-first hotel. I really wanted to break my five-star record and last more than a month, but you ruined that for me."

She runs her fingers down and over the pages, absorbing the details.

"So you just up and leave and start again, over and over?"

"Yep," I say, proud of how strong I sound.

"Are you going to leave the Magnolia now?"

I nod. She gives me a sad look.

"And you've never been caught?" she asks, wistfully.

"Nope. You're the first person to catch me. And before you say it, yes, you're the first person to do a lot of things to me."

"And it really gives you that much of a buzz?"

"Not so much since I met you. You distracted me."

"Glad to hear it," she says. "Right, you have to stop doing this now, today. It's too risky and you will get caught eventually."

I take the book from her and return it to its pouch. She looks on, uneasy, as I close the lid, slide the lock through the loop and click it shut. She jumps up, running her hands through her hair, which I love to watch her do. Her hair always falling perfectly back into place.

"You have to break your pattern. Like Mali needs to learn to let people touch her trolley, you need to stop taking things."

"I don't want to stop taking things," I say. I'm surprised she even thinks that's an option.

"I know someone you could talk to. A professional."

"I don't need to talk to anyone."

"Noelle, this isn't normal behavior."

"So? Who's normal? Mali's got OCD. Gaby hates her life so much she'd rather her son was brain damaged so she can be a brave warrior mum. And as for you." She raises her eyebrows. "Well, you don't know what or who you want."

"Lots of people are like that," she says, matter of fact.

"Then you should come with a badge or something with a warning on it," I blurt out. Phil sighs.

"Okay, so most of us aren't normal and thank fuck for that. But this," she says, pointing at my trunk, "is way out there freaky."

"I don't mind being freaky."

Phil puts her fingers to her temples. "If you're not ready to talk to someone, will you at least stay and try to stop taking things? I'll be your sponsor. If you feel like you're having a bad day, you can talk to me and I'll keep you on the straight and narrow." I'm touched she wants to do this for me. "It's time to stop, Noelle. You can't go on like this for the rest of your life."

My stomach sinks as the weariness from hotel 20 returns.

"This is your chance to break the cycle and stay at the Magnolia." She paces now as she works out a new reality for me. "Will you try it for me? I'll help you." She leans over and kisses me softly. Her soft lips melt my defenses away.

"I'll try," I say, and I'm surprised I actually mean it.

Chapter 23

I push my trolley along to room 709. My hair is tied back and I've added a dusting of blush to my apples. Mali noticed my slightly brighter appearance this morning when I arrived at work. She said it suited me and that I looked alive instead of like a corpse. I took it as a compliment.

It's been three days and Phil's very pleased with my progress so far. She's feeling good about helping me and even mentioned going back to college herself to study psychology. She wants to be a savior, which surprises me, but I don't mind as long as she's my savior.

I promised her I'll do my best not to take anything and that I'll tell her immediately if I have the urge. But with Phil's full attention on me again, I have no need to take things at the moment.

"Still coming tonight?" she calls out to me across the corridor as I exit the room to get my mop and bucket. She's talking about the work night out.

"I'll be there," I say. She smiles at me and goes back into room 712. I'm really connected to Phil now, and to Mali, Rose and Gaby. I even feel connected to the Magnolia and it makes my chest swell with a warm feeling. I wonder if my life could be different. Could I settle in one place? With Phil and the girls on my side, I feel like anything is possible.

Nothing sexual has happened between me and Phil since the morning after the disastrous dinner party, so I'm hoping we'll reignite things tonight. I've already been shopping for a new outfit—a coffee-colored minidress with a plunging neckline. I also bought a pair of tight jeans, that I tried on first, and a black eyeliner pencil. According to my online teenage makeup guru, a black line applied to your inner lower lid makes you look irresistible.

My sole intention tonight is to take Phil's breath away when she sees me. My secret has given us a special bond that will never be broken. We are soulmates too now, so Freddy better watch out.

I've never been to a bowling alley before and I'm struck by how noisy it is. Every lane is occupied with groups of people screeching and laughing. The thundering noise of rolling balls and smashing bowling pins echo and bounce around the huge space.

I know I have to get bowling shoes, so I wander up to the reception desk and give them my shoe size. In two seconds, the shoes appear on the counter as if by magic. I swap them for mine and spot Rose in the distance dressed in pink silky flares, twirling around doing a celebration dance. Her glossy silver hair hangs loose around her shoulders. I head over. As I get closer, I see Mali, Gaby and Phil sitting in a bay, cheering Rose on. Rose does an elegant sweep of the ball and knocks down all the pins except two.

"Beginner's luck," yells Mali.

"I ain't no beginner, baby," says Rose, doing another twirl.

Mali gets up, grabs a bowling ball in her right hand and runs at the lane, lobbing the ball onto the runway with great effort. The ball bounces and then rolls into the outside track.

"Aaaaah, look what happened to my ball?" she wails.

"You can't just chuck it at the runway," says Rose. "You need to listen to what I told you."

"I don't need to listen to anybody," shouts Mali.

"No need to raise your voice," says Rose, smiling.

"Take the shot again, Mali. We don't mind," says Gaby kindly.

"Hey? I'm not a charity case," yells Mali. Gaby shakes her head. She tried to help.

I glance at Phil, doubled over, tears in her eyes from laughing. I love seeing her happy. I wander up, my jacket over my arm, hair sleek and falling around my face, wearing smudged eyeliner to give a smoky effect. I say hi to everyone and they all turn to look at me. Mali does a dramatic dropping of her lower jaw.

"Excuse me. Has anyone seen Noelle?" she says. I shoot her a sarcastic look and quickly sit next to Phil. Phil's eyes travel over me, impressed. She's wearing skintight jeans and a fitted black shirt with big cuffs. Gaby touches my dress and tells me it's beautiful.

Gaby wears a long floral skirt and a blouse with a jacket over the top. I'm sad to see she's tired around the eyes again. When we've asked how her son's doing since he got out of the hospital, she simply says he's recovering, which just means he's at home all day, and that she's finding it hard. Tonight though, she's beaming, her cheeks flushed, delighted to be out. Rose tells me it's my turn to bowl.

"I've never done it before," I admit.

"I'll help you," says Phil. I shrug, acting like I'm not bothered but I'm secretly thrilled.

Phil shows me how to hold the ball, inserting her fingers into the holes. I carry the ball to the front of the bowling lane and Phil stands behind me, demonstrating how to swing the ball low toward the ground and then let it go on the upswing, propelling it forward.

I'm not really concentrating on her instructions. I'm too distracted by the closeness of her body to mine. She stands back and indicates I try it on my own. I swing the ball back and forth and then release it onto the runway with a loud thud. It immediately veers off and plummets into the outside track.

"That was useless, wasn't it?" I say.

"Good first try," she says.

Rose comes back from the bar with beers and shots for everyone. I don't question the alcohol this time and down my tequila like a pro. Rose wants to have one more game and then move on to the pub. I'm up for that.

It's Phil's turn to bowl. She swings the ball effortlessly, releasing at just the right moment, sending it straight down the middle of the lane for an almost total strike. She's disappointed two pins are left standing.

She sits down beside me, grabbing her beer, then nudges me as Mali goes up to bowl again.

Mali swings the ball back and forth, back and forth, really concentrating and then drops it onto the runway, where it just sits, not moving. Rose and Gaby burst into peels of laughter. I'm giggling too. Mali marches onto the runway and tries to push the ball with her foot. A security guy rushes over and orders her off the lane. Mali argues with him, her arms flailing, pointing at the ball, like it's the ball's fault.

The security guy picks the ball up and gives it to her and Mali marches back to us.

"This ball is a dud. It doesn't roll properly," she says. But Gaby and Rose can't speak for laughing. I turn to Phil, wanting to share this funny moment with her but she's not there. I look around but don't see her anywhere.

I enter the ladies' room to find a short queue for the stalls. Women stand at the sinks, washing their hands and touching up their faces and hair. Phil's not standing there. I go to one of the sinks and fiddle with my hair, watching as women come out of the stalls, but Phil isn't one of them.

I leave the bathroom and scan the area. To the right is a burger restaurant, half full of people. I run my eyes over all the tables, but she's not there. To the left is the big reception desk, with all the bowling shoes stacked up behind it.

Then I see her, but only because I see him first.

Freddy. He's holding Phil's hand and they're heading toward me. I'm immediately hot in the face and my mouth is dry as sandpaper. I drop my head and attempt to scurry back to Mali, Gaby and Rose, but Phil calls out to me.

I have no choice but to turn, as they walk over to me. Freddy scoops me up in his arms and hugs me.

"Hello, lovely girl," he says. I pull away from him, forcing a smile and manage to say hi. He drapes his arm around my shoulders and gives me a squeeze. "You look stunning," he says, crinkling his eyes at me. He means it, but while I appreciate the effort to be nice, I don't really care what he thinks. It's Phil I care about.

"Thanks," I mumble.

"I asked Freddy to come in and say hello before we head off," says Phil, like this is totally acceptable.

"What about the pub?" I blurt out.

"Me and Freddy are going for dinner, but the rest of the girls are up for it."

The hollow echoes of the bowling alley slip into the distance as the sound of my breathing fills my head, like I'm underwater and running out of oxygen. I try to swallow but there's a lump in my throat.

Phil asks us what we want to drink. Freddy says a G&T. I manage to say I'm fine. Phil saunters off to the bar. I swing my head to the right to the exit doors. I swing my head back the other way and look over at the girls engrossed in their game.

"It's good to see you," Freddy says. "I was saying to Phil the three of us should go out together. I owe you a dinner anyway."

I stare at him, not really hearing what he's saying. All I can think is, how could I get it so wrong? Phil's not interested in me the way I am in her. All she cares about is being a savior so she can feel good about herself. She'll never belong to me and I'll never belong to her. I don't belong to the team and the girls either, or the Magnolia.

"Hey, are you alright? You look peaky," Freddy says, concerned.

"I have to go. I don't feel well," I say and, without looking back, I run for the door, passing Phil on her way back from the bar two G&Ts in hand. I plow on past her, head down.

"Noelle? Noelle?" she calls after me.

I run onto the road, throwing my hand out at every passing taxi, but none of them are free.

"How are you going to pay for a taxi without your bag?" I turn to see Phil holding my jacket and bag and my cream trainers. "The guy behind the desk said if you don't return the bowling shoes, he'll call the police."

I look down at my bowling shoes, feeling even more foolish. She hands me my stuff and I quickly change into my trainers and give her the bowling shoes mumbling my thanks.

"It's not me and Freddy, is it?" she says.

"What? No, of course not. It's nice to see him," I lie, but I'm in "tell them what they want to hear" mode. She lets out a sigh, relieved.

"So you're really okay with us just being friends?" she asks. She's trying to be kind, but it just sounds patronizing.

"Totally. Friends," I say.

"Good, because you're doing really well and I want you to stay at the Magnolia, okay?"

I look at her, reading her. She means what she says, but there's an ulterior motive here. She wants to fix me. I'm her fucking project. I bet she lies in bed with Freddy discussing how to make me all better.

"Today at work was a bit of a struggle," I lie.

"Why didn't you tell me? That's the deal," she says, full of concern.

"I need to start coping on my own. I can't be relying on you all the time."

"I'll come home with you," she says.

"What about Freddy?"

"He'll be fine. I'll tell him you need me."

"I'm not ruining your night," I say, sounding very mature and friends-like, but the thought of having Phil at my side as a "concerned friend" fills me with a sickening dread. "I'll see you tomorrow at work," I say, waving at another taxi, which pulls over. I clamber into the back seat and shut the door.

"I'll pick you up in the morning," she shouts at me through the window. "We'll get coffee before work."

I give her a thumbs-up as the taxi pulls away. I keep my smile going until she's out of sight.

The taxi plows on ahead through a green light. It's the green light I need too. It's time for me to leave the Magnolia and Phil and the girls behind.

Chapter 24

I lie on my mattress, staring at the ceiling. It's the last time I'll ever have to look at those damp stains, although I've come to respect their persistence and permanence.

My phone beeps with a text. It's Phil, telling me she'll be here in thirty minutes to grab coffee before work. I text back that I'm not well, a stomach bug. I need today to organize my trunk and my general getaway without Phil or anyone else at the Magnolia knowing about it. I have my excuse for Julia all ready: my father has died suddenly and there's no one to mind my sick mother. I'll call her when I'm on the train and on my way.

I've already researched hotel cleaning jobs online and there's a new hotel, just opened in Scotland, that is looking for cleaning staff. I've even bought my train ticket, as I like to be prepared. It's an open ticket, so I can use it whenever I like. The idea of Scotland appeals to me. It's a new country and a new Noelle, with all my secrets safe and nobody trying to be my "friend." It's also a very long way from here.

A banging and knocking comes from my front door. I blink for a moment. Whoever it is must be at the wrong flat. They'll realize in a minute and move upstairs. But the knocking comes again. I never have visitors, apart from Phil over the last few days. But it can't be her, she only just texted me and I told her not to come.

I stay lying in bed. Whoever is outside will go away in a minute. But they knock again and this time a voice calls through the door.

"Noelle Moore? We're looking for Noelle Moore?" I turn over in my bed, eyes wide. They're using my full name. Not even Phil knows that. I climb quietly down the ladder to avoid it creaking and creep over to the front door. I'm curious about who they are but I have no intention of opening it. They knock again. "Noelle? It's about your mother."

What does that mean? What could they possibly know about her? And I'm not interested whatever it is. They knock again. They're certainly persistent, like the damp stains on my ceiling.

I unlock the door and pull it open just enough to poke my head around it. Two female uniformed police officers stand outside.

"Noelle Moore?"

"Yes," I say.

"Is it okay if we come in?"

"Look, I don't see my mother, okay? If she's in trouble it's nothing to do with me."

One of the officers, sporting tight, short hair and blue eye shadow, pulls a concerned face.

"I'm afraid your mother passed away two days ago. You're down as her next of kin. It's taken us a while to find you."

I squint at them for a moment.

"My mother's dead?" I say, still not sure that's what they're saying.

"We believe she suffered a cardiac arrest."

"Oh, well, okay, thanks for letting me know." I go to shut the door on them.

"As her next of kin, you need to go to the hospital and take care of things, like the funeral arrangements," says the officer with blue eye shadow.

I open the door a little wider and gawk at them. And then it dawns on me. I was all my mother had in the world.

At the hospital, I'm ushered into a small, stuffy room by a young woman in a suit with a well-meaning smile.

"I'm sure this is a terrible shock."

I nod my head. It's far more of an inconvenience, but I don't say that.

"Would you like to see your mother?" she asks in a soft voice. It occurs to me that she's probably been trained to speak that way. I tell her no. I wonder what my mother looks like dead. Maybe she looks better than she did when she was alive. I doubt it though. An image of her gray, slimy corpse lying on a cold slab swims before my eyes. The thin skin on her eyelids stretched over her bulging sockets about to split open at any moment. Her downturned, twisted mouth and her lips the same pasty color as her distorted face. But it sounds like she had an easy death, completely unaware she'd finally met her end. It's unfair when you think about it. But I don't wish pain on anyone, not even my monster of a dead mother.

"Here are some numbers of funeral directors in the area," she says, passing me a piece of paper with names and numbers printed on it. "They'll take care of everything for you. I believe the one at the bottom of the list is the most reasonable."

"Reasonable?" I ask, wondering what on earth she means.

"Least expensive," she says to clarify.

"I have to pay for the funeral?" I ask, aghast.

"There are all kinds of options," she assures me, making her voice even softer in case I might lose it.

"What if I don't have any money?" I say.

"Then the local authority will take care of it for you. But there's no service or anything like that." I feel dizzy and clammy. She jumps to my side and helps me take a seat. "There are grief counselling services and they're free." She gives me a leaflet with *Have you been recently bereaved?* printed on the front. I stare at the leaflet, not sure what to think.

How am I supposed to feel about my mother being dead? I'm not happy or sad. I search my body for some emotion, anger, relief, something. But I feel nothing.

The woman puts a hand on my shoulder and says she'll get me a cup of tea and leaves the room.

My phone beeps with a text. It's Phil again. *I'm here. Where are you?* She must be at my flat. I text back: *My mum is dead and I have to sort it out. Can you tell Julia for me? Thanks.*

I'm relieved I don't have to tell Julia myself. In fact, this is all working out rather well. I have the best excuse not to be at work and then I can just tell Julia I had to go back to Devon or wherever to support my family. It's perfect really and I never have to see Phil or the other girls again.

But the thought of not seeing them again sends a sharp pang to my heart. Am I sad about that? At least it's an emotion. But I need to ignore these feelings. I work in a hotel for as long as I can and then I move on. This is my life, no matter how weary or emotional I might feel. Nothing will ever change that. Maybe the shock of my mum dying is causing me to have strange thoughts. As much as I don't care that she's dead, it did come out of the blue.

I gaze into space, aware of the soft cushioned chair holding me up. I do have some money saved—about seven thousand pounds the last time I checked my account. That's the result of working for eight years and not spending money on anything but cheap rent and beans on toast. I could pay for a funeral, if it's not too expensive. My cheeks suddenly get hot. I'm annoyed now.

She's dead and now *I* have to deal with it? I have to organize and pay for a funeral? I decide quickly that I'm not going to do that. Let the authorities take care of my mother's carcass. I don't care what happens to her remains. I know she wouldn't have cared what happened to mine, had it ever come to that.

My phone rings. It's Phil. I bounce the call and switch my phone off. I don't have time for work issues and anyway I'll be gone soon. My plan to leave for Scotland is still in play. This was a little hiccup in my day, that's all. I can still make my train.

I drag myself up the stairs to my flat. I was exhausted before the police came knocking at my door, now I'm wondering if I can even make it up the last flight.

"Jeeeeesus! What the fuck?" a voice yells. I look up to see Mali leaning over the banister, dressed in her work uniform. She runs down to meet me on the stairs. "We came as soon as we heard about your mumma."

"We?" I say, confused to see her here. Then Gaby, Rose and Phil appear across the top of the stairs. Gaby's eyes are moist. Rose has a kind look on her face. Phil, on the other hand, is frowning—maybe she's annoyed by the inconvenience too. They are all dressed in their Magnolia uniforms. Mali puts her arm around my waist, her head coming up to my shoulder, and helps me up the stairs. Her strength is impressive. I'm sure she could have carried me over her shoulder if she'd had to.

"Shouldn't you be in work?" I say.

"Your mum died," says Rose, like that answers all questions.

"You should have called us," says Phil.

"We would have come to the hospital with you," says Gaby. "Was it horrible?"

"No, it was fine," I say, still a bit confused as to why they are all here. I glance at Phil.

"You look like shit," she says.

"You should see my mother," I say. They all look at me, surprised. I realize it's probably not the most appropriate joke. "Sorry, it's been a long morning," I say, a little feeble. "And I didn't see the body."

"What? You didn't say goodbye?" says Mali, shocked to her core.

"Not everybody wants to see a corpse, Mali," says Phil. "All it does is confirm that the person is definitely dead, just in case you were kidding yourself they weren't."

"You're not doing that, are you?" asks Rose me, eyes wide. I assure her I'm not. We're all silent for a minute. I'm wondering what I'm supposed to do or say next.

"Don't you have to be at work?" I say, awkward.

"Julia said as long as we're back this afternoon and finish all the rooms, we could come and see you," explains Gaby. "Julia sends her best wishes by the way."

"I'm fine, so no need to mess up your day," I say, wondering why on earth they're making such a fuss. I want them all to go, but they're not making any signs of leaving.

"For God's sake, Noelle, open the bloody door," says Phil. I scramble for my key in my backpack. Thankfully the door opens on the first attempt; Phil's big boot kick before must have sorted it out.

They all wander in. Mali says she'll put the kettle on. Except I don't have a kettle. I'll leave it to her to work out the saucepan alternative. I watch as Mali flicks her head around taking in my pathetic flat.

"Whatever you're paying for this place is too much," says Mali, heading into my cupboard-sized kitchen. Rose and Gaby pause in the living area, looking around.

"It's okay, I know it's a dump. It's all I could find when I got to London."

"I've seen worse," says Rose. Phil comes up beside me, puts her arm around my shoulders and pulls me into her. She says she's sorry about my mum. Rose says they all are, and Gaby, who is dabbing her eyes, says it's very sad. I'm about to tell them that it isn't really that sad when Mali sticks her head out of the kitchen.

"You've got curry powder and stock cubes but no kettle and only two cups?"

I raise my eyebrows at Phil, Gaby and Rose, a sheepish look. Then all at once we burst out laughing. Mali waves a hand at us, like we're useless, and tells us we'll have to share mugs. Rose teases her again about catching her OCD germs and gradually the tension begins to seep out of me. Phil, Gaby, Mali and Rose have waltzed into my flat and somehow made it their own and I like that.

Rose and Mali sit on my trunk, oblivious to the hoards of secrets beneath the hard wooden lid. Phil slumps in one of my armchairs, Gaby in the other. I am perched on the armrest of Gaby's chair. We are rotating my two mugs filled with black coffee, taking a sip from one and passing it on. Phil watches me, analyzing me, at least it feels like that.

"When's the funeral?" says Rose.

"I don't know," I say, dismissive.

"We'll need to get time off work for that too," says Gaby.

Why do they need time off for that? I won't be here myself, not that there'll even be a proper funeral.

"What do you mean, you don't know? What did the funeral director say?" says Mali.

"I haven't spoken to them yet," I say. And I'm not planning to either.

"You haven't spoken to them yet?" Mali peers at me, like there's something wrong with me. "You need to know when it is and where it is so you can tell people."

"And I'll do that, but you don't need time off to help me."

"But we'll be coming to the funeral," says Gaby. They all exchange a worried look, like I'm not making sense. Just tell them, I say to myself. Tell them your mother was the most hideous human being who ever lived and you're leaving her remains for the local authority to dump in a hole. But I stall. I can't get the words out so continue to lie.

"Don't be silly," I say, "you don't have to come. It's not like you knew her."

"Of course we're coming. We're your friends," shouts Mali.

"Do you want us to call the funeral director for you?" says Phil.

This is not going to be as easy as I thought. They expect me to have a funeral for my mother, so I suppose I'm going to have to look like I'm at least making the effort.

"I'll call them now," I say, grabbing my phone and the list of names and numbers the woman gave me in the hospital. I step outside the flat onto the landing.

Leaning on the banister my head throbs with the pressure, as I go over my options. I could go back into the flat, pretend I've spoken to the funeral director and say the funeral is next week, date to be confirmed, then leave for Scotland, no explanation, never look back, who cares what they think. Or I could call a funeral director and arrange my mother's stupid funeral.

I try to conjure up images of my mother while she was alive, drunk, violent, vile. But I can't. The only image that springs to mind is of Tesco Erica, drying my hair with a tea towel and handing me a Mars bar from the vending machine.

But that wasn't my real mother. That was a fake person. She was empty inside, so scorched with evil that she didn't even know how to appear human unless she was pretending to be someone else. And now she's gone, forever. Why aren't I happy about it? Surely this is a reason to celebrate. But it's not. It was a meaningless life that caused so much pain and misery that to say it's over, well, is simply a relief.

Fuck, I mutter to myself, kicking one of the spindles in the banister, which splits and splinters. Fuck, I say again and try to put the spindle back the way it was. Looks like my mother's getting a funeral after all.

Chapter 25

The modern chapel is chilly and smells of newly varnished timber. The minister, a jolly-looking woman dressed in a suit and tie, steps down from the podium. She managed to say nice things about my mother based on the few bare facts I gave her, so she did well, falling back on clichés about the privilege of motherhood and a life of hard work and friendship. It mostly made me feel nauseous but I comfort myself that if there is an afterlife and my mother's looking down from wherever she is, she will know it's bullshit too.

Organ music blasts from the speakers, as the basket-woven coffin—the greener and cheaper option—starts to shudder and move along the conveyor belt. A single lily tied with a pink ribbon, lying on top of the coffin, nearly slips off as it shunts through the open curtains and stops. A wooden door drops down to signify the end of the coffin's journey and the velvet curtains slide shut.

I let out a long sigh of relief, pleased that's over. And they really need to do something about the woeful organ music. They did ask me if I would like to choose a song to play out at the end, but I couldn't think of anything. My mother never listened to music. We didn't even own a radio. I stare at the closed curtains. Goodbye and good riddance.

But something is gnawing and nagging away inside me. I want to be angrier—I feel like I owe it to myself—but I just can't muster it.

There are about twenty people at the service most of whom I don't know or recognize. I'm surprised at how many showed up. I had an excuse prepared to explain why there might not have been anyone here, a story about emailing the wrong date and time to people, but they must have found out about her death some other way. A group of five women sit together, drying their eyes and comforting one another. One of the women waves over to me. I turn away. I don't have a clue who she is.

The smart black jacket I'm wearing belongs to Rose and Mali has booked a corner in the local pub for us to go to after the funeral. Phil helped me pick the flower to go on top of the coffin and Gaby arranged for a charity collection at the door to the chapel. I was worried the bucket would be empty because no one would come so I'm even more relieved there's an okay-sized congregation. At least I think it's an okay size. I've never been to a funeral before, so I have nothing to compare it to. The truth is, I could never have organized this without the girls' help. In fact, I wouldn't have done it at all if they hadn't pushed me, not that I'm resentful.

Somewhere, deep down, alongside the troubling gnawing in my gut, I'm pleased I've given my mother a decent send-off. It was my one last act of defiance. At least I'm not like her.

I become aware of hands on my shoulders and arms. I'm not sure how long they've been there, but they feel warm. They belong to Mali and Phil sitting either side of me. Rose and Gaby are seated behind me. Even Julia is here a few rows back. She gives me a strong smile, like I can get through this. Good old Julia, always the mentor.

Mali releases her arm from my shoulder to get a fresh tissue from her bag and blows her nose. She was crying a lot through the service.

"Funerals rip my heart out," she says. I put my hand on her arm and squeeze.

"You are being so strong," she says to me. "But it's not good. You need to cry, okay?" I give her a sad look, or at least my best attempt at one. I never cry for real. I trained myself long ago never to give in to it and now, all these years later, I barely remember what it feels like to even want to cry. But I'm not going to tell Mali that. Today is no time for honesty. I've been baring my soul way too much lately and all it's done is got me into trouble.

Mali throws her arms around me and hugs me tight. I glance at Phil. Phil shrugs—that's Mali. I twist around to look at Rose and Gaby and give them a sad look. I hope my sad expression is hitting the mark and I don't just look like I have a headache. Gaby blows her nose rather noisily. Rose smiles at me, strong and dignified.

"Excuse me?" We look up to see the five women who were sitting together. Their faces are puffy from crying and a couple of them have mascara smudged under their eyes. They clearly had a bawling fest.

The woman who said excuse me holds a Tesco carrier bag. She's rather bronze-looking due to over-applied fake tan and her bleached blonde hair is piled up in a bun. She wears a fitted black minidress with a shawl across her shoulders and very high-heeled shoes.

"You're Noelle, aren't you?"

"Yes," I say, shifting a little, uncomfortable. Nobody said I'd have to talk to strangers.

"I'm Liv. I met you once, years ago, at the Tesco in Bromley. You got locked out of your flat?" And suddenly I do remember her. I'm surprised she remembers me though.

"Oh, yes," I say. "Thanks for coming."

"We all worked with Erica, although I hadn't seen her for a while, after she was sick and everything. Then she took a job in a different store. I just can't believe she's gone." She starts to cry again. I feel awkward, unsure what to do. Mali leaps up from her seat and puts her arm around Liv's waist.

"Death is tragic, and it happens to all of us eventually," she says to Liv in a soothing voice but quickly starts to blub again herself, which proves too much for Liv who manages to dry her eyes and focus on me again. Rose and Gaby shoot out of their seats and gently escort Mali out of the chapel. I sense Phil beside me, closer now, supporting me. I'm grateful she's there.

"We wanted to give you this," says Liv, referring to the Tesco bag she's holding. One of the other women pipes up about how it's the contents from Erica's locker from the last store she worked in and how the manager let them take it to give to me.

Liv reaches into the bag and takes out a folded Tesco pinafore with my mother's name badge clipped to it, glinting in the yellow overhead lights. The pinafore is pressed and clean and the badge is shiny and polished. I am totally lost for words. This is absolutely the last thing I want. Phil comes to my rescue this time.

"That's really nice of you, thank you. Isn't that lovely, Noelle?"

"Yes, thank you," I manage to say. The women smile, pleased to have brought me some comfort. Liv reaches into the bag again and this time takes out a dark brown, fake leather handbag with a large gold circular fastener.

"This is Erica's handbag. We felt you should have it."

"Her handbag?" I say, trying not to sound amused by how ridiculous this presentation ceremony is becoming.

"That's great," says Phil, stepping in again. "Thank you. Isn't that so nice, Noelle?" I plaster on my sad smile and nod.

"We loved working with her, and she talked about you all the time," gushes Liv. "Noelle this, Noelle that. She was so proud of you." Bile slips up the back of my throat. I manage to contain my urge to projectile vomit into the fake leather handbag. But Liv isn't finished yet.

"We used to say to Erica, if we could have a daughter half as lovely as hers, we'd feel like we'd done something right in the world."

"That's very sweet," I say, but my hands are shaking now. Phil gets to her feet, takes the carrier bag from Liv and puts the items back into it.

"Thank you," she says to Liv, a little more firmly now. Liv leans forward and squeezes my hand. The other women each step forward to squeeze my hand too and then finally they all walk away, comforting each other. I let out a huge sigh of relief.

"Are you going to tell me what's going on?" whispers Phil, looking down at me, hands on her hips.

"What do you mean? My mum worked in Tesco. So what?"

"Either you loved her so much you can't bear to talk about her, or you hated her guts."

"We weren't close, that's all," I say.

"Your mum obviously thought you were," says Phil. I shrug. Phil squints at me, not satisfied with my answer. She knows she's not getting the full story.

"I gave her a funeral, okay? What more do you want?"

"What more do I want? She's your mother."

"I mean . . . what more am I supposed to do?" I bluster quickly. "Can we just go to the pub now? This place gives me the creeps."

I walk on, head buried in my jacket collar. Phil catches up and links arms with me. I glance down at her arm lying in mine, like two school friends. I enjoy it for a moment. I never had a friend at school to link arms with, but I saw other girls doing it. As we near the exit to the chapel, I disentangle my arm from hers and walk out into the cold day alone.

Even if I wanted to be Phil's friend, there's no point. I'm leaving for Scotland as soon as I can.

Chapter 26

Phil, the most sober of us after Rose, grabs the key from my hand and takes charge of opening the door to my flat. She puts the key in the lock but it won't budge, jammed again.

"We might be here for some time," I say, swaying as the last Bacardi and Coke I had before leaving the pub enters my bloodstream at breakneck speed.

Rose carries the Tesco bag from Liv and Gaby munches on a packet of crisps. We spent three hours at the pub and I consumed more alcohol in that short space of time than I have in my entire life. My head is spinning and I feel sick. Although shoveling a basket of deep-fried shrimp down my throat probably didn't help.

Mali is singing and dancing to Madonna's "Vogue." She makes angular shapes with her hands and flicks her head from side to side, pouting. Me, Rose and Gaby laugh. Mali turns and wiggles her bum at us, looking over her shoulder. We laugh harder.

"Mali, you are a wasted talent, girl. You should have been a pop star," says Rose. "You had what it takes."

"Had? What do you mean, had?"

"Well, you know, maybe ten years ago. You're way past it now."

"I'm not past it," says Mali, gyrating her hips and pelvis to make us laugh.

"I wanted to be in the West End," says Gaby, licking her forefinger and sticking it into the bottom of her crisp packet to hoover up the last of the salty crumbs. She sucks the remains off the end of her finger.

"Plenty of hotels in the West End need cleaners," Rose says.

"You know what I mean. On the stage, in a big show. I used to be able to sing."

"You sing? You never told me that," says Mali, shoving her lightly on the arm.

Gaby shrugs, sticking her finger back in the crisp packet.

"Let's hear you then," says Mali.

"What now?"

We all say yes, begging her to sing something for us. She scrunches up the crisp bag and puts it in her pocket.

"Alright, I'll sing something from *Phantom of the Opera*," she says, wiping her damp fingertips on her coat. She clears her throat.

"Now, it's been a while since I even tried to sing so this could be terrible."

"Oh, stop your stalling," says Rose. Gaby takes a deep breath and then, from the back of her throat, a beautiful, soft sound escapes and floats into the stairwell.

Me, Mali and Rose stare at her, our mouths open. Phil stops trying to open the door and turns to look at Gaby in awe. Gaby, unaware of our reaction to her angelic voice, carries on. The grotty stairwell suddenly seems light and fresh, as though Gaby's singing is cleansing everything around us and making it sparkle.

She stops and pushes her glasses back up her nose. "Was that off key? It sounded off key?" She now sees our stunned faces.

"Fuck me," says Mali in wonder. "You can sing."

"I was in the school choir," she says.

"Gaby, that was truly beautiful," says Rose with tears in her eyes.

"Oh my. My singing made you cry?"

"No," says Rose, waving her away. "I'm crying because you threw your life away. All these years you've been cleaning up after people when you should have been shacking up with Andrew Lloyd what's his face."

"Really? You think I'm that good."

"We should be in a band," says Mali. "I go on stage first, warm up the crowd with my dancing and then you come on and blow them away with la la la la." Mali makes a joke attempt at opera singing. We all giggle.

"Were you ever on stage?" I ask her.

"God, no. I mean, I would have loved it, but I get stage fright. And anyway, I was pregnant at eighteen and on my own." She smiles at me, no regrets about her life. She's just delighted we liked her singing.

A banging noise makes us all jump. Phil, running out of patience, is kicking my front door with all her might.

"Stupid. Fucking. Door," she yells. She stops kicking, flicks her hair back and tries the key in the lock again. This time it opens. "Works every time," she says and marches into my flat. We all bundle in after her.

Rose goes straight to the kitchen and I hear her clanging about as she fills a pan with water to boil. Gaby flops into an armchair and looks comfortable. Phil pulls a bottle of brandy from her jacket pocket and Mali takes a small stack of plastic cups from her bag.

"We know you don't have any glasses," she says to me, matter of fact.

"Remind me to remind you to buy a kettle," Rose yells from the kitchen. Mali puts four plastic cups out on the aluminum table.

"Rose? You having brandy?"

"No, thanks," she calls back. "I can't stay too long."

Phil pours four large measures and passes one to me. I down it in one and hold out my empty cup for a refill. I'm nowhere near as drunk as I need to be to get through the rest of the day. Mali, Phil and Gaby exchange looks, eyebrows raised.

"What? I just buried my mother and I can't have another drink?" Phil gives in and fills up my cup, which I down again.

"Oh, boy," says Gaby.

"You're too skinny to drink like that," says Mali.

I wobble a little on my feet and Mali jumps up to steady me.

"You should go to bed," says Phil.

"I'm not going to fucking bed," I say, suddenly filled with an intense urge to be a bitch. "Where's my bag?" I mutter, looking around.

"On your shoulder," says Gaby, pointing to my small backpack.

"Not this one," I say, struggling to take it off as the strap gets caught in my hair. I see Phil stifle a smile. I finally get it off and chuck it on the floor where the zip splits open and the contents spill out.

"I mean my Tesco bag."

Rose comes from the kitchen with coffee in my SpongeBob mug. She tells me the bag is by my trunk. I snatch it up, take out the pinafore and unravel it to show them.

"Isn't it pretty?" I say. Gaby gives a nervous smile. Mali, Rose and Phil look confused. I put the pinafore on over my head and let it hang around my body. "How do I look?" I swish my arms from side to side, which makes me dizzy and I fall against the wall.

"Go and lie down" says Phil. I ignore her.

"And there's more in the goody bag." I give them a big grin and lift my mother's handbag out and hold it in front of me.

"Do I have any takers? Bids start at 50p. 50p, anyone, 50p?" They cast their eyes down. "No bidders? Maybe if we see what's inside the handbag, you'll change your mind." I flip the gold fastener to open it. "Oooh, lucky dip," I say, dropping my hand into the void to rummage around. I pull out the first thing I find—a small black lipstick case.

"Ah, lipstick. She was a glamorous lady, this one." I chuck it behind me onto the floor along with the contents of my backpack. Phil comes toward me.

"Stop, Noelle, okay?"

"But I'm only getting started," I reply. I shove my hand into the bag again and pull out a cell phone. "Better hold on to this. I might get a few quid for it." Swaying on my feet, I toss the phone onto the floor behind me as well. Phil comes at me again, but I move away from her, raising my hand like the traffic police to hold her back. I plunge my hand into the handbag again and pull out a matching brown fake leather purse.

"Hmmm, matching. The woman had style, too." I drop the handbag and stare at the purse. I don't remember my mother ever having a purse. It seems like something only a normal person would have.

"Listen, honey," says Rose, trying to calm me. "It's been a horrible day and you're doing your best to get through it." Phil, Mali and Gaby all nod, trying to reassure me.

"Give me the purse," says Phil. I look at the purse again, which suddenly seems so important, like it contains the answers to all my questions. That makes me frown because I didn't even know I had any questions.

"I need to see what's inside," I say, the sarcasm and joshing gone from my voice. Phil steps back to give me space as I unzip it. It has a middle compartment for cash and two side compartments for cards, although it doesn't have much in it. I slide out a bank card. NatWest.

"Same bank as me," I say, like this means something. I pull a few more cards out of the pockets. There's a Boots card. I hold it up to show the girls.

"She spent a lot of money on toiletries, not that it made any difference; she was still ugly." I laugh at my own comment, but the girls' faces remain still, awkward. I toss the cards over my shoulder and onto the floor with the lipstick and the phone and the rest of the carnage from my backpack. On one side of the purse is a zipper compartment.

"Oh, secret zip," I say. "Maybe there's a thousand pounds in here. That would just about cover the funeral." The girls stare at the floor again, clearly uncomfortable. They feel sorry for me, but I don't care. I zip open the compartment, slide my finger inside and run the tip of my finger over a small, smooth papery square.

"There's something in here," I say in a singsong voice. I pull it out and hold it in the palm of my hand. It's a picture of me, smiling at the camera, about age ten, although I can't be sure. I hardly remember what I looked like this morning let alone sixteen years ago. The picture is faded and grubby around the edges.

A memory floats into my head of sitting in a passport photo booth with my mother standing outside ordering me to sit still and not to move.

I had needed a photo for something to do with school. I showed her the printed note from my teacher, which she screwed up and chucked in the trash. I said nothing and went to my room.

I perched on the side of my bed, still wearing my coat and shoes, and waited. I knew she wouldn't want to attract any unwanted attention. If I turned up at school, the only pupil without their passport photo, eyebrows would be raised and phone calls made.

Sure enough, ten minutes later my bedroom door flew open and there she was, coat on, scowling like an angry cat.

"Come on then. Do you want to get your stupid photo taken or not?"

She marched out of the house and down the hill toward the high street taking long, impatient strides. I just about managed to keep up. I didn't need to walk beside her, she didn't care as long as I was following, but I remember thinking, the closer we walked together the more chance we had of looking like a family.

Half an hour later she marched into the shopping center, me trailing behind her.

"Get in then," she said, pointing at the photo booth. I'd never done this before and wondered what she meant. She pulled the curtain back and pointed at the little round seat. "Sit on that and look at the screen," she ordered.

I did as I was told, excited about having my photo taken. I'd never seen a picture of myself before.

"Tidy your hair. You look like a scarecrow," she said. I quickly pushed my hair behind my ears and peered into the black screen intrigued.

"Is there a man with a camera in there?" I asked. She looked at me in surprise and then, the strangest thing happened: she laughed. Her eyes crinkled at the corners, her mouth bent into a crooked smile, and a delicate noise I'd never heard before escaped from her lips and lightly filled the photo booth.

If someone had asked me what kind of laugh my mother would have if I were ever to hear it, I would have said gruff and cackling like a witch. But this was a playful titter, like you'd expect from a posh lady, a duchess perhaps.

My eyes widened in amazement but she quickly caught herself and the smile, the crinkled eyes and the ladylike titter disappeared in an instant.

"Of course there isn't a bloody man in there. Shut up and look at the screen, like I told you." She shoved some coins into the slot and snapped the curtain shut, leaving me on my own. I stared at the screen. "And don't move. And make sure you smile," she barked from outside.

I didn't move a muscle, except for my lips as I smiled the biggest smile I could. Flash, pop, flash, pop. My heart skipped a beat with excitement. When the flashing stopped, I remained on the little stool, still as stone, still staring at the screen with the smile on my face.

"Are you done?" she said, through the curtain. I didn't know if I was finished or not. If I turned, that was moving. If I spoke, I wouldn't be smiling. Finally, she whipped the curtain back and dragged me out by my arm.

We stood together, staring at the tray in the side of the photo booth. Then, as if by magic, a strip of four milky-looking squares slopped out. My mother grabbed them and marched off out of the shopping center. I pelted after her.

"Are they the photos? Can I see them?" I asked.

"No," she said. "They're not ready yet."

This time, I kept up with her all the way back up the hill, through the estate and into the flat, not taking my eyes off the white strip in her hand. I'd never wanted to see something so much in my life.

In the kitchen, she waved the strip around in the air to dry it and then looked at them herself. And that's when I saw it, a flicker in her eye, for a brief moment, and I mean, so brief that I can't be entirely sure I saw anything at all, but she looked the tiniest bit impressed.

"Can I see them now?"

"Don't be vain," she said and, grabbing the kitchen scissors, she cut one of the pictures off the end of the strip and put it in an envelope, which she then licked with her bobbly, alien tongue to seal it.

"I'll drop it at the school myself," she said, "just to make sure your teacher gets it." There was malice in her tone.

"Can I see the other pictures?"

Her eyes narrowed. "Two seconds," she said.

She held them up in front of me for a moment. My mouth opened in delight to see my own picture. There I was, a real person, in a photograph. It was evidence I was alive and existed.

She quickly cut the rest of the pictures up into tiny pieces and dropped them in the trash. When she left the room, I tried to fish the pieces back out, but they were too small to salvage and were already lying in yogurt-y gunk. So what? I told myself. I had my picture taken today and that's enough to keep me going.

What I hadn't noticed was that she'd kept one of the pictures for herself. And here it is. Me, happy and excited on the day I had my picture taken and the only time I ever heard my mother laugh.

I double over slightly, feeling winded, my breath quickening. Phil comes over to me and puts an arm around my shoulders, but I shrug her off.

"She had a picture of me in her purse," I say, holding up the picture for them to see it.

"You were her daughter," says Phil. "Why wouldn't she have a picture of you?"

"Because my mother was a bad person. And this is a lie," I say, waving the picture at them.

I chuck the photo over my shoulder, but it doesn't get very far and flutters to the floor by my feet. I grip both sides of the purse and yank at it hard, ripping the fake leather. I drop it on the ground and stamp on it. I pick up the handbag and pull hard at the straps, tearing them off. I pull at the sides of the bag, straining with all my might until something snaps inside it and it becomes floppy, like the smelly, amoeba beanbag in our flat in West House.

The large gold fastener is harder to dislodge but I try my best to rip that off too, but it won't budge. I put my teeth around it. I hear four sharp intakes of breath, as the girls look on, but I couldn't care less. But it still won't loosen.

I drop the bag on the floor, shove my foot on the now flimsy fake leather casing and attempt to prise the fastener off that way, but it must be stuck on with some kind of industrial glue. Giving up, exhausted now, I drop to my knees, the contents from the purse and the bag and my backpack lying around me.

My cheeks are hot and my hands are sweaty. My hair has fallen over my face in the frenzy and I imagine I look like a raving lunatic, which I probably am. Phil and Rose pull me to my feet. Phil pushes the hair from my face and smooths it back into place.

"This is what grief does to a person," says Mali. Phil lifts the pinafore back over my head and passes it to Rose and then helps me over to the ladder up to my mattress.

"I don't want to go to bed," I say.

"Stop whining. You'll feel a lot better in the morning," says Phil.

But I won't. I never feel a lot better in the morning, only worse. The only good thing about morning time is that it isn't nighttime and I can get up and go to work.

Phil pushes me up the ladder. I take one step at a time, slipping and sliding as I go. If Phil wasn't there to catch me, I'd have fallen right off.

I climb onto the top and crawl over to my mattress. Phil follows me up and scrambles ahead of me, bent over so as not to bang her head on the sloping ceiling. She throws the duvet back and helps me into bed. I put my head on the pillow, too exhausted to even talk now. The last thing I remember is Phil asking me if I need a bucket.

Chapter 27

Blasting sirens from a distant ambulance seep into my subconscious and the stark morning light plays havoc on my eyelids, which I'm keeping tightly shut. My head pounds, paining me. I attempt to lift my head, but a sharp twinge hits me in the face and I lie still again.

I try to open my eyes, but I barely get them a fraction apart before shutting them again, thanks to the sun blazing in through the crack in the curtains. I'm hot and sticky. Even my nose feels like it's on fire. Maybe I'm about to die. Maybe this is it. The end. I wouldn't mind if it was and my death was going to be quick, but this is agony.

A growling noise fills my head, like a dragon breathing flames before inhaling deeply again. I wonder if the noise is coming from inside me. I try to speak, but my throat is sore and dry. Get up, I tell myself, suddenly panicked by the heat and the ominous growling. I go to move my arms, but I can't lift them. I try my legs next, but I can't move them either. Am I paralyzed? Did I drink so much I now have brain damage? I attempt to wiggle my toes and they move. Relief floods through me. But I still can't move my arms. It's as if a great weight is bearing down on my whole body.

More awake now, I open my eyes again allowing them to adjust to the brightness. I glance down and see the duvet pulled tight around me, squashing me down. I try to move my arms again and manage to wriggle them up toward my head and force them out over the top of the duvet. The growling noise fills my head again—a rattling, unsettling sound, like grinding gravel.

With great effort I heave myself onto my elbows, dragging my body to a half upright position. A puff of air shoots across my face followed by the heaving rattle sound again.

I turn my head slowly to the left in the direction of the noise, squinting, unsure if I can trust my perception, given the state I'm in.

Mali lies beside me, sprawled out on her back, on top of the duvet, fully clothed. Her closed eyes look like huge capsules and her mouth is wide open. She inhales deeply, like a vortex sucking all life from the planet. The air whistles through her nose and down the back of her throat, releasing the hideous snorting, growling sounds. Mali is snoring.

I look to my right and see Phil, lying on the other side of me. She is on her side and facing me, also on top of the duvet, hence why I'm wedged in like a sardine in a can. Phil is fast asleep, graceful and quiet in her slumber. Her long dark eyelashes swoop down almost touching her smooth, soft cheeks. The heat rushes to my head again and suddenly I can't breathe. I need to get out of this straitjacket before I scream.

I drag my knees up to the top of the duvet, carefully pull myself out and crawl across the bed and to the ladder. I peer over the top and see Gaby below, fast asleep in one of my armchairs with her jacket pulled up under her chin like a napkin. My backpack lies on the aluminum table. Someone put all my things back in my bag and tidied up the flat. I hear stirring in the bed behind me.

Phil is leaning up now, her dark eyes barely open under her inky, slightly tousled hair.

"How are you feeling?" she asks.

"Like I've been kicked in the head," I say.

"For someone who doesn't drink very much, you were certainly able to put it away."

"What are you all doing here? Don't you have to be in work?" I ask, genuinely confused.

"You mean *we*, don't *we* have to be at work," says Phil. I didn't mean we, but I can't tell her I'm leaving today. I know she'll try and stop me, and I suppose I'm worried she'll succeed or at least delay me again. "Mali was convinced you'd puke in your sleep and drown in your own vomit."

I pull a face at the thought. Mali lets out another enormous snuffle as a gurgling sound emits from the back of her throat like a wounded animal. For a moment I think she's going to suffocate. Phil leans over and shoves her in the shoulder. Mali coughs and splutters then sits bolt upright, eyes wide open, startled.

"Morning, Mali," says Phil. Mali yawns and stretches her arms above her head.

"Morning," she mumbles. "Very comfortable bed."

Phil and I both stifle a smile. Mali must have no idea how badly she snores, if at all. Mali peers at me.

"You're alive then?" she says.

"Just about. You didn't have to stay."

"You shouldn't drink," says Mali. "You're a lightweight and it's not good for your liver."

"No more tequilas for me then," I say.

"Oh, you can drink tequila, but nothing else."

The thought of touching another drop of alcohol makes me want to gag. At least Rose had the sense to go home to her own bed.

"I'll make some coffee, if you don't mind sharing cups again," I say.

My mind wanders to the supermarket aisle with all the crockery and clean white mugs on the shelf. But I push the thought away. I'm not buying mugs for a flat I'm about to leave.

I squeeze into my doll's house kitchen. I reach down to grab the larger of my two rickety saucepans when something white and shiny on the cooktop catches my eye. It's a kettle, sitting on a base with a cord running up to the dirty plug socket in the wall.

"Open the cupboard." I flick around to see Phil leaning in the doorway. I do as I'm told and open the cupboard. Three shiny white mugs sit on the shelf next to SpongeBob and spotty.

"Rose and Gaby ran down to Asda and grabbed a few things."

"Oh, I've never been to Asda," I say, awkward, unsure how to respond. Why are they buying things for my kitchen?

"Gaby says you need at least five cups so we can all have a drink when we're over here." Do they actually like being in my flat? It feels odd to me. "You're welcome," says Phil, amused by my shock.

"Sorry, thanks, that's great. Let me know what I owe you."

"It's on us. It's a 'your mum died present.' But seriously, the whole lot cost about seven quid." I feel bad suddenly that I won't have room to pack the cups and kettle to bring with me. They'll have to stay for the next person unfortunate enough to move in here.

"Sorry about last night," I say, hoping to quickly skip over my embarrassing behavior and move on with coffee followed by everyone leaving.

"You're quite a performer," says Phil. I muster a smile and pick up the kettle, which is already full of water. I push the little lever down on the handle and a blue light comes on as it starts to hiss, warming up. I feel like it's warming me up too.

"How bad was she?" says Phil. I glance at her. I know she's asking about my mother but I really don't want to discuss it. I busy myself taking four mugs from the cupboard and finding places for them to stand around the cooktop and sink. I grab the instant coffee jar and twist the lid off. I wish Phil wasn't standing in the doorway. Heat rises up the back of my neck and I start to sweat.

"If you don't want to talk about it."

"There's nothing to say. She's dead now," I mumble, focusing on shoveling large teaspoons of coffee granules into the mugs. It occurs to me that I've never had anyone in any of my flats before, and here I am with three people on a sleepover. How did I let any of this happen?

"Those scars on your body . . . ?" she trails off. I swallow and my throat feels rough. I've never told anyone what my mother did to me, but I've also never been asked before. I put the lid on the coffee and pause for a moment. Then I shrug and nod once, hoping that's enough and that this conversation is now over.

"It probably explains why you do what you do—you know, taking things?"

"That's all behind me now," I say way too breezily. I need to shut Phil down. Taking things, my mother, my flat, they are all my own private business and I don't like her prying. I never should have shown her my trunk. I should have stuck to my plan and left after the hairbrush incident. Then I could have let the authorities deal with my mother's body.

Mali squishes into the kitchen beside Phil. Her hair sticks up, pointing in all directions.

"We have to get to work," she says. Gaby manages to pop her head into the kitchen over Mali's head, yawning.

"Thanks for the mugs and the kettle," I say.

"Do you like them?" Gaby says, beaming at me.

"Of course. I've got a fully equipped top of the range kitchen now."

Mali flips her head back, roaring laughing. She sounds less like a clown to me these days and more like, well, like Mali. Phil and Gaby laugh as well. I smile. Not just at my own joke but also at the fact we're all trying to squeeze into my tiny kitchen like it's a cool place to hang out. I imprint their faces on my memory. As much as I want to leave on the next train, I do want to remember them.

"I'll thank Rose later."

"Rose? Oh no." Mali's hands shoot to her head, clutching clumps of her hair. "Monica's cake," she squeals and runs into the living room. We all follow her as she quickly puts on her shoes and grabs her jacket and bag.

"You didn't forget it's Monica's party tonight, did you?" says Phil, grinning, enjoying Mali's total overreaction. I trawl through my memory, desperately trying to remember who Monica is.

"Just buy a bloody cake. Rose won't mind," says Phil. Monica—Rose's sister. Her birthday party must be tonight.

"Buy one?" Mali says with disgust. "I'm not going to buy a birthday cake. Is that what you did on my birthday?" Mali's eyes narrow, suspicious.

Gaby looks at her hands. Phil sniffs.

"You said you baked it," she wails.

"We got it in a proper cake shop. It cost thirty pounds," says Gaby.

"Thirty pounds?!" Mali is even more horrified. "And I ate that? Your cake of shame."

"Don't be so ungrateful," says Phil.

Mali checks the time on her phone. She delegates instructions to us, which are clearly nonnegotiable. She's going to rush to the shops before our shift starts to buy the ingredients, then leave work early to bake the cake, and we will all cover for her. Phil and Gaby mumble okay and Mali turns on her heel and rushes out of the flat.

"We'll be working late now. And all for a cake," says Phil. "Are you coming to the party?" she says to me.

"Rose will understand if you don't feel like it," Gaby adds, a sympathetic look on her face.

I was planning on leaving today, but if floor seven is going to be two cleaners down, that's not fair to the girls. I could work the day, get the storage people to collect my trunk this afternoon, and then catch the 8:15 train this evening. With everyone at Rose's house later and me, supposedly at home dealing with my grief, I can slip away quietly.

"Probably not," I say.

I've already decided I don't need to resign officially or even tell Julia I'm going. I simply won't tell my new boss about the Magnolia. It'll be like I never worked there—the phantom cleaner.

"You look perkier," says Phil, noting the healthier color in my cheeks caused by the adrenaline rushing around my body.

"I feel a bit better," I say.

I'm on the move again and I can't wait.

Chapter 28

The staff room feels warmer today and the moldy scent from the underground parking garage is not so strong. All I can smell is Phil's light perfume, which still has a tingling effect on me. I'm not quite over Phil, but I'm definitely over the Magnolia.

I tie my apron neatly around my waist, taking pleasure in the fact it's the last time I will wear this uniform in this hotel. Phil and Gaby are telling Rose about Mali's panic about the cake. I listen in, enjoying the inflections of their different voices. Rose's voice is deep and warm and reassuring but there's also a "take no shit" vibe to it.

Gaby's speech is full of heartfelt mmms and ahhs. She hesitates a lot, like she's not sure anyone's really interested in what she has to say. I'm still a little sad for her that she couldn't become the Gaby I saw in the hospital when her son was in a coma. But I'm happy she got to be someone else for a while and maybe that's enough.

Phil's smooth tones have less effect on me now, but her voice still drips gently in my ear, caressing my senses. There's a confidence in the way she speaks, slower, almost a drawl sometimes like she's in no hurry to get to the end of her sentences because she knows everyone's listening to her. I imagine her speaking at a university talking intelligently about clever things. The students swooning as she parts her inky, silky hair and points at a complicated chart on a projector. It dawns on me that I will always have feelings for Phil, although I'm not sure what they are exactly.

Mali bursts in through the door, late.

"I'm here, I'm here," she yells, like the existence of the planet depends on her being at work on time. Rose comes straight out of the traps.

"You forgot to make Monica's cake?"

Mali's shoulders shrivel and her cheeks redden. It's not like Mali to blush.

"I know, I know, but it's sorted. And it is going to be the best cake you've ever seen."

"You mad bitch," Rose says, laughing. "Monica won't know if the cake's been bought by you or baked by you."

"When I say I do something, I do it," says Mali, her head held high.

Mali's voice fills my head making me feel calm, which is strange since she's so hyper and energetic. Mali can make your heart rate increase by just saying hello. And yet there is something sad as well as joyful about her, how she expresses every raw emotion she feels in a single moment, as though every feeling she's ever had is lying just beneath the surface waiting to emerge. Even if she tried to hold back, she wouldn't be able to.

I find comfort in the reliability and unreliability of her voice, which can be shrill sometimes. There are days I can read her mood instantly and others when her mood changes so quickly it can be hard to keep up. But today it's clear, she wants to do a kind thing for Rose's sister and keep her word. To not keep her word is totally unacceptable, in the world of Mali anyway.

Phil comes up to me. "Sure you're okay?"

"Yeah. I'd rather be at work," I say, focusing on retying my apron.

"What about the other thing?" she asks, lowering her voice.

"I'm not thinking about it," I lie.

"That's progress," she says, pleased.

But I am so thinking about taking things. I can't wait to start over in my new cleaning job in Scotland. I just have to get through the day.

The moment I enter room 709 the smell hits me—a lingering, unpleasant odor. I can't place it straight away, which surprises me since my delicately honed sense of smell, and my ability to identify various questionable aromas, hasn't let me down in years.

I sniff the room. It's a man's aftershave and its thick presence in the air makes my stomach churn. The room is fairly tidy and I can see it's a solo occupancy. His striped pajamas are bundled up on the unmade bed and his small suitcase is open on the floor, still neatly packed. I pick up the pajama top and hold it up to my nose. The sickly scent lingers on the fabric and stirs my gut, not in a good way. I fold the pajamas and put them on the chair. I have an urgency now to get out of this room as quickly as I can. The fragrance, although faint when I first came in, is now overwhelming my senses.

I make the bed, pulling the covers straight and tight and bash the pillows, fluffing them up again to their full potential. I rush into the bathroom. He's only used one towel and hung it up. And his small wash bag is by the sink. I can be out of here in two minutes. But the smell is stronger in here. He must have sprayed himself before leaving. The air is stifling and sticky and makes me gag a little.

I go to his Dopp kit and unzip it with my blue-gloved hands. Lying on top of his deodorant and shaving cream is a sleek black bottle of aftershave, which I recognize immediately. I zip up the wash bag and quickly pull my sleeve across my face, letting my nose inhale the laundry smells of my clean white shirt.

His name was Roy, and for one week when I was thirteen, our flat smelled just like room 709 does today.

My mother stumbled in the door drunk one Friday night with him in tow. I was in bed with the dresser up against my door, but wide awake and on my guard. My mother, too drunk to even talk, fell into her bedroom and onto the floor.

I recognized the familiar thud and knew it was nothing to worry about. She often opened the door too fast, swung into the room, hanging off the handle and then catapulted herself onto the floor, just missing the bed.

"Get up, you stupid bint," came a hostile voice.

This was Roy. There was something about his callous tone that made my blood run cold.

My mother's bedroom door slammed shut. I lay with the covers up over my head, not daring to breathe, in case he heard me. I listened intently, hoping to hear him leave, but all I heard was some shuffling followed by grunting and groaning then silence. I did wonder for a moment if he had strangled her.

I didn't sleep a wink that night and got up early, planning to get out of the house before my mother or her visitor woke up. I knew he was still in the flat because I hadn't heard him leave.

Dressed in my school uniform, I nipped into the kitchen to grab my school bag. When I turned to leave, he was leaning in the doorway wearing a pair of pants under my mother's tacky red dressing gown. His large belly, a bulbous and solid mound, pushed its way out of the silky robe. I imagined it was about to split open and a one-eyed mutant would pop out covered in slime.

Roy had long scrawny, greasy hair and small beady eyes that peered out from behind a pair of wire glasses. His aftershave, thick and strong, wafted into the kitchen settling on everything like an invisible grimy film. It settled up my nostrils too.

"Well, well, well, what have we here then?" His mouth broke into a grin although it was more of a sneer.

"I have to go to school," I said, making to move past him.

"Not till you tell me your name," he said.

"Noelle," I mumbled.

"She never told me she had a sprog."

I shrugged, not surprised and he stepped aside to let me pass.

"I'll be seeing you then," he said.

I bolted past him and out of the house and ran all the way to school, the smell of his aftershave stuck to the inside of my nose.

He was at the flat every night that week, always with a bottle of vodka in hand. Something my mother couldn't say no to. She'd never had a boyfriend before, well not that I could remember. But I never heard him call her by her name, so I wondered if he even knew it. She started wearing more blush and washing her hair every day and dousing herself in perfume. But even that overpowering stink couldn't cover the stench of Roy.

When he was in the house, I stayed in my room with the dresser wedged up against the door. After a couple of days, their drunken sessions turned into shouting matches. I was able to work out from the odd word that Roy had stolen money from my mother. She yelled at him to get out of her flat, but two minutes later her bedroom door slammed and the groaning and snorting started again. Luckily, that bit never lasted very long.

I started brushing my teeth in the kitchen since a new toothbrush had appeared in the bathroom alongside the sleek black bottle of aftershave.

One morning, as I was sneaking out early again to avoid having to see or talk to stinky Roy, I found him standing at the front door, blocking my exit. He only had pants on this time and was scratching his overhanging belly.

I stopped in my tracks, all my internal alarm bells going off at once. Whatever it was about my mother attacking me, I knew she wouldn't kill me, not on purpose anyway. But Roy was an unknown entity.

"I need to get to school," I said, trying to sound in control.

"Yeah, well, we all need things, Noelle, don't we?" He started to walk toward me. I moved backward, away from him. My mind was racing, trying to figure out my options. If I was quick, could I get into my room and pull the dresser across? No, there was no time for that. And he was way bigger and stronger than me. He'd kick the door down in one go.

"Where are you going, eh?" he said following me as I backed into my bedroom.

I eyed the window. It seemed to be my only option. It was three stories high but I could still jump. So what if I died? Whatever Roy had in mind for me, I'd rather be lying in a pool of my own blood.

"Get the fuck away from her," came my mother's sharp voice. Roy slowly turned his head and I peered over his shoulder to see my mother, dressed in her shiny red dressing gown, looming in the doorway, broom in one hand, phone in the other.

"Oh, yeah, what you going to do?" Roy said, his voice, low, threatening. He moved toward her, his shoulders pulled forward, flexing his muscles. I looked around for some kind of weapon as well. But there was nothing in my bare room, not even a lamp. I quickly took one of my shoes off and held that.

"I'll beat you to a pulp if I have to, you dirty perv," my mother said. "And I've called the police. They should be here any minute."

Roy turned his beady eyes back on me, now holding my flimsy school shoe like a baseball bat. He was assessing the situation. Could he fight us both off? Had my mother really called the police? He squared up to my mother, looking down on her, but she showed no fear. She puffed her chest out and stared right back at him.

"Get out and don't ever come back. If I even see you around this estate again, you'll be leaving in a body bag." I was impressed with her gangster talk.

"You're a couple of ugly tarts anyway," he spat and sloped off to get dressed. My mother stayed by my door, not moving, not taking her eyes off Roy for a second until he left, slamming the front door behind him, making the whole flat shudder.

My mother dropped the broom and put both hands against the wall to steady herself. I could see her legs trembling. I wanted to help, but experience had taught me never to approach her.

"Sorry," I said, not because I was sorry but because I felt it was the right thing to say at that moment. And she was bound to blame me.

A silence fell between us. I caught a glimpse of myself in my bedroom window still holding my shoe in the air. I put it down on the floor and slipped it back on.

"Did he hurt you?" she asked, not looking up.

"No," I said. "Did you really call the police?"

"Of course I bloody didn't," she said. "Now get to school, if you know what's good for you."

I walked past her into the hallway, picked up my bag, and legged it out of the flat. I sprinted all the way to school, every now and then glancing over my shoulder to make sure Roy wasn't following me.

I convinced myself that my mother had saved me that day, that it had been a selfless act; her maternal instincts had risen from the depths of her darkness and exploded into the world to protect me like an angel in a Tesco uniform. There was hope that she did love me. That she wasn't a complete monster.

For the next two days she was quiet and not drinking, which was all very unusual. I knew instinctively that the word Roy should never be mentioned in our flat again on pain of death and figured the whole incident must have been a shock to her too.

It didn't take long for her to return to her normal evil self. Three days to be precise. Sadly, the stench of Roy took a bit longer to go.

I flush the toilet in room 709 and rush to leave, my sleeve still over my nose and mouth. I pull the door shut behind me and drop my arm, breathing in the light fresh scent of the hotel corridor.

I roll my trolley to the next bedroom, as Rose exits a room farther up and pushes her trolley in my direction.

"The state of that room," she says, nodding behind her to room 712. "Chewing gum on the carpet." I pull a sympathetic face. "Phil says you probably won't make it later."

"Yeah, I'm exhausted, you know, after yesterday."

"I don't blame you," she says. "Anyway, you won't be missing much. It's only me and the girls and my sister. And Mali's birthday cake, which will have a bigger personality than all of us put together." I'm surprised to hear this. I'd assumed it was a party with lots of people and they wouldn't notice if I was there or not.

"We'll save you some cake," she says and carries on pushing her trolley to room 714. I carry on rolling my trolley too and stop outside room 707. I glance back at Rose, now buzzing around her trolley, collecting her cleaning sprays. Could I delay catching the train to Scotland by one more day? Maybe going to Rose's sister's birthday is a way to say goodbye to everyone, even though they have no idea I'm leaving.

Beyond Rose, way up the corridor, I spot Gaby. She slides a biscuit from her apron, takes a nibble and slips it back. We all have our secrets, I suppose.

Chapter 29

The wind and rain stick to my face as I put my head down and scurry up the wide, busy road in the dark. I glance at my phone to check Google Maps as I follow the blue line leading the way to Rose's house, backpack over my shoulder. The address is 9 Wiltshire Gardens, Churchfield Estate. I wonder if it's a council estate like the one I grew up in.

The headlights from passing cars illuminate the puddles up ahead on the path, which I step around as best I can. My coat is pulled up over my head to protect my hair, which I washed and tried to make silky with a serum I bought from Boots. It didn't work. It just made my hair look slightly greasy. Still, I don't want to turn up looking like a drowned rat, although rat seems like the perfect way to describe myself since I'm sneaking off on the first train tomorrow.

A guilty knot forms in my stomach about not telling the girls. They trust me. But that's not my fault. You shouldn't trust people, not really, so it's their problem.

Google Maps says I'm two minutes away as I jump over another puddle. I'm wearing my new jeans, which don't seem as tight now as they were when I tried them on in the shop, and my off-the-shoulder top with the hole under the arm. I'm not trying to entice Phil anymore, so the pressure's off to look attractive and appealing, not that I ever did or ever could.

On my way home from work, I popped into Asda to get a birthday card and a present for Monica. My tolerance for supermarkets seems to have improved since my mother died. I settled on a bottle of sparkling wine that looked classy-ish and a box of Milk Tray chocolates. When I left hotel 9, the cleaners gave me a box of Milk Tray as a leaving present. I don't eat chocolate, but I was happy to receive it. It suddenly strikes me that I have no idea how old Monica is.

Google says to turn left. I stop and peer out from under my dripping coat. Grass verges rise on either side of the road and a big sign says CHURCHFIELD ESTATE. PLEASE DRIVE SLOWLY.

I squint up the road and see small, stumpy buildings scattered around, no more than three or four stories high. A gang of kids whizz by on bikes, powering through a huge puddle, spraying the water up in the air, soaking my jeans. I continue to follow the directions on my phone, winding through the blocks of flats. Some of the flats on the ground floor have their own front door. There are no outdoor concrete staircases, just smart-looking keypads to enter each building.

I take a right turn and find myself in a green square flanked by buildings on each side. Even in the gloomy torrential rain, the grass looks well cared for with a small flower bed in the center. A sign is stuck to a brick wall: WILTSHIRE GARDENS.

Google tells me I have arrived. I move along to the end of the block to number 9, which is a ground-floor flat. The front window blind is pulled down but a warm glow creeps out from around the edges. There's a window box with perky-looking flowers in it. I catch a glimpse of a silver chain attached to the box, which is in turn attached to the window guard. The woman who lived in the building block across from us in West House was always chasing kids with a wooden spoon as they sprinted off with her latest flower box. They didn't take it because they wanted it or because it might be worth something. They took it because they could. The chain makes perfect sense. Tie down your valuables.

I press the doorbell. It makes a short, sharp buzz sound, like it's giving out an electric shock. I step back as the door flies open and Rose, a pink feather boa wrapped around her neck and a bright pink feather in her hair, holds her arms out in delight.

"You came after all."

"I didn't want to miss it," I say, wondering now if I should have made more of an effort to dress up. She waves me into the narrow hallway and shuts the door. The flat is warm and there's a thick smell of slightly burned cheese. Light music tinkles from beyond the glass door at the end of the hall. Rose hopes I didn't walk here, and I assure her that I got the bus. She takes my coat and hangs it on a hook on the wall alongside other wet coats. I recognize Phil's and Gaby's coats. I quickly unzip my backpack and take out the wine and chocolates and the card with Monica written on the front of the envelope. I give it to Rose.

"This is for Monica," I say, a bit awkward. Rose is taken aback for a moment then hugs me.

"Thank you," she says.

She leads me to the glass door at the end of the hallway and into the kitchen-cum-dining room, which is an L-shape with double doors that lead outside. The windows are wet on the inside from condensation and the bright light overhead makes me squint for a moment. The music is louder now and the heat more intense but after getting drenched on the way over, I'm looking forward to drying out. Sparkly balloons hang from the light fitting over the kitchen table and a HAPPY BIRTHDAY banner is taped to the wall.

"Hey, Noelle," says Mali, grinning at me from the kitchen table. She too has a feather in her hair. Phil comes up to me and passes me a red drink in a plastic cup.

"You made it. Get this down you."

I take the cup from Phil. She's wearing an oversized shirt over leggings. One side of her shirt has slipped down her arm to reveal the thin strap of her bra where she has pinned a feather. She always likes to be different and I love that about her. I quickly turn my attention to Gaby, reluctant to get sucked down the Phil rabbit hole again.

Gaby also has a feather in her hair and hairpins in her mouth. She is standing behind a woman seated at the kitchen table, and is brushing the woman's long brown hair. This must be Monica. She resembles Rose, with the same thick hair and slightly heavy features. She is clearly younger, although she seems frail, with pale cheeks shining through her foundation. She smiles at me, crinkling her eyes at the corners. It's a genuine smile. I smile back. Gaby twists sections of Monica's hair and pins it up. Gaby mumbles hello to me, trying not to drop the hairpins stuck between her lips.

"Drink your punch," says Mali. "Monica made it. It's delicious." I take a sip. It's sweet and fizzy.

"Lovely," I say. Mali is busy painting Monica's fingernails bright pink. "You must be Monica," I say, surprised at my own confidence. "I'm Noelle. Happy birthday."

"Oh, Rose has told me all about you. I'm sorry about your mum," she says in a raspy voice.

"Thanks," I say.

Rose joins us, an oven glove on one hand. Rose shows Monica the wine and chocolates and explains it's from me. Monica thanks me and invites me to sit beside her. Rose gives my shoulders a squeeze and goes back to the kitchen.

Phil follows Rose to help with serving food, grabbing plates from a cupboard over the sink. I squeeze around the table to sit beside Monica and it's only now I see that Monica is in a wheelchair. She is wearing a long flowery dress with a shawl over her shoulders and a soft blanket on her lap. She must be boiling, I think. She clocks the fleeting look of surprise on my face.

"I've had a lot of speeding tickets in this baby," she says, winking at me and tapping the arm of her chair.

"Lucky you," I say, warmly. "I don't even know how to drive." She laughs out loud, which makes her cough, which turns into a loud wheeze. Rose whips off her oven glove and goes to the corner of the room. She grabs a dark blue canvas bag and takes out a small oxygen tank with a breathing mask attached to it. Monica waves her hand in the air indicating she's fine.

"Save it for when I'm really about to die," she says with a grin, the wheezing abating. Everyone smiles. Rose kisses the top of her head and Monica clicks her fingers at Gaby and Mali again. "What kind of service is this, huh?" Gaby and Mali exhale, relieved, and get back to pampering Monica.

Monica beckons to me to come closer. I lean in.

"Rose fusses but there's no need. I'm well able to take care of myself. Isn't that right, Rose?" Monica winks at me. "I used to be in the army. Didn't I used to be in the army, Rose?"

"Oh," she did, says Rose. "The army of fetch me this and get me that." Monica nods her head, laughing. I laugh too. There's something about Monica that makes me want to style her hair and paint her nails too.

"Ta da," says Gaby, holding a mirror up for Monica to see her hair, which is arranged in a twisted headpiece, like a princess. Monica says it's wonderful and thanks Gaby. Gaby beams with delight, as Mali finishes Monica's nails, blowing on them to make sure they're dry. Monica admires her nails, both hands slightly shaky.

"All I need is a date now," she says, grinning.

"Hey? You've got a date," says Mali, indicating all of us. Monica takes Mali's hand and squeezes it. She then turns to me, puts her hand on mine and taps it. Despite how warm the room is, her hand is cold and clammy.

"It was good of you to come today. It means you care about Rose."

"Of course," I say, a sudden tightness in my throat. And I do care about Rose. I care about all of them. And somehow they sneaked in under my radar and shoved themselves into my life like pushy, noisy uninvited houseguests. But now that they're here, it's hard to remember what life was like without them, not that it makes any difference to my plans.

I pat Monica's hand back, like I appreciate her comments, which I do, but it doesn't change anything. I can't survive in this world without taking things and there's no point in trying.

For a while, when I believed Phil was going to be my girlfriend and I was part of floor seven, part of the group, I thought I might be able to leave it behind me. But I'm not destined to live a normal life, the kind where you fit in or belong somewhere or to something or someone. The only place I ever truly belonged was in the flat with my mother in West House and that didn't work out too well for me. My mission in life is to keep moving until the day I can't anymore. When that day comes, I will hang up my apron and disappear for good.

Phil and Rose put two big pizzas on the table and a stack of plates. Rose tells us to help ourselves.

"Ooh, I had a huge lunch," says Monica, a bit flustered. Rose puts a comforting hand on Monica's shoulder.

"Just eat what you can."

Monica rolls her eyes at me, doing her best to distract from the fact she probably doesn't eat enough.

"See? Fussing," she says to me.

I glance at Monica's wrists, which are delicate and thin, the skin blotchy with a tinge of blue.

After pizza, I wander out onto the back patio to find Phil. It's stopped raining now and everything smells like wet wood. There are no lights on the patio but the street lamp on the road behind the back fence throws an orange glow across the stone slabs and potted plants.

Phil, wrapped in a blanket, sits on a bench against a garden shed with her legs pulled up underneath her, finishing a bottle of beer. I sit beside her. She passes me the bottle and I take a swig and pass it back. I'm overwhelmed for a moment that this will be the last time I ever see her.

"What happened to Monica?" I ask.

"She was born like that. When Rose turned eighteen she adopted her. She was in some kind of home until then."

I'm struck by Rose's commitment to her sister and suddenly I'm intensely jealous of Monica. I imagine what it must be like to have a big sister like Rose who loves you that much. A coldness shoots down my spine and I shiver in the night air. Phil lifts the blanket offering to share it with me but I say I'm fine, reluctant to get too close or comfortable.

I wonder if I should have come to the party at all. I could be on the train to Scotland instead; in fact, I could still make the last train if I hurry. I'm about to say I have to go, when the back door slides open and Mali and Gaby stick their heads out.

"Your turn, Noelle," Gaby says, beaming.

"I'll do your nails. Gaby will do your hair," orders Mali.

"No, you're alright. I was about to go," I say. But Rose appears at the door too.

"You can't leave. We haven't done the cake yet," she says.

"And we can't do the cake until we all have feathers in our hair," says Mali. "Now get your butt on a chair." I look at Phil, who doesn't have any feathers in her hair or painted nails.

"What about Phil? Do her first."

"I have a feather," says Phil, pointing to the feather in her bra strap. "And anyway, I have an exemption."

"What kind of exemption?" I say.

"It's personal," she says, grinning. I look at Mali, Gaby and Rose. I'm about to say that I'm entitled to an exemption too, but their faces are so full of expectation and kindness.

"Looks like it's my turn then," I say, caving. Gaby claps her hands together in delight as they all disappear back inside.

"You made it, you know?" says Phil as I head for the back door to follow. I turn and look at her, confused for a moment. "You beat your five-star record of one month. Congratulations," she says with a cheeky smile. I smile back, genuinely pleased. I'd totally forgotten all about the original challenge I had set for myself. Suddenly I don't mind sharing my secret with Phil so much, but maybe that's because I know I'm leaving.

"I have you to thank for that," I say and enter the house.

Twenty minutes later, I'm squished between Monica and Mali. Mali is painting the nails on my left hand bright pink and Monica, with a rather shaky hand, is doing my right hand in a silky beige. Gaby tugs at my hair with the brush, twisting and pinning it up. Phil sits across the table watching, amused by my obvious discomfort.

"I can't believe you have an exemption," I say. She grins at me.

"You have lovely hands," says Monica. "Not like a cleaner's at all."

"What's that supposed to mean?" yells Rose from the kitchen, as she carefully lifts Mali's huge chocolate cake from a tin.

"That you don't wear your blue gloves enough," says Monica. "She never listens to me," she says to me. Rose smiles over at Monica and shakes her head.

"There you go," says Gaby, putting the last pin in my updo and adding a feather. "You're one of us now."

I swallow at Gaby's words.

Monica and Mali finish my nails. Monica struggles to get the brush back into the nail polish bottle but she manages finally.

"Cake time," says Rose, distracting us all from Monica's shaky hand. Gaby grabs birthday napkins from the sideboard as Phil pours everyone more punch. Rose carefully slides the chocolate cake onto a cake stand. Mali comes to her side to supervise.

"It's gorgeous," says Rose, putting an arm around Mali and pulling her tight to her.

Rose carries the cake to the table and puts it down in front of Monica. On the cake it says *Happy Birthday, Monica* in pink icing. Phil reaches over and scoops a blob of chocolate cream from around the bottom of the cake with her finger and sticks it in her mouth. Rose smacks her hand away.

"Tasty," says Phil.

"You really shouldn't have gone to all this trouble," says Monica, looking up at Mali, her eyes shining with delight.

"There's no one else I'd rather bake a cake for," she replies, smoothing loose strands of Monica's hair behind her ears.

Rose starts singing "Happy Birthday" at the top of her voice and we all join in. Monica, delighted, nods her head along to our terrible singing. Even with Gaby's angelic voice, we still sound like a tuneless choir. We finish singing and all cheer and clap. There aren't any candles on the cake, and I figure that's because Monica would find it hard to blow them out. Rose passes Monica the cake knife. Monica puts the end of the knife in the middle of the cake, closes her eyes to make a wish and then pulls it down slicing into the soft, rich sponge. We all cheer again. Rose takes the knife from Monica and starts to carve out big slabs of cake that she then puts on napkins. I'm not a food person let alone a cake person, but something about the fact that Mali made it makes me want to eat every last crumb.

Monica goes to put a piece in her mouth, but her shaky hand gets the better of her and a smudge of chocolate icing appears on her cheek.

"Ah, bugger," she mutters. Mali immediately copies Monica and accidentally on purpose smudges icing on her own face too.

"Oops," says Mali. Gaby does the same and turns to Mali.

"Is there something on my face?"

Mali goes to clean Gaby's cheek with her napkin but smears it around instead, making it worse.

"Thanks," says Gaby, pretending she's all cleaned up. Phil puts a dollop of cream on the end of her nose and then flicks a piece of cake at Rose, which lands on her neck. Rose giggles. Phil looks over at me and flicks a piece of cake into my hair. I laugh, picking it out, cake on my fingers. Monica giggles now too. She goes to put another piece of cake in her mouth and this time gets it in, no problem. We all cheer as she dips her head from left to right, taking a bow. Mali, of course, takes it too far and stuffs a massive piece of cake into her mouth.

"I think it's my best cake ever," she says in a muffled voice, as crumbs spray from her mouth all over the table. Monica roars laughing and we all join in. I look around the table at everyone. Mali takes a big gulp of punch to wash the cake down as Gaby pats her on the back, on standby in case she chokes. Rose has her arm around Phil's shoulders as they cry laughing at Mali.

And then there's me. The outsider. The misfit. The one who doesn't belong, not just here but anywhere.

Phil glances at me. *You okay?* she mouths. I nod, forcing a smile, but a prickly heat creeps up my spine and into my head. A strange pressure is building behind my eyes as my gut contracts. What's happening to me? I'm gripped by a sudden urge to get out of the kitchen. I get up from my seat.

"Loo's in the hall on the left," says Rose, assuming that's what I need.

I shut the toilet door behind me and lock it, catching my breath. The mounting pressure behind my eyes is more intense now, pushing and pulsating. My chest feels like it's going to implode.

I know what this is. I remember the feeling from when I was a kid. I'm on the verge of crying, and I mean properly, for real, but I have no idea why. Nobody hurt me or tried to make me feel bad. If anything I was enjoying myself, celebrating Monica's birthday with everyone.

I lean on the sink and peer at myself in the mirror. I quite like my updo, feather and all. No crying, I tell myself. It shows weakness and I can't be beaten, not in my head anyway. My mother tried to make me cry, but I never gave her what she wanted. My refusal was all the power I had sometimes.

Thoughts of my mother invade my mind. The photograph of me in her purse. Her tittering laugh at the photo booth. The fact she named me Noelle when I was born so close to Christmas. The time she tried to dry my wet hair with a tea towel in the Tesco staff room. And saving me from Roy.

I turn the tap on, splash cold water over my face, and look at myself again in the mirror. Are these memories, these moments from my past, proof that she cared about me, even the tiniest bit?

My limbs feel weak. I sit on the toilet seat, my hands in my lap, breathing deeply, trying to regain control over my thoughts.

Is it possible that under the dense black sludge that surrounded my mother's heart, there was a microscopic speck of love for me? All humans love something or someone and not because they try to but because they have no choice. Maybe my mother had no choice but to love me, even the smallest bit. She just buried it under a mountain of self-hate and confusion and ugliness and cruelty.

But is a miniscule amount of anything even significant? Was my mother's love for me, if she did have any, too small to matter? It's worse to know that she'd loved me but was unable to feel it, to dig for it, to try as hard as she could to show even a smidgen of kindness. It took Roy to bring it out in her. It took seeing a photograph of me, for her heart to be warmed. It took a funny comment, for her to find me amusing. And only Tesco Erica, her fake persona, could take care of me for a fleeting moment when I was soaked through from the rain.

Had she been aware of these moments herself? What was it about me that made it so hard for her to love me? Maybe I did cry all night as a baby. Maybe it was all my fault.

Familiar panic shoots up my arms, as the walls of Rose's small bathroom close in around me. I pull the neckline of my top away from my body, hot and short of breath. I need to get out of here. I need to leave.

A knock on the bathroom door snaps me out of my thoughts.

"Just a minute," I manage to garble.

I pull myself together and swing open the door to find Phil standing outside.

"What's going on?" she says.

"I was having a wee," I say, like she's being weird. I go to leave, but she blocks my exit. I feel more hemmed in as the panic inside me swirls faster, gaining momentum.

"What's wrong?" she says.

"I buried my mother yesterday, remember?"

"Oh, the mother you loved so much? That mother?"

I push past Phil, shoving her out of the way and burst into the kitchen to get my bag. Kylie Minogue now blasts from the speaker and Mali is turning Monica around in her chair, dancing. Gaby and Rose stand on chairs, swinging their arms over their heads.

"It's a rave," shouts Gaby.

Phil comes in behind me. I know she hasn't finished asking me questions yet. I grab my backpack and shout over to Rose that I have to go, putting on a tired face—although I am exhausted so I wonder why I'm pretending. It occurs to me I've been pretending for so long that I don't even know how to be real anymore. I can't just be me, whoever that is. Suddenly I'm stricken to my core. Am I like my mother? An empty, fake person with no identity? My hands go cold and tremble.

I wave over to Mali and Monica. Mali waves back. Monica blows me a kiss. I turn to Phil, still in my way. I duck past her into the hall, heading straight for the door.

"I know there's something wrong," Phil calls from behind, following me. "Just tell me."

I stop for a moment. Even if I wanted to tell her what was wrong, where would I start? I'm not a real person. I'm not your friend, just an imposter. I don't know how to be part of anything or belong in the world. All I care about is taking things.

"I'm tired. I'll see you at work tomorrow," I manage to muster.

"I'll come home with you, if you don't want to be alone," she offers, reaching for her coat.

I nearly laugh out loud. I've been alone my whole life. My problem isn't being on my own, it's not being on my own.

I mumble something about needing a good night's sleep and open the door. I glance back at Phil one last time, wanting to remember her beautiful, perfect face, and shut the door.

In the square outside the air is crisp and the estate seems strangely quiet, especially for a Friday night. I take several deep breaths, filling my lungs to the brim. I look back at Rose's front door. I can hear the distant sounds of the party still going on.

The pressure mounts behind my eyes again. I dig my fingernails into the palm of my hand, squeezing hard until the sharp pain dominates my thoughts and the pressure ebbs away.

I put my head down, my collar up and run out of the estate. The feather in my hair bobs about and then takes flight. I turn to see it float to the ground. I leave it and plow on, determined to catch the morning train out of London.

Chapter 30

I never get attached to the places I live in. I'm normally there for so little time that I barely remember the address let alone the décor or furniture. I view every flat as a shell I inhabit for as long as I need to. But for some reason this grubby, dilapidated hovel has grown on me.

There is an indentation in the worn carpet where my trunk was before the storage people took it away. I'll arrange to have it sent to Scotland once I've found a place to live. It looks empty on that side of the room without it there. The clothes rail seems barren and lost without my crisp white shirts on the hangers.

My eyes sweep around the room, taking in the disgusting armchairs, which seem characterful now, and the wobbly, stained aluminum table. Memories drift into my mind of Gaby slumped in one of the chairs asleep with her jacket pulled up to her chin and Phil perched on my trunk, smiling at me, holding the Sponge-Bob mug in her hand. I shake my head, ridding myself of these pointless thoughts.

I check the time. It's 8:00 a.m. The girls start work in half an hour. I imagine them putting on their aprons, laughing and joking. Rose winding Mali up and Mali reacting just the way Rose wants her to so she can start her day with some playful banter. Work for Rose is a respite from home and Mali probably knows that.

I know they will wonder where I am and try to call me. But they'll get on with their shift, thinking I overslept or I'm running late. And my phone will be switched off, of course, and then once I get a new SIM card, my old number won't work anymore. I don't always change my phone number when I leave a hotel and move on, but I'll have to this time.

I wonder about leaving a note for the girls or at least for Phil. But I don't have to. Phil knows this is what I do. She'll explain it to them, and they'll move on too and forget about me soon enough. I don't think I'll be back to London for a very long time, if at all.

My suitcase trundles along the concourse behind me, the grid-like ceiling of King's Cross station hovering above, like the underside of a giant mushroom. It's half an hour until my train leaves but I want to be on the platform early, so I'm in the right place at the right time, no mistakes.

Platform eight looms ahead as I weave through the crowds toward the entrance, my one-way ticket in my hand, which I had bought earlier, in preparation.

I look up at the screen to double-check it's the right platform. It says 9:15 Edinburgh. I feed my ticket into the front of the turnstile and it spits it out at the top for me to retrieve. The two upright flaps shoot open and I walk through, dragging my suitcase behind me.

The train is already at the platform, waiting. I normally feel a spring in my step when I see the train or the bus I am about to board to a new destination, as it means the journey is real now. But all I feel is heaviness in my legs. I'm tired, I tell myself. It's been an exhausting week after all.

I wander down the platform, eyeing the empty train as I go, deciding where I'd like to sit. The main doors at the end of each carriage are open welcoming passengers to board.

I carry on walking until I'm halfway up the platform at the middle section of the train. A few people bustle past me and climb on board but I'm not ready to step off the platform yet. I sit on the empty bench facing coach H.

I lean forward, forearms resting on my thighs, staring at the concrete platform by my feet. I gaze at my painted fingernails for a moment—pink on one hand, beige on the other, then screw my hands into a ball to hide them. I squeeze my eyes tightly shut and imagine arriving at my next hotel on my first day. The familiar hotel smells and noises. The unfamiliar faces and staff room. My mind wanders to Phil, Gaby, Rose and Mali laughing together in the staff room at the Magnolia, and the pressure builds behind my eyes again. I shove my nails into the palm of my hands and the pressure ebbs away.

I need to face the truth. I'm sad about leaving, but it can't be helped; staying is not an option and never was. Phil and the girls are not my friends. They were just useful colleagues, like in every hotel I've ever worked in. I became friends with them to make sure they defended me when I was accused of stealing, so I could leave that job and move to the next with a clean record. Maybe my experience with Bernadette in hotel 20 tricked me into thinking I need to belong, but I don't.

The girls were never supposed to come to my mother's funeral or stay overnight at my flat or invite me to special birthday parties. Suddenly, I'm angry. Why did they have to do all of that? Why couldn't they just leave me alone? All this messing around has set me back and wasted my time.

I sit up, feeling my strength return. It's time to bury the memories of the Magnolia along with my mother.

I look in my backpack and check I still have my ticket, ready for inspection on the train. I hear footsteps running along the concourse and look up to see a little girl, about six years old, wearing a red jacket and a red dress. Her hair is tied up in a ponytail with a red ribbon in it and she has a little blue rucksack on her back. She smiles with delight, as her light legs carry her up to the open door to coach H.

Running along to keep up with her is a man in a baseball cap and jeans, wheeling a suitcase behind him, and a sporty-looking woman in leggings and trainers with a baby strapped to her front. They are laughing. He calls out for the little girl to slow down. The little girl stops, moving from side to side, wiggling on the spot, unable to contain her excitement. Mum and Dad catch up with her. Mum tells her she's a very fast runner and the little girl's face lights up, delighted with the praise.

Dad takes the little girl's hand and helps her up into the carriage. Then he stands aside, protective of his wife and baby as they climb on board. He follows with the suitcase and the little girl bundles into a seat on the train. She squishes her face up against the window, putting her lips on the glass and moving her head from side to side. I smile at her. Her naughtiness and sense of fun remind me of Mali.

Mum scoots in beside her and gently pulls her away from the window, telling her not to put her mouth on the dirty glass. The little girl looks out at me and waves. I wave back. Dad sits down across from his daughter and they look out to see who she's waving at. I feel my cheeks redden, not because I'm waving but because they're all looking at me. They smile at me too.

Mum produces a carton of juice for the little girl and helps her open it so she can drink it. She takes a huge mouthful and some dribbles down her chin. Dad wipes it away. They're a real family, I think. But not everyone has that.

"The train now at platform eight is the 9:15 to Edinburgh," booms the announcer's voice, echoing around the station.

Passengers stream down the platform to board the train. Some run past me toward the front of the train, worried the train will leave without them. An older man stops and beckons to his wife trailing behind him. She waves him on, irritated by his fussing. He carries on past me. The couple remind me of Monica and Rose.

A train guard walks along the platform jangling keys on his belt, getting ready for the train to depart. It's time to get on the train, but I'm glued to the bench.

A whistle blows—the first warning. The next whistle will signify the doors closing. A huge hissing sound escapes from underneath the train. Get on the train, I say to myself. You've got nowhere else to go.

I look at the little girl in the red dress again. She has a book out on the table now and Dad is helping her put stickers in it while

Mum tends to the baby, who is also looking out of the window or at least its face is turned toward me.

The pressure behind my eyes builds again, stronger this time. I dig my fingernails into the palms of my hands. But the more I watch this family together, the more the pressure mounts. I flinch with pain and look down at my hands now gouged and bleeding from my nails. I need to get on this train, but my body won't respond to the instruction.

The whistle blows again followed by a loud beeping sound as the sliding doors to the carriages all shut at the same time, synchronized and perfect, like the family sitting in the window.

The train creaks and then emits a quiet hum as it launches forward, gathering speed, snaking its way out of the station. The little girl waves out of the window at me. I wave back. The rest of the carriages whoosh past me until the last one whips by with a gush of wind, ruffling my hair. I look on as the back of the train disappears into the distance, on its way to Scotland.

I stare down into the tracks. I can't stay. I can't go. Maybe I'll just sit here, on this bench until I waste away. Or die from hypothermia. It happens to homeless people all the time. I'm homeless too. In fact, I've always been homeless. Having a place to sleep at night doesn't mean you have a home.

My feet are cold now. Good, I think, the colder the better. No one will bother me sitting on a bench. It's a free country. I'll just stay here until I slip away. Girl found dead on a bench from the cold. No one will care. No one will notice. And the local authority can take care of my remains.

"It's the wrong fucking platform!" A familiar voice pierces my thoughts.

"That's platform eight. This is platform six." I follow the voice, peering over the tracks to platform six across from me.

It's Mali with Phil, Gaby and Rose, all wearing their Magnolia uniforms. They're pacing and catching their breath. Phil has her hands on her hips. Gaby, bent over, wipes sweat from her brow. Rose taps her foot, mop still in her hand. Mali points to the large number six sign on the concrete pillar on the platform.

"See? Six," she yells. Rose flops down on the bench across from me, her shoulders drooped. I stay very still, unsure if I want them to see me or not. "You all need glasses," says Mali.

"I don't need glasses, you need glasses," Rose says to Mali, slightly annoyed.

"That's what I said. We all need glasses," yells Mali, pacing up and down.

I watch them, wondering what the hell they're doing here. Are they looking for me? How did they know I was here?

Gaby stands up straight now, her face all red. She pushes her damp hair from her forehead and then looks directly at me across the tracks. We stare at each other. She looks confused for a moment then—

"NOELLE!" she screams, pointing directly at me. A few people on the platform flick their head in my direction and I try to shrink into my jacket. Phil, Mali and Rose see me too now. They all move to the edge of the platform forming a line and peer over at me in disbelief.

My heart swells in my chest, like it's going to break out of my rib cage. Heat rushes to my head. I'm not sure what's happening to me. All I know is that these women, standing on the platform across the tracks, one with a mop in her hand, matter to me.

Rose puts her hands to her face, relieved. Phil, grinning, shakes her head. Gaby continues to point at me, in case I move and they lose sight of me. I raise my hand and give a rather pathetic wave. It's obvious I've been sitting here, hiding in my stillness.

"Don't move," orders Mali. "You are in big trouble." She stomps off back down the platform to the exit with her chest pushed out in front like a sergeant major. She's clearly on her way over to throttle me.

"Like the mop," I call over to Rose, sheepish. Rose holds it up to her side.

"Not much to look at but he's great in the sack."

A laugh escapes my mouth, unexpected. Rose grins at me.

"We're coming over there, okay?" she says.

"Don't be getting on any trains," adds Gaby, still pointing at me.

Rose and Gaby rush off down the platform after Mali. I'm still rooted to the spot, unsure what I'm doing or how I'm feeling. Phil has stayed where she is, hands still on her hips, looking over at me from platform six.

"Why didn't you get on the train?" she asks.

I shrug. "How did you know I was here?"

"The train ticket fell out of your backpack when you were throwing things around after your mum's funeral. I put it back in your bag with everything else and hoped you wouldn't use it. Then when you didn't show up for work . . ."

I stare at her, unsure what to say.

"You didn't think we'd let you go without saying goodbye, did you?"

My throat tightens and pressure builds in my head as the tears start nudging at my eyeballs again, desperate to be released. I fight it hard, but the palms of my hands are too sore to dig my fingernails into now.

"Julia says if we're not back in an hour we're all fired, including you," she says, walking down the platform, following the others. I feel stupid, stuck to this bench, not moving, but I really don't know what else to do.

Mali strides toward me, a woman on a mission. "Look at you, sitting there like a skinny rabbit," she shouts. She stops in front of me, peering down, arms crossed high across her chest. Rose and Gaby approach in the distance. Rose has the mop over her shoulder now, swinging out behind her.

"What have you got to say for yourself?" Mali says. "We got the taxi driver to drive through red lights for you."

"Sorry," I muster, desperately trying to keep the floodgates from opening. There's nothing else for it, I'll have to dig my fingernails in my palms. I wince with pain as my nails slice into the small open wounds.

Mali pulls me to my feet. I forget how strong she is. Her face is sweaty and her eyes wide and urgent. She's going to punch me, I think, but then her forehead crinkles and her lower lip starts to wobble. Her eyes fill with tears and she hugs me tight, squeezing the air out of my lungs, making the pressure behind my eyes retreat a little, which I'm grateful for. She pushes me back and holds me by the shoulders. I'm a good foot taller than her, but it feels like she's towering over me.

"Sorry isn't good enough," she says, shaking her head at me. "You think that's how you treat your friends? Running away without telling us?" I don't want to point it out to her, but that's what running away means.

"It's time for me to leave, that's all," I say, but I know it sounds flimsy.

"You think you've got problems? We've all got problems," she says, wiping tears from her dripping nose. I sit back down, feeling drained and out of excuses. Gaby and Rose rush up and plonk themselves on the bench either side of me.

"Too bad you missed your train," says Rose, with a grin. Gaby puts her arm around me and pulls me to her.

"I'm pleased you're still here."

The pressure of tears returns to my head, even more forceful this time, threatening to explode and flood the entire station. I quickly scramble to my feet again, grabbing my bags, keeping my head dipped, so as not to make eye contact. I mumble something about getting the next train, turn on my heel and walk straight into Phil. She takes hold of my arms to steady me.

"I have to go," I whisper.

"Look at me," she says. But I can't bring myself to. "Noelle, look at me," she says again, softly. I look up this time. She takes my tender hands and holds them tight, like they've found a safe place to sit for a moment.

"Everything is going to be okay," she says.

I stare at her, trying to make sense of her words. It strikes me that nobody has ever said that to me before. A simple sentence: Everything is going to be okay. And suddenly I wonder if that could be true.

And then it happens: the dam finally bursts and the tears come gushing out, let loose from their holding bay. They stream down my face, like someone left a tap on. My gut convulses and I lean over to help myself breathe through the sobbing.

Looking down at my hands, I'm shocked by how drenched they are from my tears. My nose is running too now and I watch in wonder as huge drops fall from my top lip and splatter on the ground. Phil puts her arm around me. Rose, Mali and Gaby hug me too.

I feel myself being led back along the platform to the exit. I hear my suitcase trundling along behind me. One of the girls must be pulling it. My head is still bent over and I'm unable to see clearly due to my wet, sodden eye sockets.

I manage to get control of my breathing and the flow of tears reduces to a slower trickle, sliding from the corners of my eyes and down the side of my cheeks.

"We got her, thanks," shouts Mali to the station guard at the turnstile, as we pass through the wide exit.

We walk out into the brightly lit concourse of the station where passengers scurry around, grabbing snacks and running for their trains. Everyone's going somewhere, I think. I'm aware of an arm holding me and I look up to see Phil.

"Where are we going?" I ask.

"The pub, I think," she says.

Mali, Gaby and Rose walk by taking the lead. Mali is pulling my suitcase, Gaby has my backpack over her shoulder and Rose drags the mop along behind her. They are chatting with each other. I don't know what they're saying but I can guess. Mali wiggles her hips and flicks her head from side to side, probably singing a Kylie song. Rose is laughing, probably telling her she's making a show of herself. And Gaby is looking at her phone, most likely to see if Julia has called.

"What about Julia?" I say to Phil, meekly.

"We'll get the cleaning done later. She's not going to fire all of us, is she?" All of us. The words echo in my mind.

Mali struts on ahead of Rose and Gaby shouting, "Tequila time, baby." Rose turns to us and rolls her eyes, indicating there will be no tequila.

Gaby joins in with Mali, wiggling her hips and shouting "tequila time."

I look from Phil, to Rose, to Gaby, to Mali. What a collection of oddballs we are.

I disentangle myself from Phil, able to walk on my own now, and run up to Mali and take my case from her.

"Tequila time, baby," I shout. Mali throws her head back and laughs.

Hotel 21

5-star. London. Feb 2019-
Total stay

Items

Condom x 1 (first day)

Tweezers x 2

Hair comb x 1

Tester tube of eye cream x 1

Handkerchief with butterfly x 1

Chapstick x 1

Hairbrush x 1

Acknowledgments

With love and gratitude to my husband, Dave, and my son, Miles, for their unwavering support in all my writing endeavors, and who both read the first 4,000 words of *Hotel 21* and told me to drop everything else and keep going. Thank you to my mum, Deike Begg, for our lengthy discussions about Jungian psychology—long may they continue. A huge thank you to Kirk England, who painstakingly reads everything I write—your early feedback on this book was invaluable. Massive thanks to my other early readers, Nick Wilkinson and Lisa Kinsell—your feedback was so appreciated. A very special thank-you to Rachel O'Flanagan— the very first editor on the book—your brilliance and support was also invaluable. Huge gratitude to my agent, Marianne Gunn O'Connor, for believing in *Hotel 21* and for your excellent insights into the book. Thank you to the awesome team at Bloomsbury—it was an absolute pleasure to work with you all, including Emma Herdman, David Mann for designing the perfect cover, Francisco Vilhena, Sharona Selby, Ros Ellis, Tabitha Pelly, and the entire sales and marketing team. A big thank-you also to the wonderful team at Union Square & Co., including Claire Wachtel, Barbara Berger, Kristin Mandaglio, Richard Hazelton, Melissa Farris, Jenny Lu, Daniel Denning, and the rest of the team. And now, some "behind-the-scenes" thank-yous, including François and Jean-Christophe of

Villa Extramuros in Portugal (where I wrote my first 4,000 words), my lovely sister, Connie, Vivienne Luke of Dubray Books, and Lili Motea. Every one of you helped bring *Hotel 21* into existence. Thank you x.

About the Author

Senta Rich began her career as an advertising copywriter. During this time, she also wrote radio plays and magazine articles, before moving into the world of screenwriting. She now writes regularly for film and TV. She is originally from London but now lives in Dublin with her husband and son.

2198232079805